IN THE VILLAGE OF THE MAN

Also by Loyd Little

PARTHIAN SHOT

Loyd Little

IN THE VILLAGE
OF THE MAN

THE VIKING PRESS

New York

FIC
L7785in

c.1

LIBRARY OF CONGRESS CATALOGING IN PUBLICATION DATA
Little, Loyd, 1940
In the village of the man.
    I. Title.
PZ4.L7784In   [PS3562.I7829] 813'.5'4   78-27285
               ISBN 0-670-39705-9

Printed in the United States of America
Set in Fototronic Baskerville

Dedicated to

My mother and father, Reba and Sunshine Little

CONTENTS

IN THE VILLAGE OF THE MAN

CHAPTER I

THE FIELD OF FURTIVE LABOR

SHAY of the Lahu tribe shivered, although the spring night was warm. The field of ashes was funereal and indistinct in the argentine light from the moon, now in its first quarter. Behind him, his wife said nothing as she shifted the cloth, full of year-old, first-harvested seeds, from one hand to the other. She knew he was examining the mood of the *phi,* the spirits, as well as the shadows on the field. It was important to do so.

"Po-nagar," said Shay loudly, "look with your usual benevolent sagacity on our incompetent efforts to grow the plant of dreams. Should these insufficient words of praise also reach the spirit of the rain, may his seasonality be even more precise and our opium reach a memorable height, and stream an abundance and richness of sap. Some of these seeds are for you, some are for the lazy, some are for our old, some for the thieves, and what stunted ones are left will be ours."

He turned. "Come. Let us begin. It's only a few hours until the sun rises."

They began working their *kamu klaik lava,* their field of furtive labor. It was the hour of the tiger on the day which was the fourth past the waking of the insects, in the fifth month of the year of the snake. The spirits, summoned by rituals taught by every Lahu father to his son, had selected this night for Shay and his wife to secretly plow and sow three rows of opium. After the sun rose, he would wander by this field and discover the new furrows. He would exclaim, "Who labored secretly in my field during the night?"

Then he would rush home with the news, prepare offerings and bring them back to the field, for land which cultivates itself must indeed be consecrated. After more prayers to Po-nagar, the field would be sown openly.

The field of furtive labor came to be because, in the old days,

1

plowing and sowing were associated with the crime of sexual violation—or so said an ancient woman in their village, who also sang the stories of their tribe coming south from China, long before it was known as China.

But tonight the ritual would not be completed. Before Shay and his wife had finished the first row, they heard a noise from the sky. They knew what it was: one of the half-machine, half-man creatures that flew sometimes in their universe. No lights were visible, though the noise became louder.

Ki, ki, ki, thought Shay. Perhaps it isn't the flying creature. He held his wife's hand tightly. The noise came from the cinereous clouds directly overhead. Suddenly, his wife squeezed his hand and cried, "Ahee! Look there!"

High above them floated a being. It was black and shaped like a large mushroom topped by a smaller, more elongated mushroom. The noise from the flying machine grew distant, and the silence spread around them. The creature descended slowly toward them.

Shay whispered, "I don't think that is Po-nagar. Possibly it's a demon. Perhaps a mushroom god."

His wife tugged at him in fright, and they broke and ran, dropping their hoe-stick and seeds. They raced across the field of ashes toward their village.

Three days and nights later, Martin Borjek hunkered beside a clear stream and splashed water on his face. He breathed heavily, not yet acclimatized to the six-thousand-foot elevation of these Laotian mountains. His face was florid, but not only from his exertions. When he was younger and had a headful of hair, it had been just slightly darker than his complexion. Huge red eyebrows darted forth from his forehead. They sprouted from a single mass above his nose and flung themselves in greedy trespass across his face. Thick and matted near their center, loose and straggly at the edges, they leapt free of their roots and climbed, hair upon hair, beyond his eyes and over his temples, overshadowing his face.

At an even six feet, Borjek did not hunker easily; his bones were large and they carried two hundred and twenty-five pounds of flesh. Also, the priest's cassock he wore made squatting precarious. On a rock beside him lay his knapsack and carbine.

After filling a plastic canteen, Borjek pulled out a map and compass, and studied his location. As near as he could tell, he had been dropped ten miles from the village of Sop Hao. I suppose, he thought, I'm lucky not to be inside China. Another ten minutes and I would have been. The pilot had been an Air American pilot, but he was young, one of many Nam skyjockeys who couldn't leave the East when the war ended.

Borjek's mission was simple: Find CIA man George Violette, who until three months ago when his reports stopped, had been operating out of Sop Hao under the cover name Neil Treadmill. The Agency was interested in Sop Hao because it was in the far northwestern corner of Laos, on a toe of land two and a half miles from Burma and thirty miles from China. Near the Mekong, the Sop Hao area had long been a passing-through place for caravans traveling from Ching-hung, Ssu-mao and Ching-ku in China, to Keng-tung, Burma; to Chiang Mai, Thailand; and to Vientiane, Laos. The caravans came with iron, copperware, swords, silk, tea and gossip. Some returned with opium. The Western press had named this area "The Golden Triangle."

Treadmill's last reports had been littered with obscure and strange warnings: A team of revolutionaries had moved into the Sop Hao area; guns were seen; the villagers were uneasy; more opium was being grown; less opium was being grown. At one time or another, Treadmill had blamed the North Vietnamese, the Red Chinese, the Nationalist Chinese, the Corsicans, the neutralist Lao, the Pathet Lao, the Royal Lao Army and the Burmese Shan bandits. In the Agency's view all of these groups were suspect. It was the spring of 1977, and in spite of Pathet Lao control of the Laotian government in Vientiane, the CIA knew that any of these groups could control almost any given area in Laos at any given time. The CIA wanted no unknown factors; not because it was busy smuggling democracy to less than three million Laotians, but because it was keeping watch on more than eight hundred million Chinese next door.

Thus, Sop Hao was a key listening post for the CIA and Army counterintelligence, and they both wanted to know what happened to Treadmill/Violette. Find him. Find out what happened to him. If necessary, take his place, they told Borjek.

This was not Borjek's first time in the steamy jungles of Asia. In

February of 1959, when he was twenty-two years old, he had been among the earliest Americans in Viet Nam. The Geneva Conference was concluded in 1954, and France withdrew her forces as per the treaty. The United States did not sign the agreements, and before a year had passed, American agents had begun replacing the French cadre.

Borjek had enlisted in the Army in 1957, two years after being graduated from high school, years which had been spent drifting around and fighting sporadically with his father. Finding the civilian world lackluster, and rebelling against his father's insistence on college, Borjek joined the Army. It was familiar. People he had known all his life were inextricably part of the Army family. Lives crossed and recrossed. Friendships were quickly made and easily renewed over the years. Unlike civilian life, there was always the shared bond of service and the common interest of Army gossip. One of his closest friends from high school in Bad Tolz, Germany, where his father had been stationed, showed up in his class at officers' candidate school. It had never occurred to Borjek not to become an officer.

Still, after the excitement of the first year and a half had worn off, Borjek began wondering if he could really endure eighteen or twenty more years. But he also wondered what the hell he could do as a civilian. He had found he had a quick and easy ability to learn languages—his voice could create the exact sound his ear received—but beyond that his skills were vague and certainly not technical. However, in his youth he was not seriously worried about a marketable talent in the civilian world.

His father had sensed Borjek's discontent in those early Army days and arranged, without his son's knowledge, to have him assigned as an adviser to one of Prime Minister Ngo Dinh Diem's personal ranger companies in Saigon. His father was of the make-or-break school. The promotion to first lieutenant came quickly and the promise of promotion to captain even quicker. Borjek re-enlisted for five years.

By the time he returned to Viet Nam in 1969, he was a major and the Indochina conflict was a nondeclared war. He was in intelligence and, as head of "Thunderbird," launched a hidden campaign of assassination and terrorism against the Viet Cong.

4

For a while. Then politics, swollen and fevered in response to the anti-war sentiment in America, overrode attainable results, and the program was halted: A Harvard schoolteacher was meeting secretly with Mao Tse-tung, and President Nixon wanted no embarrassing incidents. Borjek had pinned his career to a falling star. In addition, he became disgusted with the conduct of the war, like many Army men. The war was questionable to begin with, but the political shackles on the military were a burden that grew heavier almost daily.

His mother died of leukemia in 1969. His father retired the next year and was dead of a heart attack five months later. At last relieved of any obligations, even to a figure whose authority he had always resisted, Borjek requested, and was given, a transfer to the Joint Military Command in Thailand. But the promotions and the action were in Viet Nam, so after six years as a major, finding his name no higher on the roster for lieutenant colonel, Borjek joined the CIA in 1972. His pay grade and fifteen years in the Army all counted toward retirement.

At first he was a paper shuffler in Bangkok, but the night clubs were too close. Borjek had always been a heavy drinker, and the inactivity and boredom of doing a routine job made drinking easier. Finally the Agency noticed. Borjek was an agent going sour, and standard procedure was a change in assignment and surroundings. He was demoted to the level of a senior field agent, moved to Udorn and notified that he was on probation. A man was no good to the Agency if he was terribly happy or terribly unhappy. And Borjek had not been happy.

He looked at the jungle surrounding him. Christ, I need a drink, he thought. I should never have let Willard talk me into this dumb cover as a priest. The bastard is probably yukking it up every time he tells someone. Except for my brilliant pilot, I could have been in and maybe out by now, he thought with frustration. Borjek stood, shrugged on his pack and slipped the carbine under the cassock into a specially designed rifle holster.

Less than a hundred yards away, thirty-seven-year-old Reverend George Saint Sareno of the Foreign Baptist Mission of the Southern Baptist Convention was urinating on a small fig tree. Along with his six-feet two-inches of mainly skeleton, Sareno had inherited a weak bladder from his father. Together they had probably urinated on every square foot of their twenty-five acre farm in the Tennessee hills. Sareno had also inherited his father's haunted face: big, washed-blue eyes and high cheekbones under alabaster skin. His nose was too small for his wide mouth and thin lips. Long black hair served the contrast well. A friend at theological school once told him he was half-way to being a saint because he already looked like one.

Sareno had been visiting with the Nam family a few dozen yards up the trail in Sop Hao, trying once more to explain why Jesus Christ had died for their sins. Today, he thought he had been able to persuade them that Jesus had personally known their ancestors, but they steadfastly refused to consider that any of their relatives had sinned. Sareno was unusually patient with the Nams because their oldest daughter, Tanna-li, was becoming a full-bodied woman with dark eyes and dimpled mouth. He had also noticed the trim of her brown ankles and the firm muscles of her calves. His memories were turning into fantasies when he heard nearby the noise of a person or an animal.

Sareno was trying to shuck the image of Tanna-li from his mind, stop urinating and button his pants when a man wearing a black robe pushed through a stand of bamboo.

A Catholic? Here? thought Sareno, at last pushing his top pants button through its hole.

Borjek dropped his knapsack and said, "Good morning. I'm looking for the village of Sop Hao."

"Right back there," said Sareno, waving behind him.

Something was vaguely familiar about the tall, thin man. On a wild hunch, Borjek said, "George?" He looks terrible, thought Borjek, but the photographs I saw were two years old.

"Yes?" said Sareno, puzzled and suddenly afraid that the notorious Catholic conspiracy had penetrated the jungles of Laos. He had a silly vision of himself holding up a cross to ward off the priest.

"My God, man, what a coincidence. Meeting here, like this," said Borjek.

"Yes?"

"What the hell happened to you?"

Sareno said, "I hardly think it calls for that kind of language, father. I accidentally urinated on myself. It's embarrassing and . . ."

"No, no. For the past three months?"

"I don't recall peeing on myself in the past three years, much less three months," said Sareno, realizing that the man before him was one of those legendary renegade priests. He's gone mad out here in the mountains. There's no telling how long he's been like this.

"The mission? Have you forgotten your mission?"

What does he mean? thought Sareno, almost giving in to panic. "That's exactly what I'm doing here, father. Carrying out my mission—"

"Urinating?"

"Father," Sareno began uncertainly, "there are heathen up the trail. I have just come from their home. They—"

"Why haven't you contacted us?" What kind of heathen is he talking about? wondered Borjek. No one told me about heathens up here.

Sareno held himself taller. "I am a Baptist missionary. Frankly, I see no reason why I should contact you. No offense, father, but my directions come from the Southern Baptist Convention in Chattanooga, Tennessee, not the Vatican." One must be firm with madmen and Catholics.

"Oh," Borjek chuckled. He realized his mistake but still wondered why Violette had changed his cover. "I've not identified myself." He lowered his voice and spoke the code. "Greetings, eyetooth gordian knot."

"Greetings, Father Knot. I'm George Saint Sareno, a Baptist missionary in God's service among the natives. And I must say that it is my impression that according to the last Asian Mission Ecumenical Council, this territory was awarded to the Southern Baptists. If I'm not mistaken, you Catholics have the burden of the Jeh tribe, some fifty miles southwest of here. 'For unto you it is given not only to believe in Him, but also to suffer for His sake.' One: twenty, Romans."

Suffer? thought Borjek. "You're not George Violette?"

"Sareno. George Saint Sareno, Father Knot."

"No, not Knot—Treadmill!" said Borjek, suddenly remembering Violette's cover name was Treadmill. He'd almost blown his own cover in the first five minutes in Sop Hao. He was reacting like a novice.

"Treadmill? That's odd. We used to have a Treadmill here. Unusual man. Your kin, Father Treadmill?"

"No, I'm not Treadmill. I'm sorry, reverend, your name confused me."

"You brought it up first."

"Of course I did. That's why I was confused," said Borjek. Get a hold on yourself, man. That didn't make any sense. And no one told me anything about a territorial division between the Catholics and the Baptists. "I am Father Borjek. I am new to this area—there must be a simple misunderstanding about our areas of mission—and Treadmill and I were friends in college. Come, let's go into Sop Hao. I've come a great distance."

"Certainly."

Borjek picked up his knapsack and followed Sareno along a narrow path. They were on the side of a hill which was part of the Muong Tha Mountains, the southern leg of the Himalayas. The mountains were sharply drawn, rising and falling great distances within a few thousand yards. To their right, the land dove quickly toward the Mekong. The mighty river itself was invisible in its own valley, but a long shelf of fog hung above its winding course. To their left, tall oak and chestnut trees abruptly concealed the mountain's peak.

Sareno asked, "How did you get here?"

"I caught a ride with a government official to Xieng Luang in Thailand. Then I hitched a ride across the river and up to Ba Kok. The rest of the way I walked. 'He that walketh must walk even as He walked.' One John eight: twelve." I remember a few things, Borjek thought.

"Uh, that would be One John two: six, and it goes, 'He that saith he abideth in Him ought himself also to walk even as Jesus walked.' " As soon as he finished, Sareno remembered the Catholic Bible was different. He coughed in embarrassment.

The trail and the hillside turned sharply to their left and Borjek looked at a scene as old as the mountains. Bamboo huts perched on stilts, and tidy paths strolled casually around an ice-green hillside. Terraced rice paddies stepped downward in unison. It could have been the fingering of a harp chord carved into the landscape. In the distance, Burma's Pangnao Loi Mountains rose above the mists.

"Our land," said Sareno simply. Even though he'd been here for nineteen months, the beauty of this ordinary village still astounded him. Possibly it reminded him of his own Tennessee hills. Parts of the Smoky Mountains were like this—sudden hills rising around primeval valleys. Sareno called up a memory from his childhood when he played hide-and-seek with his three brothers and one sister, all older. He would hide in the big apple tree and look out over his father's farm which was nestled in the elbow of a great blue mountain. The blue haze was the effluvium exhaled by a million pine trees. Later, Sareno realized his family had been money poor, but then, when he was growing up, it was his land and they were his family. He remembered telling himself when he was nine to memorize the farm and to remember it's niggardliness as well as it's beauty because he would leave someday and it would never be the same again. He had not been a well child—thin blood, the doctor said—and he knew, and his parents knew, that he would not stay to work the farm. His father, Heziakiah Sareno, began reading the Bible to him when he was still a baby. Heziakiah was a strong man, determined and proud. One of his boys would be a minister, and he decided that George would be called. No one questioned it.

George was at the Memphis Baptist School of Divinity when his mother died of tuberculosis. Less than six months later, his father and the farm were also gone. The government was going to build a dam to make power for the textile mills two hundred miles away, and they needed the Sarenos' twenty-five acres. Heziakiah had spit on the six-thousand-dollar check, then had ripped it up and thrown it in the face of the federal man. Later, when they came with the condemnation order and the bulldozers, Heziakiah climbed to the top of that old apple tree and, with his bolt-action .30 rifle, held them off for two days and two nights. On the third day, he fell asleep on a limb and tumbled off onto a goat, breaking both their necks. The bulldozers were already working by the time the ambulance arrived. Heziakiah died as he had lived: suffering. George clung bitterly to the church.

Perhaps that was why he loved Laos and the Man tribe. They suffered, too. Every day's living had to be stolen fresh each morning from the jungle, from the animals, from sickness and from other tribes. At the end of his first year in Laos, Sareno asked that his tour be extended another year. His need to suffer was obviously greater than any other Baptist missionary who had served God in Laos, and his request was granted.

Of course, that request came not long after Sareno realized that his interest in Tanna-li encompassed not only the future home of her soul, but the well-being of her spirit and the body that housed that spirit in this world.

With another turn of the trail, the two men of mission were in Sop Hao.

CHAPTER II

A VISIT TO TREADMILL'S GRAVE

SOP HAO nestled on a lopsided ledge that measured one hundred yards across. When India smashed into the continent of Asia one hundred million years before, pushing up the Himalayas and the Muong Tha, a rock plate had slipped backwards here and a shelf had been created. The village was hidden in this mountain's belly button, like treasure stashed in a child's secret place, which he knows adult eyes can never see.

Several dozen huts rode bamboo stilts as tall, on the downhill side, as a man. In the space captured underneath, children, chickens, pigs and water buffalo tolerated each other with an old caution. Women and teen-agers sat on the porches, sorting and arranging seeds in preparation for the new season.

"The planting begins soon," said Sareno as they entered the village. "The monsoons are close and everything—look out!"

Borjek whirled to see a clay pot hit the ground a few feet away. Not far behind it came a thin, middle-aged man leaping from the porch of a house. Borjek reached for his carbine, but the cassock bedeviled him. He clawed at the robe.

Sareno, watching Borjek's spasms with dismay, said, "Please, father, relax. It's only Tsao and his wife having an argument."

Tsao landed near the shards of the pot, threw the men a quick smile, then ran underneath his house and into the bushes. Seconds later, his wife rushed onto the porch and shouted at the disappearing form until she noticed Sareno and the stranger. She bowed quickly and returned inside.

"What was that all about?" asked Borjek as they resumed walking.

"No one would tell me for a long time. Then I found out that Tsao likes to . . ." Sareno cleared his throat. ". . . have at his wife—who is a niece of the village chief, by the way—once or twice a day.

This happens," he waved a large, pale hand, "when he's too persistent. His physical stamina is remarkable. The other men watch Tsao to see what he eats and what ceremonies he performs to gain his strength."

"Does he have any secret methods?"

"I don't know," said Sareno stiffly, appalled at the implication.

The villagers stared at the white men as they passed. In the sudden quietness, Borjek became aware of attitudes of curiosity and suspicion. He sensed no hostility, but as they walked he grew self-conscious, first because of his robe and then because of his size. The scrutiny of the people disquieted him because he should have foreseen it; he should have expected this reaction and been prepared for it. I have been in offices too long, he conceded.

Borjek matched the Man with their description from a two-month-long crash course on Laos. Between five-feet and five-feet six-inches tall, they were similar to the Montagnards with whom he had worked in Vietnam. Their ethnic background, too, was similar. The Green Beret instructors in Udorn told Borjek that the Man, or Yao, as they were called in China and North Vietnam, were one of the oldest tribes in southeastern Asia. They were a mixture of Chinese and an ancient race of people who, from the archeological evidence, resembled modern Indonesians. Their hair was black and straight. Some had the single Mongolian fold above their eyes. Others had round eyes. Small, flat noses separated high, sharp cheekbones which rose above powerful chewing muscles and strong jaws. Their faces tended more toward longness than the roundness of the Chinese. It was a visage that was rough and primitive, and belonged to an older time on earth.

There were a quarter of a million Man living in the Himalayan foothills of Burma, Laos and the Vietnams. And they had little understanding of, and even less allegiance to, any government that was less than three thousand years old.

Borjek noticed that the young Man women were slender and handsome. They wore long blue or black saronglike skirts fastened near the waist. Breasts, tipped with chocolate nipples, grew in all shapes and sizes. The men wore a *suu troany*—a long sash, pulled between their legs and tucked in at the back. The younger boys and girls were naked except for amulets made from bones and animal claws. Most adults wore their hair long in a chignon at the back of the neck.

Sareno, undecided about what to do with the priest and unable to think of any alternative, said, "Let's go to my house for some tea, and you can rest. It's beyond those last huts. The Man Lan Mien, which is what these people call themselves, do not let an outsider move into the village until he has lived nearby for several harvests. That is to ensure he does not have, or attract, bad spirits." When Borjek said nothing, Sareno continued, "It's not a bad idea, actually. It gives everyone time to see if they like each other or not. Bad spirits could be an allegory."

Borjek lifted one of his massive eyebrows.

"Not that I go along with the spirits and all, being a Baptist," said Sareno, offering a small laugh to cover the realization that he'd gotten deeper into the subject than was necessary, "but I have seen many unusual things here."

Borjek changed the subject. "Tell me about my friend Neil Treadmill and where he is."

"You say you were friends in college?"

"We knew each other."

Sareno pointed to a hut off the edge of the path. "Here's my house. I suppose it must have been the same Treadmill, but how long had it been since you'd seen him?"

Borjek stared at a miniature building of some kind on a pole about four feet tall beside the house. Damned if it isn't a tiny church, he thought. Made of bamboo, it was finished with columns and a steeple tapering into a cross.

Sareno saw his look and said, "My *kham nua phoan,* my house to the god of the land. It's there to honor the custom of building a small house to the spirits before building the permanent home. Since I am a missionary, I thought it fitting to build a church. They believe my Holy Ghost lives inside."

Borjek said, "I haven't seen Treadmill in a good many years. He went into archeology and I, uh, went into the Church. I've seen him only a few times since."

"I dare say he probably changed a great deal. Come inside."

The house was simply furnished, almost devoid of any personality. Borjek wondered if its sparseness was a deliberate deceit or a reflection of its inhabitant. The front room contained a small bamboo table with a Bible on it, a clay jug covered by a bark slab, a woodpile and a few blackened stones.

"Please sit down," said Sareno, gathering wood and making a fire on the stones. From the back room he brought out a soot-covered brass kettle and balanced it on the rocks.

Borjek sat awkwardly on the floor, the hidden carbine forcing his right leg straight out. Underneath him, the bamboo slats creaked.

Sareno prepared tea for both of them. "You don't look very comfortable. Can—"

"It's nothing. My back is a little stiff." Borjek waited until Sareno had sipped his tea before drinking his own. "About Treadmill . . . ?"

"Father Borjek, I'm terribly sorry to tell you that your friend passed on. It happened about three or three-and-a-half moons—months—ago."

Borjek looked into his cup. He was not surprised to see bits of leaf floating on the pale citrine liquid. So the bastards got him. "How did he die?"

"In sin, father. In sin." Sareno's eyes sought Borjek's, unsuccessfully.

With a woman? wondered Borjek. A heart attack at the supreme moment? A commie trap? "You mean with—"

"Yes. Without knowing Jesus Christ. I had spoken with him only the day before about being saved. He had laughed. 'Christ died for the ungodly.' Romans five: six."

"I'm curious, Reverend Sareno—"

"Call me George."

"George, exactly how did he die?"

"Poison gas, as best we can tell."

Borjek scratched his knee to dissipate his reaction.

"A strange death," Sareno continued. "It happened late of a night. Dugpas Seng, our village chief, found the body the next morning. Treadmill had died horribly in his bed."

"Are you sure it was gas?"

"We are fortunate to have a young American doctor here, Dr. Caen, and he spent several days establishing the cause. There was no doubt. The Man are quite adept at various poisons, including

14

gas. Someone blew gas into his room while he slept. I am sorry."

So, Dr. Caen is still here, thought Borjek. "I hadn't seen Treadmill in a while, and we weren't all that close. Did he leave any books, personal belongings? I think he had a sister in Cincinnati," he improvised.

"A few clothes, which were buried with him. Some scribbled notes to himself, I believe, and several books. Dr. Caen has his effects. We tried to get word to the Red Cross or someone, but communications are difficult up here . . ." The sentence trailed off long after the thought had ended. Sareno always found it awkward to talk about death. When he was an assistant pastor in Tennessee, he fretted over the emotions and platitudes surrounding funerals. Perhaps that was another reason he liked the Man: Their rituals were carefully defined and exact; the intent was clear.

"Who killed him?"

"There was no one accused," Sareno said.

"Suspects?"

Sareno sipped his tea. "Nearly everyone. Treadmill was not well liked. He was a coarse, loud, abrasive man. We all knew he was supposed to be an agent for the CIA."

A few drops of tea slid unnoticed over the lip of Borjek's cup. "Supposed to be?"

"It was so obvious he was an agent that it became clear he couldn't be. I doubt the CIA would hire anyone that inept. Dr. Caen suspected he was involved in the opium trade, possibly a middleman for someone."

Shit. To get my hands on Treadmill's neck, thought Borjek. "Who?"

"I don't know. There have been many pressures on these people. By the way, Father Borjek, please don't say anything to the Man about how Treadmill died. We gave the impression it was a natural death."

"Why?"

"We wanted to flush the killer out, but it didn't work. And we didn't want the village to move again. A violent death, such as Treadmill's would be enough cause to abandon Sop Hao and move a mile, five miles or ten miles. Nobody really wants to move. Sop Hao has been here only a little over three years as it is."

15

Borjek grunted. "So everyone thinks Treadmill died of a heart attack or something like that?"

"Oh no. Everyone knows he died of poison gas. But as long as we—we being the village chief, Dugpas Seng, myself, Doctor Caen and his woman—make it publicly known that we think he died a natural death, no one will dispute us. If we believe it and if the villagers believe it, perhaps it will become so."

Sareno poured more tea. "Tell me, father, what brings you to Sop Hao?"

Borjek plied his cover story: The Thai archbishop wanted to expand the work of the Church into Northern Laos. He, Borjek, was on a fact-finding tour to examine the susceptibility of the natives, the climate of religious thought and, frankly, the state of the competition.

Sareno listened carefully and perceived the suffering ahead. Not only did Borjek represent the international cassock conspiracy, and not only was the man possibly mentally ill, but it was hard enough working for the Lord up here without having another missionary underfoot. He thought with a familiar shame, I've only made two converts in a year. Well, honestly, only one real convert. Perhaps if this priest understood the true difficulties, the hardness of the life, the problems of reaching these people, he would seek his mission elsewhere. There was also the fear that this Catholic might make more converts than he had. Sareno heard the echo of his father's voice, "Suffer while you can, boy. Suffer while you can."

Borjek finished his explanation. "So, if you could suggest somewhere I could stay for several days, I would be grateful."

If only I hadn't been standing there when he came out of the woods, thought Sareno. "There are very few places. Treadmill's house was closed to keep the evil spirits inside. That wouldn't do." There was no way around it. "You're welcome to stay with me for a few days. I'm very busy, though . . ."

"That would be fine," said Borjek. "Where is Treadmill buried? Out of friendship, I would like to see the grave, if possible."

"Not far. Up the mountain. I was planning to go that way this afternoon to visit one of my good Baptists. I could show you."

They chatted a while longer. Sareno left once to urinate, and Borjek quickly searched the house. He found a copy of the *Baptist*

16

Missionary's Guide to Southeast Asia, a book of Chinese poetry and
four Bibles, one of which was small and white with a zipper and
the words, "In His Service George Saint Sareno" embossed in gold.
A diary, nearly filled with pinched, awkward handwriting, was
hidden under the low, wooden bed. Borjek flipped through the
diary, finding long, rambling sentences about Sareno's apparently
constant concern over his success as a missionary. In places,
Sareno-the-man wrote of a vague weariness, a personal angst
which would be answered in the next sentence by a Biblical
quotation from Sareno-the-missionary. Borjek replaced the diary.
There was no mattress on the bed, only a thin reed mat. Hanging
on the wall above the bed was a cross, handcarved from the wood of
an apple tree and polished from long handling.

They left for Treadmill's grave in the early afternoon. Borjek
walked easier now, having cached his carbine under a cinnamon
bush near Sareno's house. As they walked, Sareno explained that
mir cultivation, which the Man practiced, meant cutting and
burning the forest to provide crop land. The Man called it "eating
the forest." The trees and underbrush were cut in January and
February, during the first months of the dry season. Trees too large
to fell were girdled with axes and died before the forests were set on
fire in early May. The woods still smelled faintly of ash and fire.
The ashes supplied mineral fertilizers and the cleared field would
provide good crops for two, maybe three, years. Then the process
would be repeated.

They climbed higher on a trail which fought a losing battle with
the thick hardwood and evergreen trees. Borjek recognized rhodo-
dendrons and laurel. In the open areas, heavy underbrush crawled
over itself.

Less than a half hour later, during which Borjek reckoned they
had covered not quite a half mile, Sareno said, "Through here.
One of my flock." They ducked under a tree and stepped into a
small clearing which contained a single hut.

They stopped and Sareno spoke in the Man language, a
stuttering, single-syllable, tonal language similar to Chinese,
Tibetan and Polynesian. "There seem to be lowly and insignificant
travelers admiring the craftsmanship and beauty of this worthy

house," he said loudly. Turning to Borjek, he said, "I said, there seem—"

"I know," interrupted Borjek. "My missionary training included a course in the Man language. I caught most of what you said."

Hmmmm, thought Sareno. Rome is even more organized than I thought.

A toothless, potbellied man emerged from the house. Only his stomach itself was a round ball; the man's chest, arms and legs were thin and sinewy with age and work. "This one is inexcusably rude not to be waiting for potential guests. Clearly the many sins of my life reside in my ears." Ek Tho climbed down a bamboo ladder to the ground and greeted the men with a bow.

Borjek stepped forward, returned the bow and said in halting Man, "It is an honor for such inferior hunters as ourselves, who deserve no better than the leaves remaining after three teas, to breathe the same air as the exalted one before us."

Sareno caught himself smiling at the unexpected preciseness of the priest's greeting. The Man used specific gambits of conversation. In addition to the usual Asian tribal disdain for directness, the Man often spoke in the third person; generally, the more serious the subject, the more obscure the words.

Sareno, using his left hand, shook hands with Ek Tho, who used his right. But Ek Tho wished to be even more beneficent with the stranger. The act of shaking hands should take place to indicate welcome, but it would be presumptuous to demand that this man touch him; therefore, Ek Tho shook hands vigorously with himself. Borjek paused and also shook hands with himself.

Ek Tho was a Baptist and proud of it. His wife had joined her wretched ancestors many seasons ago, his daughters had married dullards in the next village down the Mekong, and his only son had been killed by foreigners in fighting two years ago, so Ek Tho was relieved when he found Christianity. It had started before the white Baptist came to save him. Three rainy seasons ago, Ek Tho had been walking back to Sop Hao from his fields when he saw Jesus on a piece of paper in the path. Jesus was sitting under a tree, his arms open to a group of children, his spirit streaming from his hair in golden rays. Ek Tho had been struck by the beauty of the man's face. In spite of his paleness and the length of his nose, Jesus was beautiful.

Underneath the picture were markings which Sareno later told him represented the days and months. At the bottom of the paper was a picture of the Coca-Cola. He had observed the bottle on the calendar and suspected it was an elixir to keep away the *caaks,* the demons. Then he found a Coca-Cola bottle in the muddy bank of the Mekong after the winter floods, only days before Sareno arrived in the village. Ek Tho's mind reeled from something he knew could not be coincidence: Jesus was calling him. The other Man did not understand Ek Tho's new covenant, and eventually he moved up here away from Sop Hao. He was past middle age and found the solitude agreeable. He knew the pathway to life everlasting was through Jesus Christ, affirmed by Holy Baptism in the water and signified by the Coca-Cola.

As he shook hands with himself, Ek Tho thought that something seemed familiar about this stranger who dressed in burdensome clothes and grew eyebrows as thick as chicken feathers. But he couldn't identify it.

Sareno made the introductions with a certain pride. Ek Tho was his very first convert. In fact, he had baptized Tho less than two weeks after his arrival in Sop Hao. Sareno had taken that as a sign: They would all be that easy. Only recently, in those bleak moments just before the sun rises, when neither the day nor the night is defined, had he finally admitted his ineffectiveness.

"So," said Ek Tho, "this worthy figure is another sentinel for the Lord. Baptism is surely spreading among the barbarians."

Borjek said, "A slightly different faith, esteemed one, but similar."

Ek Tho invited the men inside and seated them around a small altar, on which was a Coca-Cola bottle, a worn calendar with a picture of Jesus, and incense. The old man disappeared into the back room with the bottle. When he returned moments later, it was filled with a clear liquid and accompanied by tiny rice balls on a leaf. He handed the rice to his guests. He was humble and anxious to share the communion ceremony with his savior and his friend of the black clothes.

19

Sareno muttered in English to Borjek. "This is a little ceremony we do to reaffirm our love of Jesus."

"Whatever."

Ek Tho said, "We eat the body of Jesus" and ate his rice ball. Borjek, following Sareno, ate his.

"And now the blood of the lamb," said Ek Tho. He gulped several swallows from the Coca-Cola and gave it to Borjek. Only as the second mouthful was half-way down did Borjek realize it was not water, but liquid fire. He exploded in a coughing fit; his eyes teared up and his face flushed.

"I should have warned you," Sareno said. "Ek Tho makes a strong wine."

Afterwards, the talk settled into the vagaries of the weather and the imminent rice planting. Later, while Ek Tho was offering his guests more wine, he suddenly realized who the stranger was. The black robe was the clue. He fell prostrate before Borjek, speaking so quickly and in such muffled tones that he was unintelligible. Sareno and Borjek looked at each other.

Sareno laid his hands on Tho and spoke softly with him. When Sareno finally understood, he shook his head in perplexity. He said to Borjek, "Father, it seems this man thinks you are a god or a demon. I don't understand. He calls you 'the mushroom god.' These people, despite my efforts retain much of their animism."

Borjek was mystified.

While Tho was beseeching the phi to have mercy on his immeritorious life, he was thinking it was surely a miracle that the mushroom god, about whom he had only recently heard, was here in his home. What did it mean? Was he about to die? Had he already died? Where had he gone wrong?

Sareno, puzzled and hurt that his prize convert was falling to pieces, suggested they leave. Borjek agreed.

Sareno bid Tho goodbye and left him with a few words about calmness and peace through Jesus. Ek Tho crawled along on the floor behind them, his eyes never above their feet and his body shaking in the glory and fear of the moment.

In silence the men continued up the hill. Sareno could think of nothing to say that would explain anything. Borjek wondered if the scene had been arranged for his benefit, but that made as little sense as the apparent truth.

Clouds were forming, although they did nothing to relieve the humidity. By the time they reached Treadmill's grave, both men were wet with perspiration.

Sareno said, "There, father. In that clearing ahead. I'll stay here."

Borjek walked forward. The woods were old and thick, and the smell of plant life was so lush it was almost fetid. Ahead rose a mound of brown earth and atop it was a tiny thatched house, leaning precariously to one side. The house had begun to fall apart in the months since Treadmill had been buried because there was no one to tend the grave. Beside the house was a wooden cross.

Borjek, remembering, crossed himself. He stepped to the grave and tripped over something, almost falling on top of the little house. Regaining his balance, he looked down. There, at his feet, were another pair of feet, sticking up obscenely through the ground. Most of the flesh had rotted off, and the toe bones gleamed white.

CHAPTER III

THE WHITE DOCTOR

"MOTHERFUCKER!" said Borjek, jumping backward. What did the priest say? wondered Sareno, standing at the edge of the woods. He walked up beside Borjek. "I'm sorry. I should have said something. I didn't think about it."

The toenails that remained were long and moldy green. Several were bent and twisted into themselves, as if they had been the last to give up the struggle against death.

Borjek pointed at the feet. "Treadmill's?"

"Yes."

"Should we cover them up?"

"No. He was buried with his feet exposed so his spirit would not be angered at being imprisoned in the grave. It could thus leave at the proper time."

"Beg your pardon?" said Borjek.

"Fear is a real force in the Man's day-to-day life, as it is, perhaps less obviously, in all our lives. Treadmill was buried this way out of fear of angering his spirit. He was buried here, far away from the village, because of fear. His was an unnatural death and therefore his spirit was, and is, not at peace. Fear and dread are more than words here; they are motives."

The sun surrendered to the gathering clouds and a sudden chill dropped on the men like a discordant note in an étude.

Sareno said, "Excuse me, I must urinate."

Borjek, absorbed in the toenails and the meaning of the exposed feet, said, "Naturally. We'll pee here together. As it should be."

Sareno, startled, said, "No. That's not part of the ritual. I simply have to go. I mean, you can if you want . . ." The thought of a Catholic priest urinating on Treadmill's rotten feet terrified him. "I'll be back in a moment. Please don't urinate on Treadmill."

Borjek looked up and realized what Sareno had said. "No, I don't have to anyway." Curious, he thought, the first time I met him he was mumbling about urinating. And now, at a moment like this. Has he really been peeing all these times? Are these really Treadmill's feet? Is his spirit angry? And why the hell are his toenails green?

The day grew darker and Borjek glanced up. Heavy, low clouds covered the sky. The smell of rain was in the air. A few minutes later, as the men were headed down the mountain, Sareno explained that the clouds might not mean rain. The monsoons were almost here and the clouds appeared darker and larger each day. Higher up, where the Lahu lived, the rains were already beginning. Although its streams ran fuller, so far, Sop Hao had received only occasional sprinkles.

They passed Ek Tho's house. From within came a lonesome, soulful chant. Sareno was morose, thinking that once again he had let himself down. On meeting new people, even someone like Borjek, he was inevitably optimistic, but just as inevitably, he ended up feeling overpowered. He wanted to be like other people, to converse easily, to laugh and be spontaneous. But the truth was, he was even more alone when he was with people. He felt dull and uninteresting, and was afraid that someday someone would turn to him and say, "You're a fraud, George. You don't know nothing!"

Ek Tho's chant wound around the trees, and the tone reminded Sareno of a half-beagle, half-mutt he had grown up with, which Heziakiah had named Curtis Lee. Eventually Curtis Lee got too old and lame to run with the pack, so on frosty October nights when Heziakiah and Uncle Harley and L.C. Kenner would go fox hunting, Curtis Lee and George sat home on the stoop listening to the hunt rage across the hills. Curtis Lee would cock his head and quiver and shake with the excitement of the night. George would hold him around the neck and talk to him, but it didn't make any difference. After a while Curtis Lee couldn't stand it, and he would start calling to the rest of the dogs. "Ooooouuueee. Oooouuueee," Curtis Lee would cry in a high-pitched howl that sounded like a piece of tin being torn in half. Curtis Lee would stand there and tremble and howl and cough and shake. Sometimes, if his mother wasn't nearby, George would join in with Curtis Lee. It felt good and it felt sad. It's been a long time since I howled at night, Sareno thought.

Borjek interrupted his suffering. "I might drop by and see this Dr. Caen—to check on Treadmill's personal belongings. Where does he live?"

"Not far from me. I'll point it out."

Borjek was looking forward to meeting Caen. He knew the doctor had been a Green Beret in Viet Nam. In fact, by a coincidence, both he and Caen had served at the same camp, Gia Vuc, at different times. Caen had been there in 1968 and Borjek in 1970. Even after two years, the Jarai tribesmen talked about Caen with reverence. Borjek, who had lived a month in Gia Vuc setting up and recruiting for his assassination program, had liked the tough Jarai. They hated the Viet Cong as much as they hated the South Vietnamese. It had been Gia Vuc, and the experience of seeing up close what thirty years of war had done to a people and their countryside that finally turned Borjek against the war. The Jarai, given enough support, would have fought the VC for another thirty years, but they had become frustrated and disgusted with the lack of help from the South Vietnamese government and the constant changes in American strategies. The South Vietnamese treated the Jarai no better than savages, and the tribesmen were not about to fight the VC for the sake of Saigon. At Gia Vuc, Borjek had realized America could never win the war.

From the files, Borjek knew that Caen had been approached by the Agency when they learned he was coming to Laos two years ago. Caen had turned the offer down. The agent who talked to him wrote: "Caen is not hostile to the Agency as such. It may be a contrariness stemming from a strong belief in the independence of a man. Such an attitude may change as he matures. On the other hand, Caen appeared never to take our discussions seriously." According to Treadmill's reports, Caen had not changed his opinions.

Below them in Sop Hao, in a building twice the size of the average hut, Dr. Beauregard Cauthen Caen was preparing a surgical pack and trying to ignore a pair of teasing female hands at the same time. Sick call was finished and the dispensary needed cleaning. Bo was thirty-three years old and six feet tall, but looked as if he weighed more than his one hundred and ninety pounds. His muscled arms and broad chest made him seem more a laborer than a doctor of medicine. He wore his wavy, brown hair long and curling low behind his ears, touching the nape of his neck. His square face was creased and deeply tanned. Older, he would wear a rough, lined face. His eyes were deep brown, almost black, and the corners rose, suggesting an Indian or an oriental somewhere in his family history, although no Caen had ever admitted it, or would have. His eyes seemed cold and distant until he smiled. His mouth was slightly off center, but the effect was curiously attractive.

This afternoon, he wore cut-off fatigues and no shirt. His nipples stiffened under the soft fingertips of Sylvia Karman. She liked the game of trying to distract him. He was usually so serious about his work. Men seemed unable to move from one mood to another simply and quickly, she thought idly. They don't like to appear changeable, or perhaps they don't like to seem easily influenced, especially by a woman. Maybe it's part of the male mating dance: the chase, the aloofness, attack and retreat. Maybe it's not an act but really part of their nature. If that's true, she thought, sliding her hands across his tight stomach, I wonder how much of our sex roles is really instinctive and how much is learned.

God, his back smells good, she thought, pushing her cheek against it. Her hands drifted down his stomach to the top of his pants and tugged at the button there.

Bo muttered something, turned and grabbed her blond hair. He pulled her head back roughly and kissed her. For a moment Sylvia thought of fighting back, but instead allowed herself the pleasure of his hard body. She was not a big girl, only five feet four—but long hair, an erect posture and a large bone structure made her seem taller. She had big brown eyes and a nose that turned up perhaps a little too much. Creamy smooth skin the color of straw added to a first and lasting impression of rugged handsomeness. It was careless beauty, for it was not studied, prepared or arranged. It was the kind that comes in a few women who were not beautiful as children or even as teen-agers. Their self-image, formed when they were becoming women, is not one of glamour. Only later, and slowly, does maturing bone structure shape their loveliness. It is the type of beauty that will not fade at forty or fifty. Such women often never really believe their own radiance. It is an unself-conscious beauty, and therefore even more stunning.

Sylvia wore green fatigue pants and a white blouse. A moment later she wore only the pants. She threw her head back and felt Bo lift her by the buttocks, so that his mouth was touching her breasts. His lips encircled a nipple, and she pressed against him.

How I love this man, she thought, and these spontaneous moments of love. Sylvia remembered the first time she met him, here in Sop Hao, when she thought him self-centered and detached. Well, he was—at first. She had come to Laos as a free-lance writer, hoping to find another Dr. Tom Dooley. First, the news article to the Associated Press or United Press International. Then a longer piece with pictures for a magazine. Finally, a quick book on the man before the public forgot him. That had been the plan at least. Before this man held her in his arms for the first time six months ago. Screw a bunch of writing, she thought, giggling aloud at the image.

"Whaaah?" said Bo, his mouth full.

"Nothing. Just you, love. Don't stop."

While Sylvia held onto his neck, Bo unbuttoned his pants and let them drop. A moment later, she kicked her own pants aside. Bo shoved back his surgical packs, lifted her and sat her on the counter in front of him. He kissed her navel.

It never fails, Bo thought. The way she excites me. Each time, I think it won't be like this again. It can't be. And it always is. Is it just us? Will it fade in a year or two? Bo had never felt such desperate, overwhelming attraction, physically and emotionally, toward a woman. As a promising young student of medicine in Charleston, South Carolina, he had perfected the role of the charming, flirtatious Southern gentleman—it kept women at a psychological arm's length. If they never got close, he didn't have to worry about being hurt, or moreover, about hurting them.

All those carefully erected barriers fell like rice before the harvest knife when he met Sylvia. She ignored his defenses and his standard I-am-man-you-are-woman routines, as if they were so much chaff. In some respects, she seemed older than he, even though she was only twenty-eigh. Her personality seemed complete and intact, and her demeanor was confident and assured. For the first time with any woman, he found himself trying to deserve her approval and respect. He found himself wanting to trust her with his love.

But when she arrived in Sop Hao, Bo had been in Laos for more than a year and had touched no woman. Maybe it is only sex, he thought. Only? he asked himself. Only hell! It's incredible. His mouth caressed the soft insides of her thighs.

Sylvia opened her legs, and her hands pulled his head forward.

The dispensary door opened and Borjek stepped inside, brushing dust from his cassock.

CHAPTER IV

AN APPARITION FROM ANCIENT CHINA

I N THE dim light inside the dispensary Borjek made out a man who must be Dr. Caen, kneeling before a patient. He was giving a woman a pelvic examination and he must have terrible eyesight, decided Borjek. He's practically got his nose in it.

"I'll wait outside until you're finished, doctor," said Borjek, even as he realized that the man was naked and his nose was, in fact, in it. Good Lord, he's eating her and she's beautiful, thought Borjek, frozen by the sight.

Bo turned and said the first thing that came to mind. "Thank you. We'll be through in a moment."

Borjek made himself turn and walk outside.

Sylvia was the first to laugh. "You heard the man, finish."

Bo leaned against the counter and gave in to the absurdity of the situation. He laughed. "Did you see a priest in here?"

"Yes, and he said—very calmly I thought—that he would wait outside until we were through," she said, tucking her blouse into her pants. "I wonder who he is."

"One of my patients this morning said something about a man dressed in black. I didn't pay any attention to it." Bo buttoned his pants. "All right, Sylvia, get hold of yourself. Let's see what he wants."

Outside, Borjek was uncomfortable and uncertain about whether or not he should stay. If he left, they would know definitely that he had seen them. If he stayed, they might feel awkward, especially thinking he was a priest. The door opened.

"Dr. Caen?" asked Borjek.

"Yes?"

"I'm Father Martin Borjek. I can, uh, come back later . . ."

"No, no. Come in," said Bo. He introduced Sylvia. Borjek shook hands with her, glancing before he could stop himself at her blouse to make certain she was dressed. She looked as good dressed as naked, he thought.

Borjek said to Bo, "May I speak with you?"

"I've got to get supper ready," Sylvia said. "Good meeting you, father."

Borjek thought he saw the faintest twinkle in her eyes as she left.

"I'm a missionary passing through the area, and I'm told you have some information about the death of my old college friend, Neil Treadmill."

On impulse, Caen said, "So you're the new Agency man?"

"Agency?"

"You're here to take Treadmill's place aren't you?" Bo congratulated himself as he saw caution flicker across the man's face.

"I don't, ah . . . no." Borjek had been told to use his own discretion about breaking cover to Caen, who, as a Green Beret, had received a top-secret clearance. "However, I understand Treadmill assisted American officials with certain information about this area from time to time. He's dead and I would like to find out why, as long as I'm here."

"Are you a priest?"

"Caen, you and I both know that no white man comes to Laos without the CIA knowing about it. Tell me how Treadmill died."

Bo shrugged. "To put it simply, his lungs quit working. Respiratory arrest. He vomited, he defecated on himself, he chewed his lower lip off, and he ripped his bed to pieces. The nerves leading to his lungs were paralyzed and he suffocated. It didn't take long." Bo had expected some reaction, but Borjek only stared out from beneath those bushy red eyebrows.

"The cause of death?"

"I don't know the exact agent. The Man use poisons against animals, fish and each other. Without better laboratory equipment, I can't tell you. I think it was something he inhaled. A gas of some kind, related to the cyanide family. There was a faint odor of peaches in his lungs."

"Do you have any idea about who did it?" As he asked, it crossed Borjek's mind that Caen himself might well be capable of murder.

"I figure either the CIA or the Chinese."

"Why?"

29

"Even though many local people were afraid of Treadmill, few hated him enough to kill him with poison, which is an extreme act of violence for the Man. Those that may have hated him enough to kill him had alibis. I know that Treadmill was involved in opium smuggling, but I'm not sure exactly how. Some was going into Burma and Thailand and some into China, I think. If the Chinese found out he was a spy, why kill him? He was more valuable in place, as long as they knew who he was. If they didn't know he was a spy, why kill him? The CIA might have killed him if he wasn't supposed to be handling opium or if they thought he had double-crossed them. Maybe he had a falling out with the Burmese bandits or the Corsicans."

Borjek stared at the dirt floor. Something was still missing. "How did you get along with him?"

"Not well. He tended to bully people. Not me so much, because we didn't cross paths often, but he intimidated the Man."

"Did Treadmill leave any letters, notes?"

Bo opened a cabinet and handed over a small stack of papers tied together. "How long—"

The door opened and an apparition from ancient China, or perhaps Tibet, shuffled in. The man was small, no more than five feet tall, but because he was stooped, he appeared even smaller. He was old; no one really knew how old, but it was rumored that he remembered when Hong Xiu quan, who proclaimed himself the younger brother of Jesus Christ, tried to overthrow the Manchu dynasty in the 1860s. Hong's army had finally been beaten when the British and French supported the Manchus. In return, Peking opened eleven new ports and gave missionaries freedom of movement in China.

The man had long white hair pulled together in back, which fell past his shoulders. His nose was flat, and his stubby, black-lacquered teeth were set in a brown basket of wrinkles. But it was the shiny black eyes that held one's attention: The eyes of a five-year-old seeing snow for the first time; the eyes of an old man who knows his death is near; the eyes of a woman who has known many men. The eyes of a genius or a madman: Large, black irises with no discernible pupils surrounded by clear, white corneas.

The man bowed and said in lilting Man, "Good afternoon,

excellent doctor of men. The mildewed years of this one's dotage are to be blamed for this ungracious interruption."

Caen said, "Not at all, *kunag*." "Kunag" was the Man word encompassing reverence, respect and age. "You are always welcome as long as you can ignore the shoddiness of my dispensary. This is Father Martin Borjek. Dugpas Seng, village chief and kunag of us all in Sop Hao."

Seng bowed again. "Welcome to our austere and inelegant village, *thay mo* Borjek." "Thay mo" was the Man word for a religious leader and it was interchangeable with sorcerer.

"Thank you, kunag. The austerity of your village is but another word for hard-working farmers, and elegance is a quality unknown to my ancestors. I am honored." Borjek returned the bow.

Seng noticed the thay mo staring at his teeth, and almost said aloud, With my teeth and your eyebrows, we could make a fine demon, a fine caak. Although Seng's teeth had been filed down and lacquered in the faraway Yun-ling mountains decades ago, most of the young men and women of the Man still went through the rites. Filed-down teeth represented man's civilization. Animals have long, white, pointed teeth; men, being more than animals, do not. The lacquer was further evidence that a man was a civilized being, and it represented a certain degree of status in his village.

Seng remembered when his parents told him it was time for the *tam sur puk jook,* the rite of puberty. At that time his family lived in western China near Wei-hsi on the side of a mountain so steep that the long winters were filled with the constant rumblings of avalanches. Seng had been thirteen and his stomach felt like he had swallowed a bowl of chestnuts. His village chief had placed a piece of wood across his lower teeth while his upper teeth were grated, chipped and filed down with a rock. None of his teeth broke during the day-long ordeal, and that was a sign of good luck. The blood and bits of teeth were washed out and the stumps covered with a black gum made from the krae, than, hot, and nghik nheng plants. The lacquer also helped numb the raw nerves. Even so, he could eat or drink nothing for three days, and he could take no food that was hot or cold for weeks afterwards. Seng remembered his father was proud that he had shown no emotion during the rites. He had brought honor to the family.

So long ago and so far away, Seng thought. He tucked away the memory of himself as a young boy in China.

"Thay mo Borjek," said Seng, "this evening I am preparing a meal of miserable and skinny rat, and bananas mixed with rice. Sharing it with you would enhance the pleasure of the meal, if not the taste."

"I will be honored, kunag, if the inhospitality of my short-sightedness in not paying a visit to you earlier can be overlooked."

Caen listened to the exchange, now almost certain that Borjek was a CIA agent because of his knowledge of the Man language—a language so remote it could only be learned from someone who spoke it. Seng surely knew the instant Borjek had arrived in Sop Hao, and Caen wondered if Seng had set up this meeting to find out why.

"Are you one of Thay Mo Sareno's followers?" asked Seng, eyes bright.

"Not exactly, kunag. I am a Catholic and he is a Baptist."

"Which one of you does your God believe in?"

After wondering whether Dugpas was teasing him, Borjek the missionary said, "Both, kunag."

"It is said that one wishing to become an elephant must learn first to eat with his nose. You already speak our language. Most of the villagers are preparing the fields for the planting which begins soon."

Borjek hesitated only a moment. "Would an extra pair of admittedly unskilled hands serve any purpose?"

"Most certainly," said Seng.

Caen smiled at the laying down and acceptance of terms. Back home in South Carolina, there had been a similar subtlety in conversations. The most obvious example was "Come go with me," which meant, "I'm leaving now." It was a softer, gentler way of announcing a departure that did not literally mean "come go with me." Possibly, it was a way of not offending someone, but, it was also a code, a way of identifying a person from one's own area. If a stranger knew the words and their nuances, it was a mark in his favor. It also offered at all times a face-saving mechanism. Much like the Man.

Seng asked Caen, "How was the health of the people today?"

"Good for the most part, kunag. Thoan came in, and his foot is healing well. Your suggestion about the juice of the thistle was excellent. The cut is closing rapidly. Kho's pregnancy is progressing and good spirits are in her."

Seng came to the dispensary several times a week to talk about the villagers' health. Often he would make suggestions or explain in his roundabout fashion how the old remedies worked. Caen long ago had stopped dismissing the herbal medicines as superstition. In fact, now he tried virtually everything Seng suggested. Caen was cataloging the plants, the preparations, the dosages and the results in hopes of a book. One of his major concerns when he came to Sop Hao had been how to purchase what then seemed to be the enormous amounts of drugs needed for his practice. Now, he bought through messengers and occasional visitors only dressings, instruments, certain antibiotics and a few of the more important drugs for diseases like tuberculosis and leprosy.

Caen said, "Kunag, I've had some further thoughts about our talk the other day concerning the *epa gie,* the measuring of the bamboo." Several days before, Seng and Caen had been discussing measuring, an ancient way of divining the truth. A stick would be cut to the exact length of a man's arm. Then the stick would be held beside his arm while he answered questions. Whenever the stick grew longer, the man was lying. If the stick remained the same length, the man was telling the truth.

"It seems to me that when a man lies, he involuntarily tenses, so his muscles contract, which would make the stick longer. The fact that the man knows he is being tested aggravates his nervousness."

Seng rocked gently back and forth. "It is said that every tree grows in two directions. Is your observation a contradiction of the belief that the spirits make the stick longer? Or that the spirits cause the man's arm to become tighter?"

Caen grinned. "Some men must take two steps to another's one. No, kunag, there is no contradiction."

Borjek, listening to the conversation, felt a curious thing: nascent respect for the old man with the white pigtailed hair. Rarely in his life had Borjek experienced an emotion akin to deference, especially on the first meeting. Strangers he usually received with reserve—even arrogance—barely concealed. Borjek recognized his own arrogance and had never been particularly displeased by it. Part of him knew it was protective coloration he used until he determined the degree of threat strangers posed. Another part of him knew it was conceit, based on a conviction, rarely challenged, that most people offered little that was new, exciting or interesting. Had he a close friend, Borjek would have admitted his own arrogance and might have described it as a fault, for even that admission concealed its own hubris.

Borjek looked at the old man and wondered if they would become friends.

CHAPTER V

THE FLIGHT OF THE WILD CHICKENS

THE monsoons began the next morning before dawn, and Dugpas Seng woke when he heard the drumming on his thatched roof. He went outside in the dark and stood naked in the unseen downpour, feeling the drops dancing on his skin and washing away the dust of the dry season. He willed his body and mind to sense the harmony of the rain. At the changing of each season, Seng took time to be alone with the weather and the spirits. It was his own private ritual.

Later, when it was light, he would meet the western sorcerers at their hih and lead them to the fields. Seng was pleased that these tall, hairy ones were adding their labors to the growing of the crops. It made the Man less wary, and no doubt exhausted any restless spirits which might hover around the white men. He wondered how long the bushy-eyebrowed one would be here, and if he was really a thay mo. At supper the night before, he had seemed friendly enough—except for a few moments when he had detected a rat's tail in the soup. But the stranger had a curious restraint in his character. At times it gave him an air of self-confidence; other times it separated him from people. Seng could not tell, yet, if the attitude was imposed from within or without the man's nature. Seng had suggested Borjek work in the large mir, the field which fed the old ones with no families and those who had no spouses or who were sickly. This mir also grew the extra vegetables which would become part of the village wealth. They would be traded with other tribes for tobacco, salt and spices.

Bo Caen and Sylvia Karman were up early to prepare the dispensary for sick call. Three days a week they opened their doors for the sixty-some residents of Sop Hao. The other days they—for Sylvia now went along—went to surrounding communities. The

35

general health of the Man was good, possibly better than the Montagnards with whom Caen had lived in Viet Nam. The Montagnards had suffered from too much contact with GIs, half-trained medics and bullets. Here tuberculosis, malaria and leprosy were endemic, but even with no hospitals and few doctors, the fit indeed had survived.

By the time the people of Sop Hao were on the way to their fields, the hard paths had dissolved into mud. Some went to the rice paddies, to ensure that the ditches and bamboo pipes were carrying the water. They would also prepare the paddies to receive the young seedlings, which had been tended in special gardens for the past month. Others went to the fields around the village and farther up the mountain. They would be planting corn with smaller crops of peas, potatoes, peppers, cucumbers and manioc. Later on, the other crops, including a variety of dry rice, would be planted. The opium would not be planted for another month, for the best sap came from plants sown in the first new moon of the rains, plants that would not mature until the first chill of autumn.

Borjek, wearing faded green pants and a black shirt loaned to him by Sareno, was already soaked from the rain which fell steadily from a blotched sky. As he trudged along in the mud to the fields, he thought about his supper with Seng last night. Not about the meal, for it had indeed been rat and every bit as miserable as Seng had predicted, but about their conversation. Seng had told him that a villager named Aung Ne Swe, who lived in a hog pen, had witnessed several people moving about Sop Hao late the night Treadmill was killed, but had not recognized them. Seng also had revealed that Treadmill used the threat of airplanes to compel the growing of more opium. Even though American bombers had officially withdrawn from Indochina, Thai spy planes still flew. And the memories of the bombings, which had stopped less than three years before, were still raw. Last season, Sop Hao had grown more opium and less rice than ever before. Only several paddies of wet rice had been cultivated.

After the supper, Borjek secretly visited Caen's dispensary and found a notebook half-filled with notes on how to prepare and use various poisons. Borjek had copied several pages:

Hsi hsin plant: Similar to wild ginger. An emetic, diuretic, diaphoretic. Side effects include high blood pressure, increased heart rate, stomach bleeding.

Yuan hua plant: Lilac daphne, related to laurel. Strong irritant. In large doses will constrict larynx; death by suffocation.

Hsu sui tze plant (caper spurge): A laxative? In large doses, death?

Peach stones *(Oleum persicarum)*, amygdalin: Prussic acid. Death by paralysis of the phrenic nerves.

Cong tree sap mixed with red pepper: Death within minutes. Antidote: Frog and chicken defecation?

Do: A powder made from ground tiger whiskers and other secret ingredients. Death by vomiting, anal bleeding and cyanosis. Antidote?

No-name poison: Made from cam tree resin, red pepper, centipede teeth and snake teeth. Death within minutes. No antidote known.

The list had gone on. So, Borjek had thought, Dr. Beauregard Caen knows a great deal about native poisons.

Borjek had also gone over Treadmill's notes and had learned little. One notebook had a series of figures, some with dollar signs, some without. But he had used a private code, and Borjek was unable to decipher it. Treadmill had also written several disjointed sentences about the "strange powers," as he called them, of Dugpas Seng. One section read: "Tibetan power. Magic knife. Seng. Burmese $55."

They reached the mir and Seng stepped to its center to celebrate the first day of planting with benedictions. When the ceremonies ended, the people set about to clear the field of accumulated branches and weeds.

Several hours later, as they reached for the same half-buried limb, Borjek met Law Dorje Oo. Oo was short, even for a Man. He was five feet tall and slim, with muscles so hard and tight that each seemed to contain its own bundle of energy. Oo wore his hair shorter than the other young men, almost in an American style. His face suggested that one or more of his ancestors was Chinese: it was rounder, the Mongolian fold more pronounced, and his skin was a lighter brown than most of the Man.

At first glance Borjek thought Oo a teen-ager until he remembered that these people changed little physically until they were about forty years old. It was as though the brutal, life-long struggle to survive kept their bodies young, even handsome, until their children could marry and attend to them. Then age irrupted, hard and fast. Men and women were old at forty-five, elders at fifty and ancient at sixty. Borjek reckoned Oo was between twenty-five and thirty-five. His eyes seemed more devious and hostile than those of the other villagers. Or was it that Oo would not look him straight in the eyes? His glance fell away constantly, as if he were nervous or constantly checking out the surroundings.

"Felicitations, tall one," said Oo.

"Thank you. The rains are indeed here," answered Borjek.

"It is hard to dispute such a shrewd observation."

Oo had seen the stranger in the field and had pointed his toes toward him. He wanted to meet the new thay mo, to see if this one offered anything more substantial than the gaunt one. It is, he thought, an indication of a lack of empathy when white people send someone the size of Sareno and this man to my country. Don't westerners have any normal-sized people? More likely, he realized, they permit only the large ones to come in order to intimidate other people. Oo remembered that for most of his youth, he was plagued and bullied by Nawng, the older and obtrusive brother of a girl named Pang. Nawng always threatened to beat him up, and Oo never knew why. The only incident remotely deserving such enmity was once when Oo, trying to win Pang's attention, showed her a foot he had cut off a dead monkey. He had left several of the tendons exposed so when he pulled on them, the tiny toes would curl into a fist, as if alive. He lured Pang aside and proudly showed her his monkey foot, but instead of marveling at his cleverness she screamed and fled to Nawng. Oo had been humiliated by misjudging her reaction as well as by the beating Nawng gave him. Pang later married a one-eyed man from another village and moved away. Nawng had been tragically swept away by the spring floods of the Mekong several seasons earlier. He had been fishing when out of nowhere there must have sprung a wind so strong that it toppled not only him but the large rocks attached with vines to his feet into the river.

After they exchanged several more sentences as colorless as the rain, Oo asked, "How do you propose to win these people to your faith, thay mo?"

Borjek was being forced into playing a role he had not imagined would be necessary. He had accepted the idea of pretending to be a priest without imagining actually being one. He improvised: "By allowing the word of God to become an example, a standard operating procedure, uh, a path without diversion in everyday life. By setting myself as His humble servant."

Oo kicked at a rock. In spite of Borjek's response, he sensed something more than the blind piety which covered Sareno's liturgies like mold. "It is easier to alter the course of the Mekong than to illuminate the minds of savages," said Oo, deliberately using the derogatory Laotian word, *kha,* meaning savages, outcasts, hill people. "Sometimes I despair of being able to educate these people to fight against their enemies." Oo had said more than he intended. This big man seems to draw out words, he thought. It's almost as if I were trying to gain his approval. Oo realized he was still trying to get Pang to look at his monkey's foot, and he knew not what to do about it.

Borjek said carefully, "Who might their enemies be?"

"It is no crime in Laos to be a Communist," said Oo with an expression Borjek interpreted as either defensiveness or self-righteousness. Oo switched to English, for the words he wanted to say had no equivalent in Man. "Rightism and imperialism are enemies to all people."

The English surprised Borjek. This little dwarf has learned English and that Marxist pap somewhere. Perhaps he knows something about Treadmill's death. "I met Treadmill in passing several years ago and I am curious about his demise."

Oo glanced around them. They were alone. I wonder where this one's course leads. Let him hoe the first row. "I, too, have been unable to quench a moderate thirst," said Oo.

"It is said he may have been assisted into the upper realms."

"Ki, ki, ki. Even the cobra enters its own den cautiously. It is also said that from time to time Treadmill secured an interest in several local crops." Even as he said it, Oo berated himself for his weakness in appearing to know something about everything.

Borjek picked up another wet limb. "Does your far-reaching knowledge encompass details of his death?"

"I was engaged in more pleasant pursuits on the night in question."

"Perhaps you could cast light on his ill-concealed bartering?"

Oo finally got himself under control. "My wisdom in that area is comparable to the fullness of the wine jug following the Festival of the Dragon Boat." He scooped up a handful of dirt. "Taste it."

"What? Taste what?" asked Borjek, leaning back.

"The soil. Here. One can taste how good the dirt is for certain crops such as *ty fong ki,* the plant of dreams. The soil is rich in, I think the word is, limestone, and you can taste the sweetness."

Borjek gingerly touched his tongue to the dirt. It tasted like a burnt potato skin. "Ah, yes. Sweet."

So you tall ones can learn from us, Oo thought. It was an odd mix of feelings that he experienced around white men. He disliked their attitudes of superiority, their basic barbarian nature, their bluntness and coarseness. At the same time, he was a little awed by their descriptions of their native countries and by the fact that they all seemed to be able to read.

As the morning wore on, Oo and Borjek continued working near one another. Borjek learned that Oo was about thirty years old and born in Sop Hao. Of course, the village had moved many times since then. Oo said nothing about his parents except to suggest they were both dead. Apparently he had been away from the village many times in recent years. Studying, he said. Oo also mentioned a girl named Tanna-li.

Before he rejoined the others, Oo asked, "Do you know about the Coca-Cola?"

"Yes."

"And?"

"And what?" Does he want a Coke? Then Borjek remembered Ek Tho and the communion bottle. "The Coca-Cola is one of the spirits of God, I suppose. Many believe that through the Coca-Cola, they will find peace."

Oo wandered away with a reminder to himself to keep an eye on this thay mo, in spite of the Coca-Cola routine.

As Borjek rubbed sore back muscles, he wondered why Sareno

pushed Coca-Cola. Of course, the man is from the South and Southerners drink more soft drinks than anybody. Maybe the Baptists own stock in Coca-Cola.

Later, during one of his self-imposed rest periods, Borjek watched the planting of the seeds which had begun now that the field was clear. One man marked parallel lines from west to east in the field. Another walked behind him and poked holes in the soil about a foot apart. Women followed next, dropping seeds through hollow bamboo tubes into the holes.

Sareno, sitting down beside him, said, "This is the second season for this mir. There won't be many weeds, yet. But there are no tools to turn the earth after the harvest, so next year we'll have to do some weeding." He spoke as if the field were his own.

"I met a man named Oo a while ago," said Borjek. "Out of curiosity, I wonder if you know what he was doing the night of Treadmill's death?"

An unidentifiable emotion, perhaps anger or pain, crossed Sareno's face. He started to say something then coughed. "He didn't kill Treadmill." He walked away quickly.

By lunch the rains had slackened to a drizzle. Borjek ate rice, which had been pressed into a tight ball, and jackfruit, compliments of Seng.

It was not long after lunch when they heard the plane, high above the clouds. Everyone stopped and looked upward, even though there was nothing to see. Borjek immediately recognized the deep throbbing of a U-2 spy plane. It must be about three or four miles up, he thought. It was headed west to east so it was going somewhere above Phong Saly province, maybe over eastern Yunnan. The unmarked planes were assigned to the Royal Thai Air Force and flown by Thais and Americans who were on leave from the U.S. Air Force. The Man remembered when, not long ago, planes had carried payloads of 1000-pound bombs and napalm. But this plane passed invisibly and harmlessly overhead.

Suddenly, a noise erupted from the woods a few yards beyond Borjek. Something was fighting its way through the brush. Borjek, his reflexes conditioned from Viet Nam, dove to the mud and cursed the fact that he had brought no weapon except his sheath knife. From out of the forest came a flock of flying chickens, leaner

41

and more ragged than ordinary chickens. As they burst through the trees and mist, they fanned out in a flight covering a fourth of the mir, heading toward Borjek, who stared at them in amazement. They flew only three or four feet above the ground and made a loud flapping noise. With legs tucked flat against their stomachs, they buzzed the field, setting up a raucous squawking. Then they banked in a tight circle and flew back into the forest, never once touching down. To Borjek the chickens' flight pattern seemed strangely coordinated, even planned.

Borjek picked himself up and slapped at the mud on his clothes. The Man were already back at work, oblivious to the episode, when Borjek walked over to Sareno.

"What was that?" he asked.

"That's our herd of flying wild chickens. I imagine the noise from the plane scared them. You'll have to watch out for them when you're in the woods. Sometimes they'll frighten you."

"I've never heard of wild chickens before."

"They weren't wild originally. They were Dugpas Seng's flock for many years. Dugpas grew tired of caring for them, or maybe he hated to keep them cooped up, so he set them free about a year ago. He took them into the woods and told them they were on their own."

While he talked, Sareno pulled a small red tin from his pocket. He opened it and rubbed his index finger in a poppy-red salve. "Want some?" He offered it to Borjek, while smearing the salve under his nose.

Borjek stared at the tin.

"It's only Tiger Balm. Most everyone uses it for headaches, to clear the nose, ease muscle soreness and to keep evil spirits away. I started using it to appease local customs, but I've grown fond of it."

Borjek shook his head. "Are the chickens considered spirits?"

"No. Just chickens. After Dugpas set them free, they learned how to fly again from necessity. They roost in the tops of cedar trees at night. Sometimes early in the mornings, you'll see an entire tree come alive with dozens of chickens flying down from it. They get up there by jumping and flying from limb to limb. They can't fly very high off the ground, but they've got good distance. I saw some soar about half a mile one day."

Borjek listened to the explanation with suspicion. These people must think I'll believe anything, he thought. Flying wild chickens, my ass. Those birds came out of that forest in formation, turned on cue and went right on with a mission. Carrier chickens, maybe. They could be carrying messages or training to deliver bombs. They had a look of intelligence in their eyes, he thought. I must not underestimate these Man. Or their chickens.

While he worked that afternoon, Borjek mentally listed the murder suspects. Dugpas Seng was a mild possibility. He hadn't liked Treadmill and had admitted that as village chief, he felt Treadmill was disrupting the life of Sop Hao. Caen was a possibility because he distrusted the Agency and he knew more than he revealed about poisons. There was something odd about Oo in spite of Sareno's statement that he didn't kill Treadmill. Sareno, himself, rounded out the list of locals. There was still the outsider theory: Laotian intelligence, Red Chinese, other revolutionaries, the stranger in the night.

One man he needed to see was Aung Ne Swe, the man who lived with hogs, who said he had seen someone the night Treadmill was killed.

CHAPTER XI

DR. CAEN VISITS CHIAO SIN

T HE morning fog flowed around the ridges, creeping through the gaps and sliding downward, as if it were about to pour into the valleys. It seemed heavy and sullen until one walked into it and found the clouds were cool, moist illusion. Bo remembered that later in the rainy season the fog would burn off by noon. Now, however, it rose and fell slowly during the day, disappearing reluctantly for a few hours under the rains.

Bo and Sylvia had left Sop Hao at sunrise with four teen-age boys. If the rains held off, they would be in Chiao Sin by mid-morning. The village was less than five miles away, and the path wound around hills so magnificent that their beauty would have curled the finest Chinese handscroll with jealousy. Ridges so sheer they were rumored to have been formed by single axe strokes soared as much as a half-mile over three hundred yards horizontally. Tumbling rivers of ice water, born of glaciers in the area called Kam on the eastern edge of high Tibet, had sliced gorges into this limestone plateau through the centuries. The name Kam itself meant "land of deep corrosions." It was the hump over which American C-47's had climbed in the final desperate years of World War II to carry supplies from Calcutta to Chung-king.

When the sun had reached the height of a young jujube tree, Bo called a break. Sylvia, looking like an awkward and errant boy with her hair tucked into a cloth cap, dropped to the ground and lifted her feet to rest against a tree. Bo sprawled out beside her.

"Do you think it's all going to start again?"

"Because of Borjek?"

"Yes."

"I don't know. It might. It got pretty hectic before Treadmill died. Seng was upset; the villagers were nervous. Then after he was killed, things eventually returned to normal. Now Borjek is here. General Yone-fu is out of the Rangoon jail, and Seng said Su-wen of the Kuomintang was seen near the Mekong a couple weeks ago. My guess is they're scurrying to line up opium contracts for the fall."

"How did it all get started?"

Bo turned the pages of his memory back to his Special Forces training for Indochina. "These countries were part of the French empire, and the cost of running them got out of hand in the early 1900s. It was the French colonial administrators who encouraged the growing of opium to raise taxes and to line their own pockets. These mountains have the perfect climate and soil for opium. It's always been grown here, originally for medicine and an occasional smoke. When World War II broke out, France put the squeeze on to raise money to support her army. The Meo, the Burmese hill people and the Man were all encouraged to grow poppies. The French government made money by taxing the crop and acting as middleman in its marketing. Then the colonies saw that an oriental nation, Japan, could fight white men. They grew restless, and France found herself sending legionaires to keep the locals in line. Once again, opium grown by the people financed the armies that kept the French here. I guess it was sometime in the early 1950s that world opinion and discontent within France forced the government to officially dump the handling of opium. But they simply turned it over to the Deuxieme, their intelligence people, who in turn, gave the franchise to the Corsican criminal underground."

"Why?" asked Sylvia, turning to lean on one elbow facing Bo.

"A political debt. The Corsicans helped the Allies in World War II. They were part of the French Resistance. They supplied information about Italy to the Allies and played a major role in the liberation of Marseille. That's why they've been able to operate, virtually at will, in the Asian and European heroin traffic."

"Weird, isn't it?" said Sylvia.

"If you think that's weird, get this: When Chiang Kai-shek was chased off the mainland in 1949, the CIA got in a panic and thought the yellow hordes would sweep all of Asia, so they sent agents into Burma and French Indochina to organize resistance. One way they paid their recruits was to handle the transportation of the opium crop. And they still do today."

"You mean our government is encouraging opium growing?"

"Not directly. But the effect is the same. Typically, the CIA offered to give villagers rice and guns, and to market their opium if they would help us spy on China or fight the Pathet Lao or the VC."

"Unreal. It all seems artificial. The Man are just farmers and family people."

"I know. The Lao state didn't exist until 1953, when the French arbitrarily drew the borders. Before that, all of Laos, Cambodia, part of Thailand and Viet Nam were considered French Indochina. There are more Laotians in Thailand—nearly three million—than there are in Laos. The original kingdom of Laos was called 'Phya Sam Sene Thai,' which means 'Land of three hundred thousand Thai,' and it included northern Laos and most of northern Thailand. But the real artificiality is not so much the boundaries, but the government, at least in the past. After France gave Laos its independence, it talked the United States into taking over the financial support of the Laotian government. Until three years ago, every man in this government got his salary, ultimately, from us. We spent close to a billion dollars in Laos from 1955 to 1974, propping up various regimes, buying airplanes and paving a few roads and a lot of airstrips."

"A billion dollars for two and a quarter million people. And of those, probably only fifty thousand live in the cities. The rest are lucky to have seen even a can of food, much less a paved road."

"Time to go," Bo said, standing.

Sylvia groaned and held her hands up to him. He pulled her up and the movement turned into the embrace she had anticipated.

A moment later the boys ran up to them. One of them, Pakse, oldest son of Tsao and Sou-ei, said, "Are you sure it is safe?" All morning the boys had talked of a strange howling they had heard in Sop Hao last night, halfway between darkness and sunrise. The creature sounded fearsome. The boys said the noise was not like that of any animal they knew.

Bo said, "The demon would not follow us in the daylight. It

might be a panther which sounds like no living creature when it is mating."

Pakse nodded and rushed into an argument about whose turn it was to carry the footlocker.

Two hours later they came to a clearing on the side of a hill, and Chiao Sin was before them, nestled in a grassy plain fringed with mountains. It was not a proper valley but a bowl of flatland well over a mile high. Thatched huts blended into one corner of the plain near them. A half-dozen buffalo grazed slowly and a little boy, who looked no more than five or six, sat on one's back, switching lazily at flies.

Bo automatically compared these idyllic mountain villages with the Vietnamese refugee hamlets he had worked in during the war. That was in 1968, when the number of refugees was estimated at between two and three million, out of a total population of only sixteen million. In America, that same percentage would represent twenty-five or thirty-five million. Bo's Viet Nam training program had praised the refugee programs: "Relocated villages concentrate population so that indigenous personnel can be protected from guerrilla infiltration and propaganda, as well as from overt hostile actions. Furthermore, the logistical problems of feeding and clothing the Vietnamese people can be handled more efficiently through the relocated-hamlet concept."

Logistics, Bo thought. That's what it had boiled down to in the end. How to count the number of people in camps, regardless of the fact that they were forced into them at gunpoint. How to feed them, regardless of the acres of rice paddies and gardens they had been forced to abandon. How to win their loyalty to the South Vietnamese government, regardless of the fact that the government was as cratered with corruption as the land was with bombs. Five hundred to a thousand people had been crammed into a few acres of worthless land. No gardens, no trees, no rivers. And the Army seemed surprised at Bo's reports of low morale; of suicide, which had nearly been unheard of, previously, in the rural population; of old men who fled at night from their new homes to return to the forests.

The favorite analogy of the Army brass was, "If we take the sea away from the fish, the fish cannot live." Bo came to realize they were right, only the fish weren't the Viet Cong, but the villagers. Without their homes, their fields and their burial grounds, they could not live.

After months of heartbreaking disappointment ("Sorry, Captain Caen, the barbed wire is there to keep the Viet Cong out; the people can't leave because they might be abducted by the VC") and frustrating red tape ("We realize these people have their own burial traditions, but we've got to store twenty-five tons of napalm somewhere"), Caen finally obtained a transfer to a Special Forces team at Gia Vuc. There, in villages almost identical to the one now before him, Bo fell in love with the people who lived on the slopes of the Chaine Annamitique. Their tribal names were aboriginal: T'in, Ngeh, So, Hre, Alak, Hroi, Ho Koho, Rengao, Stieng and dozens more. A mixture of Malaysian, Chinese, Tibetan, Mongol and Indian, they inhabited the mountains from Pakistan to China and their lives in most ways were as they had been a thousand years before.

Gia Vuc was also the camp, Caen remembered with bitter sadness, where he killed his first person. A baby. The mother was named Anha and lived in Ba To, a tiny cluster of houses ten miles up the rocky Song Be river from Gia Vuc. Bo had been able to visit her only a few times during her pregnancy because the Viet Cong held the mountaintops. She was a strong, beautiful Jarai woman with high, handsome breasts and full hips. The villagers had clucked proudly and predicted she would be a good mother. She was seventeen, and the child would be her first.

She had been healthy—the chestnut tinge to her hair meant a deficiency of Vitamin A, but that was common among the mountain people—healthy until her eighth month, when Bo found her sick with fever, painful and frequent urination, and pain in her side. Bo was as sure as he could be without blood tests that it was bacteriuria. Her term was nearly up, and Bo was afraid she would develop acute pyelonephritis, which would be fatal to the baby. He gave her sulfadiazine and made sure she understood how to take it.

Her village was excited by her round stomach. The local astrologer performed daily spells for a boy child. The young men and nearly all of the old were gone, so the birth of a boy would be a special joy. And Ba To desperately needed something to celebrate.

On Army charts it was crosshatched, a disputed area. The village had been moved four times within a year: twice by the Americans to get it closer to their camp, and twice after the Viet Cong burned it down. The crops lay dying in the fields, which had been flayed by bombs. The VC wanted the food, so American jets attacked the paddies with five-hundred-pound bombs, high explosive and napalm. The rice was finally beaten into submission. When Bo was there, Ba To huddled on a barren hillside among the rocks and rattans.

Bo saw Anha's birth by coincidence. He was accompanying a search-and-destroy patrol to a village near hers when he remembered that her time was close. He found her in a bamboo thicket outside the village, as was the custom. She was silent during the birth, for her mother had taught her well. The delivery was uncomplicated, and Bo knew he must only watch. The midwife handed the baby to her and cut the umbilical cord with a knife used only for births. It was a boy. Anha smiled and pressed the baby to her full and ready breasts. Within moments Bo knew what was wrong. He also knew that there was nothing he could do about it.

He had smiled back, praying she would mistake the tears in his eyes for happiness. The baby was jaundiced. Horribly, blotched yellow. And he made no noise.

A few days later word came to Gia Vuc that Anha's baby had died. The village suffered grievously, for it was the first male born in nearly a year. Two water buffalo, a third of the collective wealth of Ba To, had been sacrificed.

Bo had run the scene through his mind so many times it was like an endless tape recording. He had forgotten five minutes from a lecture in his junior year at medical school. Sure, he had told himself, he hadn't planned to go into obstetrics, but that didn't help; his degree said doctor of medicine. He had forgotten two underlined passages from a medical text: Never give a sulfonamide to a pregnant woman in the last three weeks of her term. The sulfur interferes with the fetus' liver function and allows bilirubin, a poison, to enter its bloodstream unchecked. It had flowed with the blood through the body and into the brain, destroying it. The baby had had no mind.

49

That was one reason Doctor Beauregard Caen was now standing on a hillside in Laos. He knew he could never bring back a life, never atone for a death, but knowing that and ignoring it did not follow.

"Hey, move it," said Sylvia. "It's beautiful, but we got a lot of folks to see."

She dodged as Bo tried to bite her on the ear. The boys giggled because the Man gesture for affection was a snort behind the ear. Clearly, this big man liked the girl, even as pale as she was.

Bo carefully checked the trail leading to Chiao Sin as they picked their way down the hillside. When involved in certain religious ceremonies, this village hung a monkey skin from a tree so it swung across the pathway, barring nonresidents as well as malevolent phi. There were no special signs today.

On the porch of his house, with his face set in a frown that Bo knew was perpetual, was Me Dong Tau-oi, the village chief. His skin was a dusky minium which stretched taut across his stomach. He had no teeth, and wore his long hair matted with an oil from the chaulmoogra plant. Bo told Sylvia to set up the medicines and begin treatments while he spoke with Tau-oi.

Inside, after the tea had been served and the formalities concluded, Tau-oi said, "*Dalam* Caen, it is said that after a long and especially excellent reign in the heavens, the mushroom god has descended to earth even to the exact vicinity of Sop Hao. Is it true that his eyebrows could nest three motmots and a great white owl as well?"

"Mushroom god?"

"The Lahu say he descended from the clouds some nights ago. Only phi or rain falls from the sky. He is said to dress in black and to have no hair upon his head."

"Borjek? You must mean a man we call Borjek."

Tau-oi nodded.

"He, ah, seems fine, although he calls himself a thay mo, a man of religion, not a mushroom god." What else were the villagers saying about Borjek? Where else had he been seen?

Tau-oi leaned over and spat a long string of betel nut juice between the floor slats.

Outside the house, the people gathered around Sylvia with

50

giggling anticipation. The visits of the dalam and his woman were great social occasions. Which medicines they dispensed, what they said, what they wore and what advice they gave to whom would be the ingredients of arguments and discussions for weeks.

Sylvia had arranged the medicines in the order Bo preferred. She examined and treated minor ailments such as earaches, cuts and bruises, ringworm, burns, colds, and ordinary fevers. Anything that looked more serious, she left for Bo.

While she coaxed an elderly woman into allowing peroxide and water to be squirted into an ear choked with wax, Sylvia recalled how her hands trembled the first time Bo had asked her to help him. She had been in Sop Hao less than a week and was in the dispensary, shooting pictures of Bo, when they brought in Pakse, one of the boys helping them today. He had slashed a deep cut in his leg, nearly to the bone, while harvesting rice. Sylvia had never seen so much blood, and all she could think was, His life is flowing out. How can there be that much blood? He's dying. She had wanted to leave, to not be there, to not watch because she was sure something awful was going to happen. Bo's regular nurse was pregnant and had been warned by her family about working around sick people while carrying a baby. Bo told Sylvia to put her camera down and help him.

She had said "Sure," and tossed her blond hair over her shoulder—an act she had copied as a child from the actress Lauren Bacall and had always used to flaunt total confidence.

Bo took charge, working quickly, surely and confidently. He had been gentle and understanding when Sylvia's hands shook so much she couldn't hold the two-by-two gauze pads.

Sylvia nourished a secret pride in her new-found courage and abilities. I'm practically a nurse, she thought.

The next person shyly pointed to her feet. The big toes on both feet were reddened and swollen, and the woman said walking was painful. Sylvia squatted and cleaned the woman's toes, using tiny wooden sticks with ends beaten to the softness of cotton. The sticks had been Seng's idea after Bo once complained about running out of cotton swabs. Two young girls devoted an hour each week to making dozens of the soft-ended sticks for the dispensary.

As she teased dirt and dead nail from the woman's toes, Sylvia felt a calmness of spirit settle on her. At these times she felt she was really being useful to someone. Sure, she told herself, it had been noble to photograph those migrant workers in southern California, but compared to these people they were rich. The Man were trying to survive. Indoor toilets? Two dollars and fifty cents an hour? Union lettuce? The questions made no sense. Here the answers were simple and basic. A man has a sore; you clean it. You grow food and you eat it. Instead of harassing the government or a businessman or the "housewives" into action, you solve the problem yourself.

After an hour, Caen came out of the house, writing in a small notebook he always carried.

"How's Tau-oi?"

"Unhappy. I'll tell you about it later. I'm writing down his cure for hiccups. It involves the ashes of a brown bean they call *yoc-sani*. We'll try it."

She made a face.

He asked, "How are you doing?"

"Great," she said, tossing her hair over her shoulder.

CHAPTER VII

THE MAN WHO LIVED IN THE HOG PEN

AUNG NE SWE crossed his legs and sank to the floor. With a banana leaf, he fanned a scanty pile of embers into flame, and balanced a bronze pot filled with water on them. He took his time to avoid distracting his visitor, who was having difficulty achieving the first meditative posture of Buddha. So this, Swe thought, is the new sorcerer from the West, the one some call the mushroom god. He is large and has developed significant eyebrows. There is much inner energy there. His face is like the ripening hot peppers. It may mean he has drunk a great deal of wine today, or that he is one of the red men who, I have heard, live in his country.

A strong, though not unpleasant odor of manure pervaded, for Swe's house occupied the upper corner of a hog pen. The pen itself was a bamboo-latticed enclosure, thirty feet by thirty feet, and situated on a hill behind the home of Chu-wei, a distant cousin of Swe.

Borjek looked around the tiny room that was this man's home. The floor was hard-packed dirt, one corner of which was covered by neatly trimmed faggots. Above them hung dried ginger leaves tied together with a string of black cloth. On a small box against the wall was a freshly cut rhododendron branch lying in front of a candle. Borjek saw that Swe was old, small and so thin that the veins were visible in his arms and neck, and his ribs stuck out like long sores. Wrinkles of saggy skin lay against his stomach, and his legs were shiny scars stretched over bone. His thin gray hair was pulled together with a ribbon. A flat, broad nose and black eyes made up a face which was young from ten feet away. Up close, the wrinkles were a thousand tiny lines. With a shock, Borjek noticed the old man's lips. Both upper and lower lips were split in the middle. Scars, dark with age and betel nut juice, made twin mouths that never quite closed. When Swe smiled, his mouth moved only at the corners. Borjek knew split lips were an old punishment for opium addiction. During the opium wars in China, the government had cracked down on addicts. One punishment was to pinch the addict's lips together and cut them open with a pair of scissors.

"How long, esteemed one, has the world enjoyed your companionship?" asked Borjek, finally finding the position which was least painful for his legs.

"Left on the vine too long, the cucumber feeds on itself and rots. This failing body and disordered mind learned more than they could understand many years ago. Now it is a process of forgetting. Unfortunately, it is a slow process." Seng was right, Swe thought, this one has latent powers and he hungers for something he has not tasted before.

"The Man are an old people. Your history goes back a hundred thousand years." Borjek did not mean literally a hundred thousand; like Laotian, the Man word for "a great many" was the same as for a hundred thousand.

"The Man are the oldest among the many children on earth. Would you like to hear some of the stories from the early days?"

"Yes."

Swe set his tea down. He crossed his arms and his eyes unfocused. "There was only one country of earthworms, only seven crawled on it. The . . ."

The sentences went on, rising and falling in a rhythmic, hypnotic cadence. Borjek realized Swe was in a semi-trance, reciting to him some involved story about the origin of mankind, memorized word for word from his father and his father's father. At first Borjek was frustrated by the delay in getting to the point of his visit. Then he became fascinated with the story.

Except for an occasional word which he didn't know, Borjek put together Swe's tale: The world was once covered with flat rock. There was nothing on the world but rock, beneath which lived man and the other creatures. One day a man called Tum Nduu and his wife followed a dog chasing a wild animal through a long tunnel. They soon found themselves on the surface of the world. They looked at the flat rock and they returned to their home underground. There they scooped up some earth, gathered seven earthworms and a basket of seeds, and returned to the surface. They scattered the seeds, the worms and the earth upon the rock, and then went home again. Some time later they came back to the surface and found it covered with soil and vegetation; whereupon Tum Nduu and his wife went home again, gathered all the animals and led them, two by two, to the surface of the world. In those early days, the sky was very close to the earth. So close, in fact, that trees and bamboo could not grow very tall and the moon was close and hot. One day a tall man was using a pole to pound the kernels from rice. While moving the pole, he accidentally pushed up the sky to where it is now. Life was wonderful and perfect in those days . . .

Swe stopped and his eyes returned to Borjek. "Your courtesy is more an indication of your graciousness than a tribute to the questionable melodiousness of my voice. Recitations of the old stories, while fascinating to the teller, sometimes so enrapture the listener as to usher him into a condition indistinguishable from sleep."

"Your memory is as precise as your voice is pleasant. I am—"

A loud oink interrupted. Through the open door, Borjek saw one of the dozen pigs rubbing against another one. Swe followed his eyes. "That's Ragged Ears. He's courting his favorite. She'll ignore him for a little while."

Borjek nodded and asked, "Did you know a man named Treadmill?"

"Does the goat really know the alligator?"

"Dugpas Seng said you saw strangers the night Treadmill died. Is your memory of that evening as luminous as your stories of the ancient days?" As he asked, Borjek noticed that Ragged Ears was now trying to mount the sow only a few feet from the door. She pushed him away, nipping at his shoulders. Both pigs were covered with mud from the rains of the past two days. The ears of the male were torn and notched—shredded evidence of past fights.

Swe answered, "It was a dark night; the moon did not rise until nearly sunrise. In the middle of the night the pigs became restless, and I awoke and walked past Cousin Chu-wei's house. I was sitting under a mango tree trying to find thoughts I had not thought before, when I saw a tall being move away from the end of the village where Treadmill lived. He was very tall and only a shadow. Perhaps it was a spirit. About a chew later"—a chew of betel nut lasted about thirty minutes—"another person came down the path. This one was small and thin. I decided to return to the pigs. Pigs are good at being pigs because they don't have to think about it. Men are not so endowed."

Ragged Ears and his potential mate bumped into the doorframe of the hut, shaking the entire structure. Swe shouted at them, but his words were as the wind. Borjek shifted discreetly to face the door. Ragged Ears had apparently decided to woo the sow with songs of love, and the courtship became more vocal. He tried to mount her again, and they wobbled precariously.

Borjek said, "I met a young man named Law Dorje Oo in the fields; he did not seem to have been good friends with Treadmill."

"Two elephants of the same temperament rarely stay in the same herd."

"I wonder if you know where he was on the night in question."

Swe raised his voice above the grunts of the pigs. "It is said that he and Tanna-li, the daughter of Kwan Nam and Nai, were discussing the loveliness of the squash blossom."

"Are they planning to marry?"

"Dugpas Seng is of the opinion that their love is still a tadpole."

The pigs backed completely into the hut. The animals were only a few feet away and Swe could no longer pretend they weren't inside. The tempo of their grunts increased. Swe glared at them.

Borjek said, "I heard some unusual howling last night from the woods outside the village."

Swe threw a stick at the pigs. "Possibly a caak telling us the rains will be heavy this year or that some other disaster is being readied."

Ragged Ears closed his eyes, folded his ears flat against his head and finally mounted the sow, but his aim was less than successful. Borjek stared at the pale pink penis slamming against her rear. Good God, he thought, a pig's root really is shaped like a corkscrew. I didn't believe the old jokes. For a moment, he thought about slipping it in for the old dude, but a sudden movement from the sow sent both pigs crashing about the hut. At last they coupled into a giant mud ball.

Enraged, Swe jumped up and began beating at them with a

piece of wood. "Get out! I have a guest. Get out and don't fornicate in my house. You miserable pigs. You filthy swine." The pigs took no notice of the man beating them. The sow had planted all four feet, one of them on Swe's altar, and stood still, stunned by ecstasy, while Ragged Ears began a paroxysm of humping.

Borjek stood and moved to one side, not quite sure what he should be doing. Swe had grabbed Ragged Ears by the rear and was trying to push the pigs toward the door. "Not while I have a guest, you stupid bugs!"

Borjek realized that the old man might have a heart attack and he knew he should help. He joined Swe and braced a shoulder against the pigs. The house was a carnival of noise with Swe screaming and both pigs squalling in urgent lust. But with two men and a male pig pushing against her fanny, the sow finally lost her grip and charged the door, pulling Ragged Ears in protest behind her. Swe and Borjek were thrown off balance and fell down.

After Borjek helped Swe up and they had brushed themselves off, Borjek decided to leave. He thanked Swe for his time.

"This embarrassed one apologizes for the disgraceful behavior of those animals. They meant no harm."

"Of course not."

"Come and go, it occurs to me that you might not have noticed that Kunag Seng does not have the hearing of a younger person. He does not mention it, but most people speak louder when they talk to him."

"I hadn't noticed. Thank you."

Outside the hut, Ragged Ears panted and stared at the two men. His sow trotted off toward the other pigs, switching her tail disgustedly.

At the other end of the village, the Reverend George Saint Sareno clutched a Bible in his lap and tried to look at Tanna-li's parents rather than the girl herself. His hands felt huge and clumsy, and he shuffled the pages of the Holy Word nervously. Sareno regretted his nose, his paleness, his hair, his bigness. When Tanna-li stood, her head came only above his stomach. She must think me gangly, he thought.

"I'll read one of the stories from the Bible." His hands stopped their movement somewhere while his eyes fell to Tanna-li's feet. They were not particularly lovely: flat, with toes splayed from going barefoot, and her soles heavy with dark calluses. Still, they aroused something touching and sweet in Sareno.

"Oh, may your breasts be like clusters of the vine and the scent of your breath like apples and your kisses . . ." In midsentence, Sareno realized what he had translated. With scarcely a pause, he flipped pages and began a recitation of the generations of Abraham's family. Am I mistaken, he thought, or is that a smile in Tanna-li's eyes? Her coffee-colored eyes were wide apart, and, though there was no fold, they were canted upward at the corners. Her nose was flat; Sareno called it a button nose to himself. Her lips were full, almost pouty, and her teeth were beginning to be stained mauve from the betel. When she smiled, a dimple transformed her face into childlike coyness. Her cheekbones were high and broad, and her skin the color of ripe corn silk. She parted her hair in the middle and let it fall simply to her bare shoulders.

That was all Sareno permitted himself to think about. What he couldn't keep from thinking about were her breasts. Sop Hao women and girls did not wear blouses, except during the sometimes chilly dry season, until after they were married and had their first child. Sometimes not even then. When he first came to Sop Hao, Sareno had suffered weeks of distress before developing a demeanor of casualness before young women. He thought it refreshingly curious that the men here attached no particular emphasis to a woman's breasts, other than observing whether or not they would be full of milk for babies. The males considered a woman's walk, her hips and her disposition fair game for gossip and jokes.

Tanna-li's breasts were high and wide. Shaped like perfect teardrops, they weren't especially large; one might fill a cupped hand. Her nipples were large and light brown, and pointed upward a little. Once in leaving the Nam house, one of Tanna-li breasts had brushed gently against Sareno's right arm, precisely two-and-a-quarter inches above his elbow. That night his dream had shamed him again. He still tortured himself by reliving that first innocent touch. Had she seen the flush in his face? Had she felt the tremble of his body?

Sareno did not understand women, and that made him awkward, uncomfortable and tense. His mother had been a meek and not terribly bright woman. His father dominated their family completely, and Sareno had never heard his mother raise her voice to Heziakiah. He didn't know his older sister, for she was six years older than he and had run away with an encyclopedia salesman when she was fifteen. Sareno remembered she was often put in charge of him when he was small, and many times since then he had asked the Lord to forgive him for the fierce and shocking hate he had felt for her. Once she had tied him to a persimmon tree while she snuck off to play with L.C.'s boy across the valley. George, who was five, tried to hold back because he knew it was wrong, but he couldn't. When she returned hours later and found his pants not only wet but filled with "number two," she slapped him back and forth across the face until he stopped crying out of absolute terror.

When Sareno looked up, Tanna-li's mother and father were preparing more tea. He glanced at Tanna-li. A muscle pulled at her mouth and that delightful dimple appeared, as if a message were being sent to him alone. What did she see in Oo, he asked himself. They had been courting for several months since their first public appearance together at the lunar New Year festivities in February. That had set the village buzzing with gossip. Oo had only returned to Sop Hao a few months before, and Tanna-li was the first girl he had courted. She and Oo were second cousins, once removed, so marriage was possible, although not encouraged. Sareno had a terrible fear that one day he would hear Tanna-li's announcement of an engagement. His only consolation was that among the Man, the woman made the proposal. She deserves someone better than him, he thought. Of late, Sareno had been toying with the idea of courting her himself. But what would the Man say, he thought. Her parents? Would she laugh? What about Oo? More important, what would happen to his mission of salvation?

Had she slept with Oo? Sareno asked himself, feeling the suffering stir in his soul. There were no taboos among the Man about premarital sex. It was as expected as the rains every spring. A favorite saying was, "You may as well leave an elephant among the sugarcane as leave a man alone with a girl." Only if trouble befell a village while a couple was indulging in each other would there be fines, for clearly they had been excessive.

Tanna-li was nineteen or twenty years old, according to the reckoning. She was born the second season in the field of som tranh, the field of flowering bananas, which was four fields ago. I'm thirty-seven, nearly twice her age, Sareno thought. In spite of his dreams, or perhaps because of them, the whole idea of sex confused and tormented him. He had never known a woman, and the moral rightness of that had given him, he told himself, the extra purity and strength to preach God's word more effectively. A man who abstained from earthly pleasures, who abstained by the power of moral resolve, should be a better man. Except . . . except where are my converts? He almost wrung his hands in dejection. Where are the fruits of this resolve? He allowed himself a hope: If she is still pure and I, too, perhaps in God's sight, a marital union would be permitted. In spite of the fact that she's unsaved and a brown-skinned woman, in spite of—oh God, he thought, his reasoning confused—in spite of everything.

Tanna-li's father said, "Thay mo, does the great one you speak of grow rice?"

"God grows rice and trees, and causes the streams to flow. He is in, and is the cause of, all these things."

Kwan Nam turned to his wife and nodded. "They are the stories of the origin." To Sareno he said, "While I slept several nights ago, my spirit met a hare in a rice paddy. Kunag Seng explained that the hare was warning me to take extra precautions this year against preying birds."

And so it went. As often as not, the villagers believed Sareno was telling them their own legends with different names. He could not openly refute their beliefs in the everyday spirits, for that would alienate them. At least, he consoled himself, Tanna-li's father will not ask questions and discuss religion. For months he did nothing but listen politely, as if he were afraid of offending Sareno or his God. Or as if Sareno were crazy.

Then, too, Sareno had come around to taking their spirits more seriously. Last year he had seen a rice crop fail while those around it grew normally—the man whose field it was had had a dalliance with a first cousin. Dugpas Seng told the man the spirits were not pleased one bit, and shortly after that the man dreamed of a four-headed snake. His crop grew sickly and yellow, and he harvested so little that he had to throw himself on the conditional mercy of the village.

Sareno stood and said, "Thank you for allowing this visit. Perhaps you will come to hear this one who speaks your language so poorly." Sareno had been giving sermons faithfully every Sunday near his hut. Sometimes a few people came; once Lahu tribesmen from the mountains came. Usually, however, his congregation consisted of Ek Tho and his Coca-Cola bottle.

"Unless the persistent and untimely leprosy reoccurs, or the crippling paralysis returns to both knees, or the temporary but painful dislocation of my arms sets in, nothing shall restrain my feet from attending you," said Kwan Nam, bowing.

Sareno bowed to Tanna-li, again catching sight of that dimple. The thought that he might be looking forward to tonight's dream caught him unawares.

CHAPTER VIII

ARRIVAL OF THE OPIUM TRADERS

THE numbness was melting away and pain was beginning to throb in his shoulder by the time Borjek saw Bo and Sylvia sloshing down the hill toward the dispensary. His breathing felt deeper and more normal with each minute. He couldn't change the focus of his eyes easily, but at least he could see again.

It was Borjek's fifth day in Sop Hao, and the attempt on his life had happened at noon, seven hours earlier. He had been outside the village on his way to radio Xieng Sen, a Thai town one hundred kilometers southwest. He had called Willard, his control, at intervals on an AN/GRC 87, which he had hidden before he first met Sareno.

The muddy path, he had been thinking as he walked along at noon, was like that interminable book by somebody Beckett about a man who spends forever crawling through mud and getting nowhere. Borjek had read it years before and had dismissed it as either being too difficult to figure out, or bullshit. But lately questions of man's self-awareness were on his mind. Was it Beckett's vision of life, he wondered, that man struggled futilely against the morass of his own consciousness? Futile because there was no end to the labor, yet constant because man's insistence on purpose, on believing in a purpose, forced him to keep on digging?

The squawk of chickens had startled him from his contemplation. Two flew wildly from the bushes to his left. Even as he froze, he heard the twang of a crossbow releasing its captive. His instincts, instincts that civilized people buried too deeply and used too infrequently, took over. The arrow grazed his shoulder before he hit the ground. He rolled and tumbled under a small tree, pulling his K-Bar knife from its sheath at the same time. I shouldn't have been caught by a goddamn crossbow, he thought.

He blamed the mud and a body that no longer could keep up with its instincts. The muscles were older and slower, the legs heavier, and the stomach softer than five years ago. Field agents, like football players, had only a few good years.

The chickens disappeared as quickly as they had come into view. There was no sound anywhere. Through the leaves, Borjek saw a silent jungle. Whoever it had been was good, and now he was gone. Borjek realized that not only was he angry because someone had tried to kill him; he also resented the reminder that he was an outsider here. For four days, he had labored beside the Man, and he was slipping into the rhythm of their life.

He smelled pepper and recognized a large pepper plant beginning to bloom near him. Borjek kicked it. No reaction. A few moments search turned up the arrow—a thin sliver of ash pointed on one end and feathered on the other. The tip was black with a gumlike substance which smelled like decaying apples. Borjek pulled his shoulder forward and examined the scratch. The arrow had torn his shirt but had scarcely broken the skin; a few drops of blood had oozed out.

Borjek combed the area and found nothing. Thirty minutes later, after doubling back several times and convincing himself no one was following, he made his call to Willard. By the time he finished, he sensed something was wrong. His movements were sluggish; breathing came with difficulty and his eyes hurt. Borjek knew then he had been poisoned, and forced himself not to panic. He was halfway through Sop Hao before he remembered that Doctor Caen was away in some village today. His breathing was labored and he had to forceably fill his lungs. His vision was foggy and his shoulder was numb; his left arm dangled uselessly. He found it hard to believe that the amount of poison which could have entered such a small scratch was affecting him so terribly.

He turned toward Dugpas Seng's house. Most of the people were working in the fields, so he was surprised to see Seng coming toward him. Borjek spoke for a minute before realizing the sounds coming from his mouth were unintelligible mumblings. That scared him. He held out the arrow, and Seng took it. Seng shouldered him into his house. Within minutes, Borjek was blind and doubled over from jabbing stomach cramps. He couldn't remember the next several hours in any kind of coherent fashion. At one point, he felt his spine arching upward violently. His arms and legs jerked and twisted uncontrollably. There was little pain, mostly frightening spasms of his entire body. Once he heard Seng speaking a language which was not Man, perhaps Chinese or Tibetan. Later, Borjek knew Seng had pressed crushed leaves and bits of cloth against his shoulder and set them afire. He knew this because he smelled the flesh. Finally, he saw flashes of light, and that, more than anything else, convinced him that he would make it.

Now, as he sat on Caen's operating table holding his left arm, he thought about something else that had happened at Seng's house. It could have been a dream, but when his vision was returning, Seng's face took on the appearance of his father's. Not so much his literal face, but a face which at once repelled and fascinated him; it demanded supplication and reverence. It was a stern, compelling face with features from Dugpas Seng, his own father and someone else. Himself? he wondered. Borjek wanted to please that face, and so he struggled against the poison. How much of it was a hallucination from the poison and how much was the surfacing of some heretofore unknown need inside himself? It made no sense now.

The door opened and Bo, throwing his pack aside, said, "They told me about you. Put that footlocker over there, boys. Get your feet on the table. Sylvia, take his blood pressure. Lay back, I'm going to look at your eyes."

While Caen examined his pupils, listened to his lungs and tested his responses, Borjek described what had happened. The wound itself rated only peroxide, a dab of Bacitracin/Neomycin ointment and a small bandage.

"Sylvia, prepare two hundred milligrams of sodium pentobarbital," said Bo.

"Why?" asked Borjek, leery because the drug was similar to truth serum.

"You're over the worst of it. This will relax you and ease the cramps. It's a small dose. You're lucky, you know that?"

"What's on the end of the arrow?"

"I don't know exactly, but I've seen something like it before. It's a curare-type poison, a central nervous system depressant and paralytic. The Man make this particular poison in the spring. They slash a cam tree—a member of the persimmon family—and collect a potful of sap. What goes into it next, I don't know. Then it's cooked until it's the consistency of an ointment. To test it, a man makes a slight cut on his forearm and drops a tiny bit of the mixture an inch or two away from the cut. If the blood stops flowing, the poison is supposed to be strong enough to kill elephants."

"Jesus," said Borjek, remembering that one of the poisons in Bo's notebook involved the cam tree.

"They say it will stop a man within five steps, a tiger within a few meters and an elephant within a kilometer. You saw what happened to you from only a scratch. In case you didn't know, Seng probably saved your life. Tell me if it starts hurting; I can give you something."

"Thanks." Borjek started to add that it had been the flying wild chickens that really saved his life, but knew it would sound strange.

Bo began cleaning up. "Tell me, Martin, why would somebody try to kill a priest?"

By then the teen-age boys had gone and Sylvia was in the back room. "I think it was the same person who killed Treadmill." Borjek fought a compulsion to tell Bo everything.

Caen leaned against a counter and crossed his arms. "Why do you put spies in these little villages? We aren't that important. And, by the way, the Lahu saw somebody parachute in a few days before you arrived here."

Whether the urge to explain himself came from the sodium pentobarbital or not, Borjek decided there was little point in pretense. "We can learn only so much from photographs. We need men in place to find out exactly what is going on."

"There is nothing going on out here except what the CIA stirs up. Is it any wonder you get blamed when something happens?"

"If we weren't here, we couldn't defend ourselves against charges like those you've made."

"If you weren't here, you wouldn't be accused of anything," said Bo.

"But," Borjek said triumphantly, "we wouldn't know that if we weren't here."

"Balls," said Bo.

"We need to know the troop strength of China along the border; we need to know about missile installations before they're built; we need to know about new heavy-duty roads. So once in a while men go in to look around. They cross the Mekong, skirt the tip of Burma and go into China. The tribesmen provide guides and guards for us."

"And somebody upset your little opium cart?"

"So we've sometimes used the transportation of opium as a favor to the tribes. But, look, if Treadmill was handling opium it was on his own. We carried none for this village last year."

Bo walked around so he was facing, and looking down at, Borjek. "I was in Viet Nam and that kind of political crap—"

"Caen, a few others besides you served in Viet Nam. Do you remember a place called Gia Vuc?"

"I was there in 1968."

"I was there in 1970."

Bo felt the anger seep from his muscles. "What was it like then?"

"Worse. By then the Green Berets had been withdrawn from Viet Nam and Gia Vuc was turned over to the South Vietnamese. But the camp was virtually in a state of siege. Men disappeared nearly every night. When I left, it was only a matter of time before it fell to the VC. They had the countryside."

Bo thought of those brave young Jarai who had trusted him. "While you were there did you hear of a little hamlet called Ba To?" He asked with apprehension, fearing that he might find out what happened to Anha.

"Vaguely. It had either been burned down or had moved. I can't remember. Why?"

"Just curious."

The next day the opium traders arrived. Dugpas Seng, having dreamed of the phoenix three nights in a row, had been waiting since dawn. The first to arrive was Colonel Ming Su-wen, representing the dread 93rd Kuomintang Division. Su-wen left his dozen bodyguards lounging in the village. The soldiers wore green uniforms and caps with the blue-and-white sun insignia of Nationalist China.

Seng had dealt with Su-wen in the past as a trader in fine cloths and metals, and he seemed noticeably older than Seng remembered. His eyes were tiny slits, and he was thinner, though the stringy arms and hands suggested a strength of tendons and willpower. He still carried the ivory walking stick which according to legend was carved from the tusk of a great bull elephant gone mad and brought down by Su-wen with only an M-1 rifle.

Su-wen could legitimately call any of the mountains within a hundred miles home. He had been a young lieutenant when his division fled from China into Laos in late 1949, with the Communists a hill behind them. Later, the KMT fought for, and took, a territory for itself in northeast Burma. With the help of the CIA, working under Truman's dictate, the KMT prepared for the recapture of the mainland. The KMT also fought the Burmese Army, which tried to drive out the fifteen thousand Chinese in their country. Truman was more sure about the KMT's loyalty than that of the Burmese government. The KMT built camps and retrained its soldiers under the necessarily far-reaching direction of Generalissimo Chiang Kai-shek, who was living temporarily on an island called Tai-wan.

Often after smoking a few pipes of the plant of dreams at night, Su-wen would relive the excitement of the early 1950s. He had been a major who commanded his own battalion. He had gone in on all three invasions of the homeland and, if only they had had a few more men and time, it would have worked, he told himself. It was also disappointing that the people of Yunnan never rose up, as Generalissimo Chiang had predicted, to throw off the obviously tenacious grip of Communism. The farthest the KMT had penetrated was sixty miles to Ching-ku in 1952 during the last invasion. Out of two thousand men, less than nine hundred survived that untidy retreat into Burma. It was said that Chiang Kai-shek wept when he was told how many men had died.

During those early days, opium was the Kuomintang's source of revenue, and the CIA openly supplied the planes and guns to keep that revenue flowing. Su-wen had not liked the plan, but the decision was not his. If the KMT could not retake China immediately, perhaps, reasoned the generals, they could extend their influence beyond the Shan plateau in Burma. In July, 1953, the Burmese Army was splintered around the country, fighting various warlords and rebel groups; the KMT moved its Fifth and Third armies across the Salween River toward Mandalay and the ancient capital of Pagan. But, reacting faster than expected and using two British Hurricane fighters, the Burmese government brought three brigades to bear, and the KMT retreated to their mountains.

The Burmese government knew that the CIA had provided the arms and put the issue on the agenda at the United Nations. While denying the allegations but conceding that a less public display of international discord would be desirable, the CIA agreed to repatriate those involved. During the late monsoons of 1953, hundreds of "Chinese" boarded C-47's and were flown to Tai-wan. Although the Burmese observers said that the KMT soldiers boarding the planes looked suspiciously like Lahu tribesmen, the American and Thai representatives laughed at the charge. Su-wen, who had watched the airlift from a nearby hilltop, laughed too. The "KMT soldiers" *were* Lahu tribesmen, rounded up at gun-point and promised many pigs and much rice in the land of Tai-wan. They were dressed in KMT uniforms and given Chinese names.

Since then the dream of freeing the homeland had grown dimmer; the younger soldiers had not even been born in China. The KMT armies were finally driven out of Burma and into the corner of Thailand abutting Laos and Burma. There, through a quiet agreement with the Thai government, the KMT kept the local Communists in line and in return were given the opium concession. The CIA gave guns to the KMT and made the contracts for the opium. A few months ago, word had come of a huge increase in demand for the plant of dreams, and the prices being mentioned were nearly one-third more than the previous year. Colonel Su-wen was sent into this area of Laos to obtain what contracts he could.

At noon, after six cups of tea, Su-wen left Seng's house. Su-wen had offered fifty-five dollars per kilo. He also suggested that the spirits would be extremely unhappy should Sop Hao fail to deliver its fall quota. So unhappy, they might instill his normally sluglike troops with the vigor of hasty retribution.

Seng had listened and sipped his tea.

The second trader to arrive, less than two hours later, was pudgy, bandy-legged General Liou Yone-fu. His five bodyguards, armed with a variety of rifles and grenades, hunkered on Seng's porch and said little.

General Yone-fu was born the son of a Chinese farmer who had relocated to Burma to escape a murder charge. Also to escape from what he saw as a death sentence in farming, Yone-fu joined a rebel warlord army when he has fourteen years old. The first week that he carried a gun he was part of a platoon leading a white man named Frank Merrill, an American brigadier general, and three thousand soldiers to a Japanese stronghold in the Burmese mountains. Yone-fu was impressed by the pipe-smoking, mild-mannered general and his deranged soldiers. He was even more impressed when the favor was returned by a parachute drop of fifty M-2 carbines.

Yone-fu never forgot that Merrill's Marauders had driven six regiments of Japanese out of the jungles. In 1959, when he heard the Central Intelligence Agency was hiring mercenaries in Laos, Yone-fu and one hundred and fifty Burmese and Chinese crossed the Mekong to sign up. For two years, Yone-fu and his men fought in the secret army, launching raids against the Pathet Lao, running reconnaissance into China and trading opium on the side. But the weariness of always being disguised as a Laotian militiaman, and Yone-fu's personal dream of creating his own fiefdom became overwhelming. He and his men left the CIA's army and returned to the Sam Kiao district of eastern Kengtung in Burma. Five years later, Yone-fu, having deserved and therefore promoted himself to the rank of general, controlled Sam Kiao. Even the KMT reluctantly paid protection for their caravans when crossing his territory. He had nearly three thousand men under arms, and a standing contract with the CIA for guns in exchange for guides and intelligence.

Then came 1967. Yone-fu knew he was gambling, but he also knew he should have won. The demand for opium was rising—

rumor had it the American government was pressuring Turkey to cut back production—and Yone-fu decided to challenge the KMT. His timing was good because the commanders of the KMT's Fifth and Third armies were feuding. Yone-fu figured he could slip through the gap. By June of 1967, he had assembled one of the largest caravans of opium ever seen in northeastern Burma: three hundred and fifty mules carrying sixteen tons of raw opium. He would have been able to buy a thousand rifles and ammunition. And that meant another thousand soldiers. But he miscalculated the strength of the blood ties of the Kuomintang. When the warring generals heard of Yone-fu's caravan, they closed ranks and began marching toward Ban Khwan, a small Laotian village on the Mekong where Yone-fu was planning to sell the opium. A Laotian general named Sai Kong owned a large refinery there.

In late July on the outskirts of Ban Khwan, the two armies met. The noise from the recoiless rifles, the .50 machine guns and the sixty millimeter mortars could be heard seven kilometers away. Both sides were double-crossed by General Kong, a man Yone-fu hoped to meet someday alone in the jungle, so that their inequality would be rectified. While the two armies were hammering away at each other, Kong and six T-28 fighters attacked both sides. When the smoke cleared, Yone-fu had lost one hundred and fifty men and sixteen tons of opium, the KMT had ninety dead and was fleeing across the Mekong, and General Kong had his nation's highest decoration: "The Grand Cross of the Million Elephants and White Parasol." Kong had proudly turned in two tons of opium to the Laotian government.

Yone-fu not only lost the opium, he lost the trust of his men and his own prestige. Three years later, he was arrested for trying to convince other Shan State rebel leaders to unite behind a single commander whose courage, leadership and physical abilities fortuituously coincided precisely with his own.

Yone-fu finally escaped the Rangoon jail and was proud that he already had found eight hundred men to follow him. They weren't as good as those he had once commanded, but they could be beaten into periodic fearsomeness. All he needed was one good year of sales and he would have enough men to retake Sam Kiao, now in the hands of his worthless, one-eyed cousin. So, Yone-fu came to Sop Hao, a village which, he remembered from the days of the secret army, grew some of the purest sap in the mountains. He had also heard that Treadmill, the local CIA man, was dead.

Yone-fu, looking as drawn and tired as he felt, came out of Seng's house in the late afternoon and disappeared with his men into the woods. The mole on his left cheek had been blacker than usual. He had offered Seng sixty dollars a kilo, protection of Sop Hao from the ravages of marauding bands—including his own—and a goodly supply of sugar and iron.

Seng had listened and sipped his tea.

Borjek, exhausted from his bout with the poison, had slept the entire day. He first heard of the visitors when Sareno returned from the fields at supper. Sareno didn't know who they were, only that they were opium traders. Borjek decided to see Seng. Willard had left it up to his discretion to get pledges for the opium crop if it would secure the people's loyalty. He could offer up to seventy-five dollars a kilo.

Borjek arrived at Seng's house shortly before dark. With circuitous care, he inquired about the visitors and Seng, with even more circuitous charm, declined to answer. Finally, Borjek suggested he could arrange the payment of sixty-five dollars a kilo, plus a guarantee of additional rice.

Seng had listened and sipped his tea.

CHAPTER IX

YOUTH AND AGE ARGUE

THE fog seemed heavier that night, and Seng felt a cooling from the day. He slipped on his light cotton robe and wandered around his house, touching an ivory carving, his father's knife, his fern. He remembered the first time he had seen a plant living in a pot inside a home was at Doctor Caen's dispensary. Maybe I'm getting as foolish as Swe, living with his pigs and his plants, thought Seng.

He looked into the black night. Po-Nagar revealed nothing tonight, and that boded ill. The air was misty and moved gingerly, distorting sound and vision. From somewhere in the dark came the faint moans of the caaks and *nats* making their spiritual rounds. It was a night for phi, not people. Seng forgave the window, and looked inward at the years he had studied as an anchorite on the cold slopes of Mount Chung-yun. Living in a stone cave in a climate that warmed the air enough to bathe only three moons a season, Seng had studied the mystic powers and beliefs of the ancient Bon religion, a religion whose origins were so distant in the past that Buddhism was considered its offshoot. Bon was a psychic mysticism formed in the beginnings of time and passed on by the tsam khangs, the strict recluses who lived in the barren Wu-Liang of eastern Tibet. As was customary with the young men in his family, Seng became a helper at a *gompa* when he was fifteen. Later he elected to become a novitiate among the Bon lamas. He studied under the precious jewel, Kushogs Pabong, one of the most ancient and revered of the Bon shamans. Seng allowed himself a moment of unworthy pride by toying with the knowledge that he could still create *tumo*, the heat generated within the body to warm the flesh. That had been one of his first accomplishments, and the two winters he lived alone in a mountain hole three miles high in the Wu-Liang with only a thin, patched robe were a tender memory.

The vast knowledge and awesome powers of the shamans—and they were very real powers—had been attractive to him. But in his sixteenth year at the gompa, his father sent word that his family was moving south beyond the Great Snowy Mountains toward the Shan and Yunnan plateaus. Seng decided to go with them. He never regretted that decision, for he came to love his people, as well as his two wives, with a deep, permanent love, a love which he knew he could not have allowed himself as a Bon priest. But he was always curious about what his life would have been like had he lived as a shaman. And there was a sense of sadness and loss when he remembered the day he left, for all time, the gompa of Kushogs Pabong.

Seng also wondered when Oo would speak. He sensed that Oo had stepped into his home some minutes before and had been standing in the shadows, silently watching him.

Seng turned and said, "It is truly rewarding to this crumbling old man that the young Law Dorje Oo will overlook the barrenness of his hovel and attend to his veneration."

Oo bowed, though not quite enough to satisfy tradition. "Father of our village, perchance in your beneficence you would share a cup of your exquisite tea with an intruder?"

"One as close to me as you is never an intruder in this house. Make yourself comfortable admist the poverty of these furnishings." Seng served cups of rice tea and lemon. "It has been many days since you brightened my home," he said, motioning for Oo to sit down.

"The time of the spring planting is at hand, kunag, and the hands are as full as the mind preparing for the growing season. It is also wearing of late to forgo sleep in order to discuss the comings and goings of so many strangers in our village."

"The giving of seeds to the earth is upon us," Seng said cautiously. "It is surprising that enough time has been found for farming and for the necessary homage to our ancestors, when some of our village deviate from their labors to ensure that visitors are familiar with the working of the crossbow."

"The mushroom god was unfortunate indeed to be in the vicinity of a moving arrow. I heard about it myself late yesterday. Of course, should I myself attend to a distant village, I would be

73

unfamiliar with whatever hunting practices those natives might use. It is said that the spirit of one who is far from the home of his ancestors finds no respite," said Oo.

The time has come to straighten the course, Seng decided. "A number of moons ago, another man who came here as a stranger was hurried on to his next life, and I doubt that it was because of his artless personality. The person who violated his being insulted the phi of this village and, therefore, my spirits as well. Whoever the worm was, is forever obligated to me."

"We have exchanged these words before, kunag. Had I not been with a certain female that night in question, I would surely be of help in your search," said Oo.

"Perchance since then you have heard an explanation of the events of that night?"

"If the mango is spoiled, does one blame him who discards it?" Oo smiled tightly.

"Granted your wisdom has usually exceeded your youth, but surely the difference between a person and a mango has not escaped your normally keen vision?"

Oo took the rebuke with no show of emotion. "Esteemed one, in my ignorance I was not aware of the brotherhood between yourself and the one who traded in the plant of dreams."

Send said, "The nefariousness and treachery of the long-nosed one was as well known as his rapidly increasing supply of paper money. Perhaps it was the attraction of the latter rather than disgust with the former which brought about the use of the *open pit gam.* From your travels you must be knowledgeable about such poisons."

"Speak more exactly, oracle," said Oo, setting his cup down with pointed deliberation.

Seng pushed back that part of him which clamored that his suspicions were built on sticks. "The abundant consequences of becoming a merchant was a subject about which you frequently inquired as a boy. Sop Hao is a small village with not enough goods to satisfy two such appetites."

"The obscureness of your remarks confirms your age."

"He who would eat the muskrat would well remember to boil

the meat twice. Oo, my son, will you let the bamboo measure the truth?"

"I am not old enough to be your son. Like much that is of this village, the epa gie is antiquated. There are new ways, new thoughts. Since your youth, rivers have changed their courses, much less customs."

"And Tanna-li?"

"A girl. She is a child who talks of flowers," said Oo.

"It is then curious that one so refined enjoys her company."

"The pleasure of her touch overcomes the simplicity of her thoughts. But let us discuss mountains, not swamps. The plant of dreams must be sown shortly, and the people await a decision from you, kunag, on the number of rows to be marked."

To delay a growing apprehension about the purpose of Oo's visit, Seng withdrew an ivory snuffbox from his robe and placed a pinch in each nostril. "The sweet taste of the apricot is hardly worth the savagery of the tiger that lives nearby."

"Perhaps that is why it is so sweet," said Oo.

"Men from beyond the Mekong come here to talk of the ty fong ki. Because ten-times-ten rows of the Yunnan poppy were planted last season, this village now has no surplus of rice. Still, they ask for more. If one's home has no pleasurable view, one should take down the wall."

"Elder, let us pull the weeds. I am instructed to pledge a payment of sixty thousand kip per kilo of poppy, five baskets of spices and several guns upon delivery at the end of the growing season."

Seng stared at Oo. He attempted to rise, but stumbled. Oo caught him as he fell forward. When Seng regained his balance, he placed his hands on Oo's shoulders and looked into his eyes.

Oo was uncomfortable at the closeness, and could not bear the touch of Seng's hands or the look in his eyes. "Is your selfhood intact, patriarch?"

"The withered legs of this decaying body fell asleep sitting on the floor. But were that the problem, I would sacrifice them in exchange for what I heard."

Oo stepped back. "Do not be deceived by the lack of white in my hair. I do not speak to perfume the air, but to encourage the flowers of decision."

"Then you should reap an excellent harvest, beardless one, for flowers grow well near refuse pits."

Oo rubbed his hands together but could not hide an angry countenance exposed by the candlelight.

Seng reached out one hand, palm up. "You are not one with yourself, Oo. You have bad *san pa-ku*. The whites above and below your eyes are showing. Your soul is divided against itself. Let us talk as we once did."

Oo clipped his words with impatience. "My boyhood fat is good, and I am no puppy. Last year, Treadmill and I entered into an agreement for the delivery of the poppy. The *farang* is not here and I make the terms."

Seng breathed as though the air burned his lungs. "It is unusual that the Pathet Lao would finance the purchase of the poppy. They—"

Oo laughed. "Your knowledge should grow even as your age. I am a cadreman in the People's Army of China. I have studied in Kochiu, Yunnan. And I have returned to this village of my childhood to prepare the way. I want Sop Hao to grow four hundred and fifty kilos of opium."

"That is almost two times that which we grew last season," Seng said in amazement.

"Diligence and hard work produce more than their own reward."

Seng turned his back and walked to the window. In the night, he imagined he could hear the roar of the Mekong as it crashed and raged through its stone confines. Or was the noise within his ears? Seng's eyes fell to a long, curved knife which hung between the window and the altar below. The blade was mauled with Tibetan words and the handle was inlaid with seven shades of ivory.

"What is the purpose?" asked Seng without turning. "For generations, this village and its people have grown rice and lived properly. We have not had, until recent times, pestilence or great fear, beyond the occasional tiger or stray elephant. Now, guests are attacked; fire has fallen on our land; and spiders weave webs across the mouths of our rice baskets. The phi roam the hills at night and of late, howls from a strange caak disturb our sleep. Strangers bring guns, and our children are afraid to laugh. Is this right? When I was younger, only a row of the poppy was sufficient. Perhaps a return—"

"The ways of that life are as remote as your youth," Oo said in frustration. "Gather your wits and tell the villagers how much to plant."

Seng faced Oo. "I saw a white cobra three sunrises ago."

Oo shuddered involuntarily. The white cobra at sunrise was a powerful omen signifying a death before the next full moon. "The old ways, kuang. It was only a snake." Nevertheless, he stole a look around the room.

"Listen," Seng said, nodding toward the door. "The phi are restless and unsettled, no less than we humans."

"Snakes and phi. Come, old man, do not let the corn grow up around your dilatory feet."

"Others have approached me, even the one called the mushroom god. I am not sure the opium should be grown."

"The mushroom god? So, he is the one. It might not be prudent to enter long-term contracts with that one."

Seng's face darkened. "Oo, I have too rarely spoken harshly with you. But do not allow me to discover you are involved with the intimidation of my guests or my phi, or that you are planning to be. I am old, but not without power."

For a moment, the widened eyes of Seng reminded Oo of his Bon powers, and Oo shrank before the memory.

Seng continued, "Are you failing to observe the spirits of your parents, Leua and Tsapos, even as they observe you?"

"My parents! They were killed by the farangs and their airplanes. Their spirits are always with me."

"That happened during the season of the thistle, nine or ten seasons ago. Your mother was running to the village Naan Tow, where your father lay incapacitated by rice wine, to tell him the creatures that fly were going to drop fire there. Your father was a strong man, especially when wine replaced his normal food, as it often did. I don't know if you knew that your father was not himself that day, as on many other days. Tsapos was unwilling or unable to move, even though he had fended off three villagers to the extent that one's arm was broken and the others suffered many pains. Everyone had left the village but your father. Leua heard of the fight, and she went to take him from Naan Tow. As she approached the village to warn him, the flying creatures appeared. There were clouds, and the creatures were far on the other side of them. The fire fell indiscriminately."

"The hairy farangs are all devils," Oo said angrily. "They are like fowl—early in the procession of life. You speak of disruptions; they are the disruptors. They must all be destroyed. I . . . I loved my mother."

"I, too, loved your mother, and, while her choice for a husband was curious, I loved him too. Your mother was tolerant, for otherwise she could not have stayed with him. Your san pa-ku is alarming. I plead with you to take the epa gie."

"We are superior to the farang. They are destroying our country. Old man, you will someday join your ancestors, and I will assume my place. Do not hasten your own future."

In anger, Seng raised his arm, and, as if that were the signal, an unearthly howl began in the night. It quivered and grew louder. Both men stopped and looked out the window. The howls sounded like a dog's, lost and forsaken, screaming into the face of fear and death. But the throat that formed the noise was no dog's throat.

Tiny bumps raced across Oo's neck and shoulders.

Seng let the cry press deep into his stomach, and for a moment it became his. Its loneliness spoke for all of them—for a time that was lost and perhaps for a future that was lost. After uncounted minutes when even the flicker of the candles were stilled, the howl died away, slowly and in pieces.

The men were thrust back into the same room; each was tense.

Oo spoke, "Just as the Mekong flows downstream, so the opium continues to flow."

"Go. You are not one with yourself and until you are, you cannot be one with anyone else. A chicken's head will hang from my *wudang* tomorrow and I will ask our ancestors for guidance." Seng turned and knelt before his altar.

Oo hesitated to go into the dark so soon after the howling.

Seng said in a voice scarcely loud enough for Oo to hear, "One must know how to protect oneself against the tigers to which one has given birth as well as against those begotten by others."

"You speak to me, old man?"

"No, Oo, to myself."

CHAPTER X

THE BAPTISM OF EK THO

AFTER Oo left, Seng prepared a pipe of opium and smoked it, something he hadn't done in months. The howls of the strange caak had not been repeated, but other phi scurried around in the dark, muttering and whispering to themselves. Seng reminded himself that even as a youth he had been impatient. Once he went to Kushogs Pabong with a question, the content of which he no longer remembered. He had waited at the entrance to Pabong's house for nearly two months, and, finally unable to repress his impatience, went into the woods. One of the other novitiates came to Seng and asked why he had left. The novitiate said Kushogs had already asked that supper be prepared for an extra person. Seng was to have been admitted that very day.

Perhaps I'm being impatient with Oo, Seng thought. Do I respond to a truth that I do not know, or to the impudence of a young man that I do know? Time passed, and his thoughts circled on themselves like birds trapped under the roof of a house. His mind searched for the black in the white and for the white in the black—for an answer to a question he could not frame. His body was heavy and cumbersome.

He recalled one of Kushog's teaching questions: "A tree moves. Which is it that moves? Is it the tree or the wind?" Seng had answered the wind, but the correct answer had been neither the tree nor the wind. It is the mind which moves.

Seng began the breathing exercises. He imagined his central artery to be as thin as one corn silk but filled with fire and trembling at the top from the air currents in his lungs. He began the chants and concentrated on increasing the size of the artery. His thoughts grew lighter.

Hours went by, and the slow rhythm of his breathing never

changed. Each step in the ritual seduced the next, and finally he felt himself rising, quickly at first and then slowly as he gained control. He opened his eyes. Below him he saw an old man sitting crosslegged on a mat with his gray head resting on his chest. He's becoming so old, Seng thought. So alone. He wanted to take the man in his arms and tell him that he could be young and with hope again.

Seng roamed through the mist, fighting to keep the link with his body, searching to find some new perspective on his problems. He encountered only fleeting shapes and sudden shifts of light in the hoary ether. As he was becoming weary and afraid of losing his way, he heard the soft voice of Kushogs Pabong swirling from the grayness. The precious jewel spoke the same words he had uttered to Seng the first time Seng had traveled from his body: "Is a visionary a sudden transformation? Or, rather, is it that one had been blind and can now see all that was always there to see?"

Seng sensed a coldness and a change in the quality of the light. He let himself fall backward into his body.

When Seng shook himself and rose, it was near dawn, for the fog was restless and the bats were darting to their secret caves. His muscles were stiff, but he felt refreshed. He knew he could not speak to Oo, but perhaps the spirits of his ancestors could. He poured his cold tea back into the kettle and waited for sunrise.

George Saint Sareno, his dreams having turned abruptly to images of a waterfall, was behind his house urinating when he heard the chicken leave the flock. The mottled red fowl escaped from a stand of trees on Sareno's left and, turning slightly around the hillside, crossed not far in front of him.

Standing silently in the doorway was Borjek, who had risen after Sareno in hopes of finding the reason for the preacher's nightly departures. Seeing what Sareno was doing, Borjek was about to return to bed when he saw the chicken careening past an oak tree. The bird sailed through the sleeping village.

There was enough light for Borjek and Sareno to see Dugpas Seng standing in front of his house near the middle of the village. In his right hand was a sparkle of reflected light. The chicken curled its wings and tail feathers and settled at Seng's feet.

Seng stroked the chicken's feathers and called it by name. "Gi, thank you for coming. This sacrifice to my ancestors carries more significance than an ignominious death at the claws of a tiger."

Seng held Gi's head and, with a quick movement, severed the neck from the body. Instead of flopping about, it tottered for a moment and fell over, as if still in a trance.

"Good God almighty," said Borjek.

"I didn't hear you come out," said Sareno, who had been thinking that Seng in his sometimes gory and sometimes quiet way affected the villagers far more than he ever could.

"George, your lizard is out," said Borjek, pointing. The man is certainly absorbed with his penis, he thought.

Sareno's face burned hotly as he buttoned his pants.

Borjek said, "Was it my imagination or did that chicken fly over there deliberately?"

"Yes. I've seen Seng do many strange things, and this may be the strangest yet. They say he was once a Tibetan priest. They're supposed to have incredible powers, such as telepathy and the ability to choose when they will die."

Later that morning as the people headed out of Sop Hao, some on their way to Sareno's Sunday services, some on their way to the fields, they all stopped to look at Seng's wudang. The wudang was a tall, intricately carved pole, made from a cedar tree. It served to remind the phi that certain sacrifices had been made and to remind the villagers that it was Seng who performed them. From Seng's wudang hung a dozen buffalo skulls, two tiger skulls and one humanlike skull which no one could identify—it had always been there. Several dozen tiny, woven baskets were tied on the pole, corresponding to the number of chickens sacrificed in the past. Baskets were used because chicken skulls disintegrated in time. Today a freshly severed chicken head swung from the top of the wudang.

The villagers knew why bowls of chicken blood were on Seng's porch and on his family altar inside. Word of the argument between Seng and Oo had spread quickly. As they passed, the people muttered words of sympathy for Seng and directed prayers toward their own ancestors.

No one noticed the five Lahu tribesmen until after Sareno, dressed in a black shirt, black pants and white collar, had begun his sermon. Fifteen Man, more than usual, were attending the Sunday services because they had heard Ek Tho was to be baptized again and that the stranger named Borjek, whom many now called the mushroom god, might also be present. Sareno had built a small baptismal pool on the hillside northwest of the village, one hundred feet down the hill. To carry water to his pool, he had dug a miniature race, like those which once diverted water to power the grain mills in Tennessee. The creek, which ran not far away, supplied the village with water and fed the rice paddies through a series of dams and ditches. The creek was also named Sop Hao because the Man considered a village to be all those homes supplied from one source of water. Sareno had first wanted to build his baptismal pool higher up the mountain, so he could be assured of fresh water. But when the Man found he intended to submerse people in it, even though he promised not to kill them, they insisted the pool be placed below the village, just in case.

The Lahu tribesmen, hair frizzed and faces white with ashes to disguise themselves from the spirits, had crept out of the woods above Sop Hao and hunkered at the edge of the cleared area. So unseen was their approach that later that day, Seng had long words with those who lived at the perimeters of Sop Hao, who were to watch for strangers at all times.

The first to see them was Tsao, who had turned around to stroke the satin skin behind one of his wife's knees. "Lahu cannibals! Savages!" He jumped up and pointed. A few people moved for their knives and someone screamed, but they were quickly calmed by Seng, who saw that the Lahu had already laid their crossbows on the ground several feet in front of them.

Borjek, too, had started to rise, but was restrained by Bo. "It's okay. They mean no harm," he said.

"Are they cannibals?" asked Borjek, sitting down.

"I don't think so. Anymore. Maybe occasionally."

"What are they doing here?"

"I'm really not sure why they come. They came once before to Sareno's services. They live higher up and are mainly hunters. I don't think they stay in one place more than a year or two. Last time, they just sat staring at Sareno, talking among themselves and then, after giving Seng a bunch of bananas—a gift for letting them visit—they disappeared."

Above them, Chom, the oldest of the Lahu and a man who was such a good carver of wood that his birds were said to stay aloft for three days, spoke to his fellow hunters. "I believe the man we came to examine is sitting down there beside the dalam and his mate. What hair he has is the color of ripe sumac, as was foretold, and he wears the flowing garment."

"Yes, yes," said Shay with nervous excitement. "That is the one I saw flying through the air."

"The legends said he would come in the form of a less-than-handsome white man with a black cloth that covered his entire body," said Luba. He closed his eyes and started to chant, "Chyanun-Woishun was the first and gave birth to Ka-any Duwa, chief of the middle land, who mated with an alligator and their first son was Kang—"

"Luba, be quiet," said Chom-the-carver, after seeing that the chanting had caused several of the Man, timid though the lowlanders usually were, to turn around. "I know the stories, too. Chyanun-Woishun is to be reborn in the body of a white man, and we are here to see if this mushroom god is the creator spirit."

"We were mistaken once," said Li. "We came to see the false Chyanun-Woishun, who even now is making coarse noises to those below us. Although he was white and clearly less-than-handsome, his hair was unfortunately black. Furthermore, it is said that he is interested in a girl of the Man, scarcely an indication of heavenly discrimination in taste."

Chom-the-carver said, "It is taught that when one wishes to use one of one's skills to the fullest, such as seeing, one should use less of one's other skills, such as talking."

Li muttered to Luba, "I think he just made that up."

The morning was half gone and the day grew hotter. Far to the south, a low ridge of clouds was beginning its journey toward the huge deserts of northern China. After the spring equinox, the winds, pulled by the swirling air above the Chinese deserts, raked the moisture from the Indian Ocean and spread it across southeastern Asia.

Sareno began his sermon with the story of Noah and the ark, for the Man seemed especially fond of accounts of the flood. He was more nervous than usual because the Catholic priest, Borjek, was present along with Tanna-li and her family. She sported a white orchid in her raven hair. It was the first time her family had attended services. And there were the Lahu mumbling to each other on the hillside.

Why is a priest attending the services of a Baptist minister? wondered Sareno. How am I supposed to concentrate? When is he leaving, and what if the villagers think he's with me? Perhaps my technique is being studied? What if Borjek starts holding services?

The shame that his only true convert was sitting before him, grinning like a goon in anticipation of his baptism and clutching a Coca-Cola bottle, nearly brought tears to Sareno. I shouldn't have promised Ek Tho another baptism, he thought morosely. Is this his fourth? Or fifth? After getting over his initial terror at being held underwater, Ek Tho had become infatuated with it. When Sareno explained that baptism was normally held only once to signify being born again, Ek Tho was dejected for days. Then he came to Sareno and told him he had returned to his sins and that only through another baptism could he be saved again. If only I hadn't agreed that very first time, Sareno thought. But without Ek Tho, I wouldn't have even one convert. The residents of Sop Hao enjoyed Ek Tho's rebirths and the turnout for these Sundays was always better.

"But that he should be made manifest to Israel, therefore am I come baptizing with water," Sareno concluded, closing the Bible. The Man were silent with anticipation.

Ek Tho held up his Coca-Cola bottle and pointed at the bottom. Sareno wished that Ek Tho had forgotten—this was so embarrassing. It had started out innocently enough, but now was out of hand and there was nothing he could do about it without risking the salvation of Ek Tho. He lowered his voice, hoping that Borjek couldn't hear him.

"And I did not know him, but he who sent me from Tuscaloosa, Alabama, to immerse in water, that one said to me, 'Upon whom you see the Spirit descending and remaining upon him and the Coca-Cola, this is the one immersing in the Holy Spirit.'"

Ek Tho was excitedly showing the villagers near him the words "Tuscaloosa, Ala." on the bottom of his bottle. They could not read them, but, knowing that Ek Tho was harmless, they smiled back.

Sareno stepped around his bamboo podium and took Ek Tho's hand, leading him to the pool. Everyone but the Lahu formed a circle around them. Ek Tho, one hand tight around the Coca-Cola bottle, waded to his thighs in the pool. Sareno placed a hand on Ek Tho's head.

"I baptize thee in the name of the Father . . ." Sareno pushed Ek Tho down. Instead of merely dunking his head, Ek Tho collapsed beneath the water. After a moment, Sareno released the pressure on Ek Tho's head and, when he didn't come up immediately, snatched a handful of hair and pulled him upright. Ek Tho, delighted, beamed a toothless smile.

" . . . and of the Son . . ." Down again, and again Ek Tho refused to surface. Sareno could not look at Tanna-li. His ego was torn between believing these people had come to learn the way into the Kingdom of God and believing that they thought he was staging a show for their entertainment. Behind Tsao and his wife, Sareno spotted Borjek donning a faint smile.

Sareno jerked Ek Tho up again.

" . . . and of the Holy Ghost."

As the water closed over his head, Ek Tho, who was already in a state of religious ecstasy, hit his knees with his hands and the Coca-Cola bottle slipped away. Sareno felt Ek Tho moving away and grabbed for his hair, but missed. Sareno tried to remain calm and casual as he leaned over into the water. His hand searched under the surface. Why are you doing this to me, worthless Ek Tho? He felt a piece of cloth and captured it, but the man wouldn't budge. He must be holding on to something. Abandoning all pretense, Sareno reached both hands under water and seized the material.

Ek Tho's feet popped up nearby, flailing and kicking.

The Lahu tribesmen shifted their attention from Borjek to the two men thrashing about in the water.

"I've never seen this ritual before," said Li.

"Maybe they're mating with an alligator," said Luba.

Chom-the-carver said, "This is a true test of the saying, 'If there is piety, even a rat's claw acquires a golden sheen.'"

"Maybe the tall one is going to eat the other one," ventured Shay.

In the crowd below them, Borjek asked Caen, "Does this go on every Sunday?"

"No, Ek Tho likes to be baptized. Sareno seems to have lost him just now."

The struggle continued in the pool. Sareno, water dripping from his head, braced his feet in the mud and gave a mighty pull. The cloth ripped free, and Sareno toppled backward, pulling Ek Tho's loin cloth with him. Oh my God, he's naked now, Sareno realized. He's ruined the entire baptism. This is not the way to do it. He stood and wiped water from his eyes. You reprehensible, deceiving old man, come up! Sareno leapt toward a brown toe peeking out among the waves.

Sareno hollered, "Damn it, Ek Tho, come here! That's enough."

Borjek said, "That man may be drowning. It's been a couple of minutes. I'm going to help." He rushed to the pool and waded in toward Sareno, who saw, with horror, the Catholic priest coming at him. Within seconds, Borjek had located an arm and by then Sareno had a firm hold on a naked leg. The villagers crowded closer to see the men through the windmill of splashing water.

Borjek said, "Get him up, pull."

"Go away," shouted Sareno. "He's mine."

"He needs air. Let's save him."

Sareno spit out a mouthful of water. No priest is going to get his hands on one of mine. Borjek has been waiting for this, he thought. "No! I'll save him. I've already saved him four or five times. Go save your own."

Sareno released the leg and dived at Borjek, who fell back under the sudden attack. The two grabbed each other like wrestlers and disappeared under a muddy foam.

Suddenly, Ek Tho rose, naked and smiling, and held up his Coca-Cola bottle. He saw the two men struggling with each other and sloshed toward them. In a moment, he had pulled them apart.

On the hillside, Chom-the-carver said to the other Lahu, "Yes, indeed. The mushroom god may be the spirit of Chyanun-Woishun. This has been an amazing occurrence."

CHAPTER XI

A COBRA BITES THE PRIEST

THE monsoon rain gossiped with the thatched roof, whispering news from Sumatra and Malaya to the bamboo in the gray afternoon. Borjek lay on the operating table with his shirt off and one arm across his eyes, protecting them from even the dim light. When was it Sareno and I got in that stupid fight? Yesterday? Two days ago? I'm losing track of time; it's meaningless up here in the mountains, he thought. Nothing depends on time here; only the seasons mark it. No deadlines, no workweek, no television. It's curious, if you take away the demand for time, it eases off, meanders around like an old slow river. When was I in Vientiane? Two weeks ago, I think. Drinking beer on the rocks. He could imagine the warmth of alcohol spreading over his mind like a blanket. An alcoholic? Of course not, he answered himself. Maybe toward the end there in Bangkok, I was drinking more than usual. More than usual, hell. I was clearing my lungs every morning with a little glass of vodka and then a beer or two at lunch "to relax." By Thursday nights I was ready to start a weekend of steady drinking. I called it partying, fun, R&R, but it amounted to an alcoholic haze from Friday through Monday morning. Then he remembered the blanks, the times where there was no memory and the self-flagellation was too frightening to be amusing. A man close to self-destruction. Borjek's image of himself, the image he imagined he presented to others—that of a tough, straight-talking agent, a lady's man with no obsessions, a man not afraid of men or situations—was changing. In its place appeared a picture of a beefy-red face and a pot belly on a man who called drunkenness having a good time. A man getting old and everyone but him knowing it. Toughness now seemed inflexibility. Straight-talking became crudeness. A lady's man became a man who slept only with prostitutes. A man with no hang-ups became a man who had no beliefs. A man not afraid of men or situations became a man who refused to involve himself with others. I never saw it happening, he thought. That scared him.

The fact that he was thinking about his life scared him, too, for he had never been an introspective man. He operated close to the surface, on instant reaction to people and situations. On instinct. He rarely thought things over, and when he did, he wasn't sure he trusted what other people called rational thought. In Sop Hao, he was forced into working and living with others according to their standards of right and wrong, not his. He was involved in their lives and he was not used to it. Several days before, Chu-wei, who lived above Swe, had asked Borjek if he had any advice on how to grow larger potatoes. One day Tsao had wondered to him if it would be rude to ask a neighbor to return his hoe-stick, which the neighbor had borrowed several weeks earlier. Nai, Tanna-li's mother, had expressed concern to Borjek that Tanna-li was not married. He had answered them with gentle common sense, not certain at all of his replies. They expected him to make decisions and to give opinions far beyond the ones he had been issued by the Army and the Agency, ideas he had accepted for years without question. Borjek envied these people's beliefs, or, more precisely, their ability to believe.

The dispensary door opened and Borjek did not want to uncover his eyes.

"How are you feeling?" asked Caen.

"Better."

"Don't move. I'm just checking your vital signs." Bo put his fingers on Borjek's hairy wrist and began counting.

"What kind of powers does Dugpas Seng have?" asked Borjek. The words sounded slurred. His tongue was heavy in his mouth.

"You mean the chicken yesterday?"

"Sareno and I saw it fly to Seng and sit there while he cut its head off."

"It's hard to put into words. I've always thought there might be something to ESP. But there's a big difference between thinking ESP might be true and actually seeing the things I've seen in this village. And some of the things I've seen here go beyond ESP. By taking the mother's pulse, Seng has been able to predict the sex of every baby born in Sop Hao since I came here. He's tried to teach me how to do it, but only once in a while do I think I detect the difference between the pulse in one arm and the pulse in the other. It could be chance. After all, it's fifty-fifty anyway."

Bo adjusted a drip valve on the plastic bag hanging beside the operating table and went on. "He's also chosen the sex of babies for families who specifically wanted a boy or a girl. It involves about fifteen plants and certain rites that have to be performed daily for months."

"What's in the bag?" asked Borjek.

Bo noted that Borjek was more mentally alert than when he had staggered in four hours before. "Cobra venom mainly affects the nervous system. That's why you had trouble walking and speaking. But it also attacks the lining of blood vessels. This is a sugar and salt solution to keep your circulation strong. We're past the crisis. How do you feel?"

"I still can't keep my eyes open, and my stomach hurts. And my hand feels like it's rotting off."

"That's all normal. Can you tell me more about how the snake got you?"

"Somebody put it there, Caen. It was no accident."

"How do you know? Cobras occasionally get up this high. We got two bites last year."

"It was wrapped up inside my cassock. It couldn't get out so I don't see how it could've gotten inside. I worked this morning in the field, planting. I got back to Sareno's house—he wasn't there, by the way—and decided to take a bath. I was going to wear my robe down to the creek. I picked it up and thought it felt heavy. That's when the cobra came out—fangs first."

The snake nailed him behind his little finger and Borjek had shaken it loose before a full dose of venom had been injected.

"Sucking the venom out and putting on a tourniquet probably saved your life," said Caen.

"First the poisoned arrow, then Sareno attacks me in his baptism pool and now this. Where was Sareno the night Treadmill was killed?"

"I think he said that early in the evening he was with Tanni-li. Later, he went for a walk in the woods. Why? You don't think it was him, do you?"

"I don't know. I wouldn't have thought Sareno would try and drown me. Until yesterday."

Caen laughed. "For a mushroom god, you sure are vulnerable."

"Is that what they call me?"

"I heard that's why those Lahu were down yesterday. When Sareno first came to Sop Hao, they checked him out, too. Not because they were interested in a man who preached about God, but in the possibility that he might, in fact, be God. I haven't heard the verdict on you."

Borjek said nothing.

"I want you to stay another day. Do you feel up to seeing someone?"

"Who?"

"Seng is outside."

"Sure. Hell, I'm okay."

As Caen left, Dugpas Seng came in. "Thay mo Borjek?"

"Yes, kunag. Come in." Borjek found himself pleased to hear Seng's voice. A genuine eagerness to talk to another man for personal not business reasons was a new and warm feeling, Borjek admitted to himself.

Seng, carrying his conical bamboo hat dripping with water, shuffled to the table. "Dalam Caen said the man whose skin is as mature bamboo to the fangs of the *beua nga* was resting, and I hope my intrusion does not disturb that."

Borjek recalled Aung Swe's admonition to speak louder to Seng. "Please, kunag, sit. I apologize for not having any tea, but the delight of your company is a far richer pleasure." Borjek was no longer surprised to hear himself speak words which would have embarrassed him a month ago. Perhaps, he thought, it was because the Man language allowed a person to put as much or as little distance between the words and the speaker as he wanted.

Seng looked at Borjek. For a moment, the thay mo had opened his eyes and, though they seemed watery and weak, the whites had retreated a little since the priest first came to Sop Hao. Seng wondered why these people from the Americas placed little faith in san pa-ku. Was this man really any different from Treadmill, General Yone-fu or Colonel Su-wen? And why was he talking louder than usual?

"How is your spirit?" asked Seng.

"Much better. Dr. Caen said it's not unusual to have a quick recovery from a cobra bite, if one doesn't die."

"You are a strong man. The snake was seen later, and it was the size of a man's arm and as long as a buffalo's horn. Dalam Caen said you do not think the cobra mistook your clothing for a sheltered rock."

Borjek described how he had been bitten.

"There were no visitors to your house this morning?"

"I don't know." Borjek hesitated, then went on. "I don't recall seeing Law Dorje Oo at the planting this morning. I gather he only came to Sop Hao recently."

"He was born here and is a Man. But he has been influenced greatly by strangers—"

"Pathet Lao?"

"Perhaps others. He, too, wishes to purchase the opium crop," said Seng.

"For the Pathet Lao or the Chinese?"

"Even a slug can soar through the skies if it hides in the tail of a phoenix. If my directness is not offensive, why do you wish to buy our crop? Surely the poppy grows in your country and the expense of transporting it must be burdensome."

"It does not grow everywhere, and some places forbid it. The plant of dreams claims the highest respect from the world's monies. People will even kill for it."

"That I know," said Seng. "But why do you wish to buy it?"

"We want to keep it out of the hands of the Pathet Lao and the Red Chinese. It would give them excessive power."

"And to you it wouldn't?"

Borjek started to answer, but realized that Seng was right in his implication.

Seng asked, "What if the Pathet Lao and the Chinese did not want the ty fong ki?"

"I suppose we wouldn't either. But that is not the situation."

"If none were raised here, none could be bought."

"True, kunag, but we are willing to give you rice and salt as well as paper kip for the crop."

"If we did not grow the opium, we would have more rice than could fill our baskets. The rice which we received from the creatures that fly last season was of insubstantial quality. As for the salt, we have always traded the cinnamon plant to the Khmu for it. The kip? Although the colors are impressive, the taste is so obscure that even the addition of onions and pimento fails to define it."

Still, Borjek, thought, it seems to make sense to me that they grow opium to exchange for far more rice and spices than their rice itself would be worth. "Have you decided how much poppy to plant, kunag?"

"No. We do not plant the opium until the far side of the moon. Soon."

Borjek's thoughts drifted, and he wondered if the corn he had planted was sprouting yet. The seeds he had dropped into the ashen earth were the first thing he had ever planted, and twice since then he had returned to see if his corn was up. It was odd worrying about whether or not it would grow, what the corn would look like, if it would be as big as the rest in the field. He had never done anything with his hands before, except kill.

Seng asked, "Are your talents as a representative of the spirits extending to a length that is pleasing?"

"Between my visits to the dispensary and the spring planting, I've not had much chance to teach. The guidance you impart is a worthy example not only for the people of Sop Hao but myself as well."

"I? I am becoming old and move along what seems to be an ever-shortening path. I had hoped that when I achieved the ripeness of age, if not wisdom, Sop Hao would be prosperous and contented, and I could be concerned with discussing various methods to cook hares. Perhaps amuse children with my stories. But Sop Hao has problems which are as murky, yet as significant, as the flood waters of the Lan-Ts'ang. My abilities to perceive the middle way are receding as rapidly as the seasons seem to change these days."

Seng had spoken haltingly. Borjek understood that these were thoughts Seng could not say to anyone in the village.

"But," Seng added, "surely you have wisdom from your travels to pass along."

Me? Borjek's throat constricted, and he felt a rush of pity. My God, it must be the effects of the venom. Sure, old man, I know how to kill with a paper clip so that an autopsy shows death by stroke. Aloud, he said, "We learn from each other."

"Rest, thay mo. It has been tiring, even for a man to whom the poison of the cobra is as rain. I am offended that it appears a corrupt person from this village has caused such suffering to a guest."

Seng bowed and left.

CHAPTER XII

COBWEBS AND BEGONIA ROOTS

GREAT rafters of steam crisscrossed the kitchen of the house in which Dr. Beauregard Caen and Sylvia Karman lived. The rain outside had trapped the moist and smoky air inside, and water condensed on every surface. The brume blurred the two figures in the kitchen; they became murky phi brewing strange potions. Sylvia brushed at strands of hair stuck to her forehead, and cautiously stirred boiling water in a brass pot on a stone hearth. In the middle of the room Caen worked with test tubes, purple berries and small pots filled with colored liquids on a low table.

Sylvia pulled a thermometer from the pot and squinted at it. "Exactly two hundred and twenty-five degrees," she said.

"Keep on stirring," said Bo, dipping a pH test strip into a vial of buffered distilled water.

"How's our patient?" she asked.

"Better. He'll make it, although he did ask for Sareno to bring a Bible—for something to read."

"Do you think somebody put the snake in his cassock?"

"I don't know. It is a little late in the year to get one up here."

"What are you doing now?" Sylvia asked with mock exasperation.

"I'm trying to make a natural pH test from berry juice. Elderberries react to bases and acids by changing color." He poured part of the distilled water into another test tube and added a drop of red juice. After shaking the mixture, he held it beside a colored chart. "Pale yellow-green. About six and a half. It just tested at six point four using a pH strip. I think we've got a natural tester."

"My, my. And I think I got me a smart one. You're making pH tests and teaching me how to make soap."

Several days before, on a medical patrol to a village which had sacrificed a pig, Bo noticed the people did not use the fat of pigs. He asked for, and was given, the fat, along with encouragement to take the intestines as well. This, the rendering of hog fat into lard, was the first step in making soap. The Man bathed occasionally in the stream and used a white sappy liquid made from the berries of the mpat tree, a member of the holly family. While finding the mpat soap aromatic, Bo wanted a stronger soap to clean his medical instruments and himself before surgery.

"Where did you learn how to make soap?" asked Sylvia.

"Until I went off to college, I spent the summers with Grand-mother Viola, who lived on the edge of the Yemassee Swamp, about thirty miles from Charleston. She taught me to make soap." And she could have taught me a lot more, he added to himself. The Montagnards with whom Bo had worked in Viet Nam and the Man here had traditions going back hundreds of years. The smallest child could recite a litany of relatives for five or six generations. Bo found himself accepting that these children were influenced, even determined, by the beliefs, the ideals and the attitudes of their parents and grandparents. Accepting the tradi-tions of the Man forced Bo to wonder why he had neglected his for so long. He regretted that he had never gone back to his Grand-mother Viola before she died to learn more of his own legends. To visit the phi of his ancestors.

"I said, O distant one, there's a bunch of brown stuff floating to the top," said Sylvia, wondering what Bo had been thinking. I think I'm beginning to love this man too much, she thought. In that moment when she sensed he was not thinking about her, she felt like a little girl again. She was all dressed up to go out to a party and she should have been excited, but, instead, there was a cold hollow ache in her stomach. I wonder, she thought, if I'm not giving too much of my trust and love to this man.

"That's cracklins. We strain them off." He sliced the top of the water with a wooden spoon. "If you don't remove them, they'll sink back down after while and burn. We can cook them later. They're not bad."

"Tetched or not, this here Yankee girl is not eating any of that stuff."

Aung Ne Swe, the man who lived in the hog pen, offered another cup of tea to his guest, Dugpas Seng. With their wrinkles and gray hair, they seemed almost brothers.

"This is excellent tea, venerable," said Seng.

"A tribute more to the courtesy of my honored guest than to his taste buds, which are said to be more discriminating."

"It has been a long time since you and I entertained one another."

"This ancient body," said Swe, "refuses to either join its ancestors or to regain the sprightliness of youth. Too, my house discourages all but the persistent," said Swe, waving in the direction of the pigs, who were wallowing in the fresh mud outside.

"More likely, dear friend, it is your outspoken and sometimes outrageous opinions that tend to terrify potential guests. I am also beyond the age of any great productivity. You and I are the oldest in Sop Hao."

Swe nodded. "At times, I wonder what should become of me if I grow sick. I would not like to be as helpless as a baby monkey, with less to look forward to."

Seng took a small pinch of powdered tobacco from his ivory box and held it out for Swe. "Our days become more complicated and more dangerous. One is not allowed to be simply a man of his own generation," said Seng.

"The foreign thay mo withstood the fangs of the beua nga. How is he?"

"I spoke with him a short while ago. He will regain his health, but he is still a confused man. Light does not always follow a night of storms," said Seng.

"That is normal during this season. Ki, ki, ki, it is said you saw a white cobra several sunrises ago and I, myself, have seen omens: A lizard one night. And I dreamed of a large fish only yesterday."

"You have heard the howls of the fearsome new caak?"

"It is truly no animal, seer. Yesterday at dawn, I—"

"Sunrise yesterday?" interrupted Seng, for that was when he had sacrificed the chicken.

"The preceding night had been a busy one for several of us," Swe said, not looking up.

Seng wondered if his old comrade knew of his astral travel.

Swe went on. "At dawn yesterday, I sacrificed three apples and three fruits from the mak giang ngay tree."

"The most noble intentions cannot stop a crazed panther. Profundity, do you persist in the ancient, though questionable, attempts to liable the phi through sacrificing plants?"

"Illustrious one, few chickens would trip a panther either. Surely an adept such as you recalls the legends of the plant sacrifices to end the great rains?" asked Swe.

"Yes, sage, but the legends went on to say that ultimately the Mot brothers had to sacrifice a water buffalo to actually achieve the cessation of the rain."

"Implying no disbelief in you who are deserving of garlands, if not feathers, but that was a mere coincidence. As our ancestors discovered, when a human being eats an animal, he acquires some of the character of the inner being, the soul, of that animal. Rarely is this good. A buffalo can impart patience and strength, but also a shortness of temper and slowness of thought. A chicken has keen eyesight, but forgets what it saw moments later. It also tends to step in its own defecation."

"There is merit in that viewpoint, eminence, although it is still my opinion that if the ritual is done correctly, the spirit of the sacrificial animal departs from the body. Thus, one consumes only the discarded flesh. In the case of a chicken, after washing its feet, of course," said Seng.

"Need I recall that it was your ritual, involving the brain of a monkey, that we performed for Tsao when he complained of no interest in marital relations during the season of the sick tiger. As you and I discovered later, the ritual was the wrong one. I had suggested a concoction of cobwebs, begonia roots and honey. We all know the condition of Tsao these last seasons." Swe laid a small branch on the fire to create more light.

"Dear Swe, assuredly your memory is younger than your words. It was the addition of the crushed tips of trembling cinnamon which you suggested, not the monkey brains I included, that resulted in Tsao's amazing virility."

Both men chuckled at the memory, unable to keep the pretense of anger any longer.

"Didn't Tsao only want extra energy for special occasions?" asked Seng.

"Yes. He came to us saying he had been poorly and wanted a temporary rejuvenation. It was no matter that the ritual was the wrong one—I think we figured out later it was to relieve stomach cramps—because he believed. Do you suppose we should attempt to reduce his energy?"

"I have not heard his wife complain more than usual. Which is unlike the comments from nearly everyone else. They are concerned about the strangers and about how much ty fong ki to plant this season. And about Oo."

Swe stirred his tea with a section of orange peel. "It is said Oo is a man who would not be satisfied with a dozen water buffalo."

"What more has escaped these moss-covered ears of mine?" asked Seng.

"He encourages the people to plant much poppy and says he can bring them many donkeys loaded with rice and exotic spices after the harvest. He says he can order warriors from the north to protect Sop Hao. It is also reported he speaks ingloriously of the white people, especially thay mo Sareno and the mushroom god, but also dalam Caen and his woman. There are those," Swe paused delicately, "who incautiously inquire if Oo already speaks for you."

"The poisoned arrow? And the cobra?"

"Rumors, like weeds in the third season of a field, grow quickly. One should discard them else they crowd out the crops."

Seng said, "But like weeds, rumors have roots and, if the earth is fertile, grow stronger." He implored Swe to say more by putting a hand on his wrist.

"I heard Oo asking a villager about a cobra in the woods. It may have been a dream they were discussing, or even the omen you yourself mentioned. Nothing more. It is difficult for me to believe the things I hear about Oo. I still see him as a boy playing with the other children. I remember one day in the game where they catch the leaves falling from the trees, he caught the most and took them to you as a present."

"Like his mother, Oo was a handsome and quick, though short, youth. Swe, what is your opinion on the poppy?"

"The legends say Ten Luong took pity on man when we knew only to eat the bark of trees and gave us rice and taught us how to grow and prepare it. Ten Luong said nothing about the poppy. If a tree is cut back every spring, soon the tree will cease to grow."

"Your recollection of duty is appropriate. Ki, ki, ki, Swe, did you tell the mushroom god that my ears are clogged with the super-fluity of old age?"

"Why?" asked Swe, his eyes round in surprise.

"He seems to speak unusually loud when talking to me. I thought of you, naturally."

101

CHAPTER XIII

THE RAPE OF TANNA-LI

FATHER, make me more understanding of what thy divine plans are for me. I am not a very good minister of thy word, in addition to being a sinner. Remove jealousy and spite toward the Catholics from my heart. Turn my eyes from Tanna-li and her brown arms and her taffy breasts with, ah, those nipples . . ."

The prayer trailed off as a picture of her body filled his mind. Beneath the small, but round, hips were long legs and thigh muscles which corded and rippled with every step. Oh, what's wrong with me, Father? Sareno leaned back on his heels and stared at the slanting rays of the sun, driven in great slabs of light through the trees. Somewhere to the west, beyond Burma, the sun was setting. Borjek was still at the dispensary recuperating from the snake bite, and Sareno had decided to seek solitude in the woods in order to sort the questions in his mind. When he was a boy, he had turned to the forest to find his calm.

The coming of the priest to Sop Hao had shaken Sareno loose from an attitude of lethargy and self-deceit. The last letter from the Foreign Mission Board contained a polite inquiry about why Sareno had not been reporting more souls converted to Baptism. Sareno found himself fudging on figures; he had implied there were several dozen, perhaps more, on the brink of the pool. But he could stall for only so long. The image of himself standing before the Board with Ek Tho and his Coca-Cola bottle filled him with despair.

Where is that missionary zeal I had when I first arrived? he asked himself. Some of the Man rituals to pagan idols don't seem so wrong to me now. I've become more interested in the everyday life of these people, in farming and in talking to Tanna-li. That troubled him, too. Could not God look into Tanna-li's heart and know that she was basically a good woman? How could it be that she, an innocent in religion who did not yet understand the necessity of being born again, would go to hell if she suddenly died, because she had never heard of Baptism until eighteen months ago?

Because, a tired and nagging voice said, of The Original Sin. We are all sinners. Perhaps next Sunday I could preach on The Original Sin. No, that wouldn't make sense to the Man because they don't believe sex is wrong, unless it is with brother, sister, parent or first cousin. If I told them the story of Adam and Eve, they would not understand how that could be sinful. Worse, they might be amused. Sex and marriage are usually in that order here. Furthermore, if I explained it, I would be insulting their mores and their ancestors. I would lose their respect, maybe even be asked to leave.

I can't tell them they are sinners because I will lose them. And if I can't tell them they are sinners, I can't save them. Sareno shook his head, trying to jar his thoughts into a new pattern. "Suffer while you can, boy," my daddy said. And my daddy knew suffering.

The raw anger that Sareno had experienced Sunday in the fight with the priest had shocked him. Until then, he had not fought as an adult, and his childhood fights had not been serious. But curiously enough, the fight had given him a new emotion, a feeling he wasn't sure he liked: a pride in his own body. Borjek had outweighed him by fifty or more pounds, yet Sareno had hurt him and he could have hurt him more. He had seen surprise in the priest's eyes; surprise at his own fury and strength. He began to understand how some men could be vain about their bodies and their ability to physically defeat other men. This must be a form of egotism against which God warned. Yet the self-confidence was a pleasant sensation, and Sareno kept touching it to find its parameters.

Perhaps I'm not meant to be a minister. He forced the thought away but it crept back, cloaked in the idea that maybe he had misread a deep religious faith for the desire to be a minister. A desire, he thought, with origins lost somewhere in my youth. If I wasn't called to be a minister, that would explain why I've not had more converts here. I honestly think that one reason why I never stayed in Tennessee long enough for a pastorate of my own was because I was uncertain how good a minister I would be. I thought these natives would be easier. Forgive me, Father. It is no sin not to be a minister. I could still love and serve you. It occurred to him that his mission could even be a disservice to the church if someone else could be doing a better job.

The light was disappearing, and night would soon chase the gray haze from the forest floor. Sareno stood, brushed himself off and walked down the hill toward Sop Hao, a half-mile away.

If I left missionary work, it would mean virtually giving these people to the Catholics, unless Borjek is not going to stay here. Sareno admitted that so far Borjek had done little to spread Catholicism. How could I ever face the Foreign Mission Board again. To return a failure. On the other hand, maybe I could stay on here. For a year or two. That might be the answer. A sabbatical from the church. A year without the pressure of reporting how many souls had been saved each month. If I weren't a minister, perhaps I could talk to Tanna-li as a person. As an ordinary man . . .

Sareno stepped off the trail into the bushes to urinate. Tomorrow, we'll be planting the field near—Sareno heard voices and squeezed his penis to stop the urine so he could listen. One voice belonged to a man. Oo? Pressure from his bladder burned, and Sareno loosened his grip and aimed the pale yellow stream to make as little noise as possible. He finished and carefully stole toward the sounds. With a sinking heart, Sareno recognized the other voice as Tanna-li's. The underbrush was thick and the shadows long. Something made a noise in a bush nearby and Sareno's heart pounded. Finally he made out several of the flying wild chickens making their roosts for the night. Slipping a branch aside, Sareno saw Oo and Tanna-li on a log in a small clearning. Tanna-li sat with her delicate hands in her lap, her arms pushing her breasts together. Oo was beside her with one arm around her waist. He wore a loin cloth and she a brown sarong.

"You know we can," Oo said. "There's no reason not to. Everyone knows we are together and probably believes we are making love. Come." He slid his other hand around her waist.

Sareno was tense. He wanted to shout, "Don't!"

Tanna-li said, "It is said one should not bake the fish until one has dug the bait."

"It is also said one should not hesitate to take the ripest of the avocados, for their succulence fades in a day. Come, my avocado, talk is for old age, which at the rate we progress may not be far." His hand crept to her thigh, each millimeter measured by Sareno.

She shrugged his hand away and said, "Is your interest that of the avocado thief in the dark or of he who plants the seeds and patiently raises a garden of his own?"

"It is a long time between the seeding and the harvesting. Leave questions of complication to others. Come closer, touch me. Here."

Tanna-li stood abruptly. Oo pulled her arm toward him, and she fell backward, tumbling both of them off and behind the log.

In the bushes, Sareno rose on his toes, trying to see past the fading light to the flailing legs the log had grown. Frustration and helplessness tasted sour. Sareno knew he was losing her, that he never had her, that it was as usual, only daydreams shielding him from reality.

He quoted to himself from Job, his favorite book in the Bible: "So I am allotted months of emptiness, and nights of misery are apportioned to me." The dream came back and in self-pity, Sareno allowed it to unroll. He had been thirteen or fourteen when he first had the dream. In it he walked outside his Tennessee home, past the wooden barrel that collected rainwater for washing, and around the corner of the house. There on the ground was his mother, naked and still. Her eyes were closed and her legs were spread apart obscenely. In the dream, Sareno would stare at her heavy sagging breasts, at her legs and the patch of hair between them. He would become sexually aroused, standing there and looking. Sometimes the dream mercifully ended there. Sometimes it would end with him ejaculating and waking and weeping with shame and fear. And sometimes the dream would end in screams, when he realized she was dead.

From behind the log, Sareno detected sounds of struggling . . . or . . . lovemaking. He almost left.

Then Tanna-li said, "Oo, do you wish to have children with me?"

Sareno wanted to cover his ears.

Oo laughed. "Children? I only want to taste the sweetness of one avocado, not harvest the entire crop."

Sareno heard the sound of a slap; the struggling grew louder and more violent. He stepped forward hesitantly. Tanna-li demanded that Oo release her. His answer was coarse and hard. Sareno saw a figure stand, only to be pulled backward. The shadows danced deceptively. Tanna-li cried out in pain, and there was the sound of flesh hitting flesh and of cloth tearing.

She needs help. She needs me, thought Sareno. He shoved tree limbs aside and stumbled toward the clearing. To the left and right of Sareno, in the smaller trees, chickens were wakened by strange noises, and their rooster clucked a warning. One of the branches bent by the Baptist swatted a chicken on the tail and with that, the flock fled toward the clearing in a great flapping and cackling exodus.

As Sareno came into the open area, he was vaguely aware that the chickens had swarmed out of the bushes, but his concern was more immediate. He barely recognized the log in the dark and jumped to it as the main body of the flock zigzagged around him. Two of the chickens miscalculated and sailed flush into the log; another glanced off Sareno's shoulder.

On the ground, the noise finally penetrated Oo's preoccupation and he let Tanna-li go. *"Sap-saang,"* he cursed, sitting up. Silhouetted against the sky in front of him was a terrible sight. Some sort of giant creature was shouting and cackling at him. Around it, smaller demons flew and cavorted in the air. Oo reeled backward as he dodged one of the lesser creatures.

"Ay! Caaks," he screamed and ran blindly into the forest.

Tanna-li, who had been nearly hysterical, turned to see the cause of Oo's flight. She recognized a voice immediately.

"Ti hak Tanna-li, my love, are you all right?"

Strong hands lifted her gingerly. Instinctively she put her arms around Sareno and pressed her face against his chest.

She is so small, so delicate, Sareno thought, his heart beating furiously. He spoke in incomplete sentences, forming soft words of consolation and kindness. He stroked her hair and listened as the crashing of Oo through the woods faded away.

After a few minutes her crying became sniffles, and Sareno became embarrassingly aware that she was naked. She would not let one of his hands loose while he searched the ground for her skirt.

Sareno saw candlelight in the dispensary as they went by, but knowing the Man women would not let a male examine them, no matter how powerful a sorcerer he might be, they continued on to the doctor's house. They found Sylvia wrapping large gray-brown cakes of homemade soap in leaves. Sareno briefly explained what had happened and left Tanna-li with her. He went to the dispensary to wait with Bo.

Over tea, Tanna-li gradually relaxed enough to tell her story in bits and pieces. Oo had tried to rape her. He managed to insert some of his penis, or perhaps all, for Tanna-li couldn't tell in the struggle. Then Sareno chased him away. Sylvia examined the girl as best she could. Only the younger women would let another woman look at their sexual organs, and then no touching was permitted. Sylvia found bruises, already turning an ugly purple against the honey skin. There were small cuts on her face and back from the rocks and limbs. The real damage, Sylvia surmised, was emotional.

After a few minutes Tanna-li was calmer and talked more openly. "This is the first time he ever attempted to, uh, do that. I am confused about Oo. He is interesting and has traveled to other lands. When he speaks of the strange things he has seen and done, I am fascinated. But part of him is stubborn, and he becomes angry over things I do not understand."

"You like Oo?" asked Sylvia.

Tanna-li looked beyond her tea cup. "I was born in the season of som tranh and nearly all the girls my age have husbands and children. There are few young men left."

Sylvia wanted to say, "Honey, I know the feeling myself."

The girl went on, "I don't think Oo wants to marry me and have a home. He speaks of many other things, of revolutions and fighting. He never talks of children and planting. He never sees us in the future."

"Is there no one else?" asked Sylvia, dabbing peroxide on the cuts.

Tanna-li glanced up quickly, and Sylvia saw a strange look in her eyes. "I'm afraid."

"Don't worry, you are safe here."

"No, not tonight. There's something else . . ."

Sylvia took her hand. "You can talk to me."

"Several moons ago when the white farang died—Treadmill was his name—" She pronounced his name in separate words. "It was the night he died . . ."

"Please go on."

"The next day Oo made me promise to say that he was with me the night the farang died. I have done that but it has given me anguish. I had been alone that evening because my parents were with cousin Pakse, who was sick."

"Pakse? Tsao's son?"

"Yes. He's a second cousin to my mother. Early in the evening, thay mo Sareno came to visit, and we sat on a rock and talked for a while. He held my hand for the first time, and it became a beautiful night. He left soon because my parents would be coming back. It was late. Later, I think he must have heard that I said Oo spent the night with me, and I think it hurt him deeply. He did not come to visit for a long time. He probably thinks that after he left, Oo came and stayed with me. I wanted to tell him it wasn't true, but I thought I was in love with Oo, and I had promised him. Thay mo Sareno never speaks of that night. I am afraid and confused."

Sylvia knew Tanna-li's parents would not have been greatly displeased to hear she spent the night with Oo because they, perhaps more than she, were worried about the paucity of suitors.

"What are your feelings about Sareno?" asked Sylvia.

Tanna-li looked up, blinking her eyes. "I . . . I like him. He is gentle, yet strong. He had been kind to me and my parents. Tonight he was fierce in the woods. And I also think"—she giggled—"he is pretty."

"How does he feel about you?"

"I don't know. I am so young. How could he like me? I am not pretty, nor have I traveled anywhere. I cannot understand things that are written. I am a *kha*. But when he shielded me from Oo, I felt his . . . heart beating very fast, and I wondered if he might like me a little."

"I think you ought to tell him how you feel," Sylvia said.

Tanna-li's eyes widened. "You do? Do you think . . .?"

"I think he likes you very much."

CHAPTER XIV

A DISCUSSION
OF BORJEK'S GODLINESS

THE Lahu village of Pok Nane was ten miles closer to China and a thousand feet higher than Sop Hao. This noon, Pok Nane's council of hunters was gathered in the hut of Chom-the-carver. He began, "We have witnessed the white, white man called the mushroom god, and it must be decided if he is more than that. If he is Chyanun-Woishun himself. I would pass around my deplorable pipe, but unfortunately it is empty . . ."

Familiar with Chom's meetings, the hunters glanced at Shay, whose turn it was. Shay said, "I happen to have some disgustingly old and probably tasteless sap from the flower of dreams, exalted." He offered a red velvet marble of opium to Chom.

"Ah, thank you, Shay. Your family deserves its edifying reputation, not only for its generosity but for growing the finest plants in these hills." From his hair Chom removed a sliver of bamboo, the end of which was frayed as fine as an eyelash from hours of chewing. He reamed the pipe with it and replaced the stick in his hair, for the tars collected on it would be smoked later.

After lighting the long pipe, Chom said, "This being fulfills many of the stories of Chyanun-Woishun. He wears a black cloth over his entire body, his hair is the color of a mango and he is a white man."

Luba, one of the younger hunters, said, "His hair has departed the top of his head and is short on the sides. Unusually short." He looked at the pipe as Chom inhaled again.

"There is nothing in the legends about the length of God's hair, although I, too, noticed its youth. God could grow his hair as short as he wished. Perhaps He doesn't allow it to grow in order to further distinguish Him from animals."

"Not all animals have long hair," noted Shay. "I was the one who first saw him, flying and whirling through the sky and—"

"We know, Shay," said Chom.

Li, who was sitting to Chom's right, said, "Then, too, his eyes are round." His hand fluttered in the air as if describing the roundness of an eye, or perhaps the movement of a hand about to receive a pipe.

"He came as a white man, and as such, his eyes had to be strangely designed," Chom answered.

"He looks not at all like an alligator," said Shay.

"An alligator?" Li asked.

Luba broke in, "What does an alligator look like?"

Shay said, "I don't know. Like a dragon, I suppose. Perhaps smaller, but similar."

"Then you're right. He doesn't look like an alligator," said Luba.

"But wait," interrupted Li. "Why should he look like an alligator?"

"Didn't Ka-ang Duwa mate with an alligator and have six sons, the youngest—"

"That was later," corrected Chom. "The alligators did mate with Ka-ang as well as with Shingra Wa and Shingra Kumja and others, but it was Chyanun-Woishun's son that mated, not Chyanun-Woishun himself. He was before all and was all, from the beginning. The shadip nats were sons of Chyanun-Woishun and the first humans were dama to the shadip nats and the mu nats."

"How do you suppose they mated with alligators?" asked Li, trying to inhale smoke as it wafted by."

Shay said, "They would have been female alligators, since they mated with men. It looks to me like you would take the alligator and turn her over on her back—"

"Enough of this talk about alligator mating," said Chom. "We have heard the mushroom god has survived the *hrup* poison arrow."

"If the poison was made by one of the Man Lan Mien, its strength would be questionable," said Li.

"But it is also said he blunted the fangs of the cobra," said Luba.

Chom said, "In a dream last night I saw two crows in a cedar tree on my left side. Naturally, this morning I placed a winnowing basket with two pieces of corn under a cedar tree in the woods. My opinion, based on many years as interpreter of events, is that the mushroom god is probably Chyanun-Woishun. God. We should continue observing him and treat him as such unless the spirits tell us otherwise."

"Your words are the morning song of the dove," said Li.

"Is the pipe well lit, elder?" asked Luba

"Ah, yes. Come and go, it was said that a great demon and hundreds of smaller flying nats attacked young Oo near Sop Hao yesterday, driving him into the forest."

Shay said, "Oo? That explains why he was seen this morning walking in the direction of northern mountains."

"They say he was with Tanna-li, the unmarried daughter of Kwan and Nai, who was strenuously resisting his charms. So much so that he had to allow his muscles to make paths where his lips could not," said Chom.

The hunters laughed.

"It is truly said that a bullfrog seeking to capture an eagle has a great deal to learn about flying," said Li, staring at Chom's pipe.

"Obtuse, but succinct. It causes me to wonder if the caaks were sent by the mushroom god. Luba, perhaps you would indulge in the pipe?"

"Yes, fount. Thank you." Luba puffed once before the remainder of the opium was consumed.

Later that day, Tsao, his wife and Dugpas Seng were hunkered around the stove/fireplace in Tsao's house. The stove, a large flat stone the size of a buffalo head, rested on four smaller stones in a bed of sand. More rocks, carried from the Mekong so as to be smooth and hard, formed the sides. The fire contrasted pleasantly with the afternoon rains falling monotonously outside. Tsao's wife was preparing *ele*, fresh trout netted that morning by Tsao in the great river. The whole fish was placed in a section of bark from the banana tree. On the fish, she put lemon peel, cardamom, which grew wild in the woods, onions and in place of salt, which was used only for religious feasts, she sprinkled cinder from the burnt bark of an oak tree.

Seng and Tsao had been chatting for nearly a full chew about the quality of trout this year, and a pause in the talk indicated that the preliminary conversation was concluded.

Seng asked, "Has Oo been seen today?"

"No, kunag, although it is rumored he left Sop Hao and headed toward the northern mountains." Tsao chuckled. "The wrath of a woman is bad enough, but add that of demons and it is terrifying. Ayi."

"Demons?"

Tsao looked at Seng. "Do you not know about Oo and the caaks last night?"

"It was my impression that Oo was stopped from disgracing himself and his ancestors even further by thay mo Sareno," said Seng.

"Thay mo Sareno? Ki, ki, ki. Others say it was a huge caak attended by flying nats that drove Oo away. It is said Oo has the enmity of the phi now, and that Tanna-li may have their special favor." Tsao watched his wife slide the ele under the large rock to steam and bake. "That is also why I did not go into the forest today. The spirits of the forest are angry and may even have prompted me to remember we had not eaten fish for some time."

"Tell me, Tsao, what are your thoughts about raising ty fong ki this season?"

"We have always grown the plant of dreams, kunag, and you have advised us most wisely through the seasons. I am but the hands and feet to your eyes and ears. On the other side of the mountain, however, there is some discontent that our supplies of rice are low because we grew so little last season. And there is curiosity about the farang who visited you."

"They want to buy twice as much opium this year," said Seng.

Tsao shook his head. "Our burden is heavy, kunag. Your hands and feet cannot grow more without growing more hands and feet. The only way would be to plant less rice . . ."

Seng did not answer.

Tsao made a sharp clicking with his tongue, a sign of disapproval. "Kunag, I don't understand. Only a few seasons ago, we grew enough rice so that even the chickens had round stomachs in the dry season."

"The farang said they would be most distressed should we fail to raise a sufficiency of opium."

"Uncle," said Tsao's wife, Sou-ei, "were these farang the strangers who carried guns into our village?"

"Yes."

Tsao clicked his tongue again. "There were those who questioned this location when we moved here. But our kunag assured us that benevolent spirits favored this ground. Now the phi are restless. There is the howling caak and the ones that attacked Oo. In such times, I find contentment at home with my wife." He placed a hand on her knee as she hunkered by the fire. She smiled and glanced shyly at Seng.

"Oo must be brought before the village for a judgment. He will take the epa gie," Seng said.

Tsao nodded while caressing his wife's leg.

"He will be tested by the phi, and they will determine the punishment. Then we can live with contentment." Seng's eyes were sad and unmoving in the firelight.

Tsao slid his other hand under his loincloth and absentmindedly touched himself.

Seng stood. "I must go to prepare my own supper." He did not expect an offer from Tsao to join them, not because Tsao was not a generous man, but because he had other things on his mind at the moment.

Borjek sat on the dispensary table while Bo examined his eyes with an ophthalmoscope. The only noticeable effect of the cobra bite was a lingering ache in his right hand.

"You can leave tomorrow," said Bo.

"Good. Where did you go today?"

"Today was our regular day at Chiang Sin. We just got back a little while ago. Look straight into the light."

"How is the girl, Tanna-li? The reverend was fit to be tied last night. Did Oo really rape her?"

"He did."

"Jesus. What are they going to do with him?"

"If they catch him, they'll hold a public trial. The punishment will be determined by what the spirits say."

"I get it. Who interprets what the spirits say?"

"Dugpas Seng, the village chief."

"Where did Oo go?"

Bo switched the scope to the other eye. "Probably into the hills or maybe into China. No one's seen him since."

Borjek was relieved by Oo's disappearance. Swe's description of one of the men who was seen the night Treadmill died fitted Oo, although the other man could easily have been Sareno. Borjek wondered what the relationship was between Oo and Seng.

"How's Tanna-li?" asked Borjek.

"She's all right. Sareno broke it up before Oo had done any real damage. A few bruises. Which reminds me. She told Sylvia something interesting about the night Treadmill died?"

"Yeah?"

"It seems Oo was not with Tanna-li that night. She said Oo came to her the next day and told her to swear that he was with her all night."

"That pretty well proves it," said Borjek.

"Oo killed Treadmill?" Bo said, putting the ophthalmoscope back into a canvas bag.

"He was the logical one all along, but everyone thought he was with Tanna-li."

"I've been reading more about poisons, and I have a theory about how he was murdered. Peach pits contain a small amount of hydrocyanic acid, also called prussic acid. It's a cyanide."

"Treadmill ate peach pits?"

"No. It was definitely a gas. All the signs point to a gas, probably a cyanide. Wild cherries, almonds and peach pits all have traces of hydrocyanic acid. If Oo collected enough of the poison, got it ignited somehow and filled Treadmill's hut with it, it would have killed him."

"That sounds like a pretty sophisticated way to kill somebody."

"Not really. Oo wouldn't have the faintest idea what it was. Generations ago, someone discovered, probably the hard way, that crushed pits were deadly, then someone else figured out a way to prepare the poison."

"I'm convinced Oo did it."

"So?"

Borjek wiggled into his shirt. "I don't know. If he's working for the Red Chinese and if anything happens to him, they'll just send in someone else."

"I think you should let the people here settle it. His fellow villagers."

"Maybe that would be best. What's your theory about Sareno?"

"I think he's having doubts about his mission. He's not been able to make—"

"Not that. About his peeing all the time."

"Peeing? Urinating?"

"Constantly. Hell, every time I see him he's got his root out."

"Really? He shows you his penis?" asked Bo.

"He doesn't show me. In fact, he's always embarrassed about it, but—"

"You go to watch him?"

"Of course not. It seems to be coincidence. Whenever I come up on him somewhere in the woods, at Treadmill's grave or wherever, he's peeing."

"Tell me, do you just stand there or do you pee with him?" Bo cocked his head.

"You don't believe me, do you? You've never seen him pee?"

"I can't say I have. Is it unusual? A strange color, or perhaps he has an oddly shaped penis?"

"Let's forget it," said Borjek.

"I wouldn't worry about it, Martin. You've been isolated out here for a couple weeks. It's probably a passing phase. Your mind can think in strange—"

"Not me, idiot. Him. He's the one peeing. Christ." Borjek buttoned his pants. "By the way, how does one get a haircut around here?"

"You don't if you're smart. The Man are afraid to cut their hair."

"Why?"

"The soul of a person dwells inside his body, but it is especially, ah, involved with your hair. At night when you are dreaming, your

116

soul is off on nocturnal wanderings. When it comes back, it recognizes you from your hair. If the hair is cut and buried, your soul will search for it and, finding it buried, will think the body is dead. It will flee to the realm of the spirits. Then you're in big trouble. If your body wakes up without its soul, it will be obliged to die."

CHAPTER XV

THE BURNED GIRL INCIDENT

THE next day was the fourteenth since Borjek had jumped from a plane into a Laotian midnight. Shortly before noon, the burned girl was carried into the dispensary at Sop Hao. Borjek had been alone. He had awakened at dawn as had become his habit. After Sylvia had brought a breakfast of fresh orange juice, water and rice with a few chunks of meat, he began reading the Bible which Sareno had sent over. He started from boredom, but found himself continuing because it was curiously relaxing. "It is good for me that I was afflicted that I might learn thy statutes. The law of thy mouth is better to me than thousands of gold and silver pieces . . . They draw near who persecute me with evil purpose; they are far from the law . . ." At times his eyes formed the words, but his mind did not absorb them; his thoughts drifted through a simple void. "Better is a poor man who walks in his integrity than a man who is perverse in speech and is a fool. He—"

Voices outside interrupted, and Borjek quickly laid the Bible aside. He opened the door to three men and a woman carrying a young girl on a litter made of sticks and rags. A torn, stained cloth spilled across the girl's body and part of her face. He motioned them inside. As Borjek helped carry the litter to the operating table, he noticed the heat of the day for the first time.

After the girl was laid down, the woman dropped her crusty brown fingers on his arm like a chain and spoke in a dialect Borjek did not recognize. They believe I'm the doctor, he realized. He tried Man, but they shook their heads. He turned to fetch Caen, but the woman, fearing that he was leaving, pulled him toward the girl. She peeled back the cloth from the girl's shoulder. Borjek stared, at first not understanding the black and green substance before him; it was curdled and cracked like drying mud. The woman gently lifted the green things, which turned out to be leaves. Borjek was frozen by what he saw. What remained was flesh, burned horribly and disfigured into charred bark.

The woman reached out to take the cloth from the girl's face, but Borjek stopped her. "Please. Sit down. Wait. I'll get the doctor," he said, not caring if they understood. He led the woman to a chair and made her sit. He gestured for them to stay.

Borjek was halfway to the house when he met Bo and Sylvia coming toward him.

"Someone was carried in?" asked Bo.

"A girl, doc. She's burned bad. I can't understand their language."

"Sylvia, find Seng and ask him to come to the dispensary."

Bo preceded Borjek into the building. He nodded at the others and went to the girl. Starting with her face, Bo gingerly removed the scraps of cloth, leaves and mud. She had been pretty—high cheekbones, thin lips, a feline face. Part of her hair and eyelashes were stubble and her right eye was hidden under a mass of exudate. The left side of her body was not burned as badly as the right.

"God in heaven," muttered Bo. "I don't know why she's alive." He scissored off the rest of the blanket and clothing. Occasionally, a piece of skin would stick to the cloth. Underneath, a gray-green mucus oozed.

"And she's pregnant, too," said Borjek. A tight, round stomach had been hidden by the coverings.

"Real pregnant." Bo's palm rested on the girl's stomach. "I think the baby is alive."

At his motion, the older woman spoke, her face grim and her voice high. Bo, guessing what she asked, nodded yes.

Borjek stared at the girl's breasts. The right one was large, plump and full, the nipple dark and swollen. The left breast was partially burned and a chalky fluid seeped from its nipple. He realized that for the first time, he was seeing a girl's body without lust, seeing her as a woman, capable of creating life. The girl's left hand uncurled and reached out. One eye opened and looked at him, and he took her hand. It felt like a child's.

Bo went quickly to work. He hung a bottle of isotonic saline on a wooden hanger beside the table and fitted a needle to a syringe.

"I've got to get to the vein in that arm," he said.

Borjek tried to release her hand, but she held him tightly. He shifted around so Bo had room to work.

A few minutes later, Seng, Sareno and Sylvia arrived. Seng tried several dialects before finding one which, though not exact, allowed some understanding. A mixture of Tibetan, Burmese and Mandarin Chinese, it was similar to the language of Seng's childhood. When the family understood Seng, they all began talking at once.

Sareno, who had been standing quietly to one side, was paler than usual. His skin was white to the point of translucence, and beads of perspiration spotted his forehead. The Bible which Borjek had put aside found its way to Sareno's hands, where it was slowly being twisted.

"Ninety over fifty," said Sylvia, reading the sphygmomanometer.

"She needs blood in a hurry," said Bo. "Martin, what's your blood type?"

"A positive."

"Sareno?"

The minister's eyes were focused on the girl; he showed no sign of hearing Bo.

"Sareno? Man, get a hold of yourself."

"O, I think. O positive. Excuse me." He left hurriedly, his tall body bent at the waist.

"Sylvia?"

"The same. O positive."

"Not a hell of a lot of choices. Sylvia, set the drip at three a second while I type her blood. Kunag Seng?"

"Yes, dalam?"

"Can you inquire if she has urinated since . . . the accident?"

A flurry of words were exchanged and Seng said, "Yes, several hours ago on the trail as they carried her."

Borjek asked, "What are her chances, doc?"

"Not good. Seng, can you find out more about where they're from and what happened to her?"

While Bo typed her blood, Seng began to translate what they said. "They are Lun Chun, a people that live three or four nights to the north. They are perhaps Tibetan, perhaps Chinese, perhaps older than both. There are not many of them left. Their home is called Ta Xai." Seng stopped occasionally to ask a question. "The girl is Lu Xi Liao and these are her parents, her brother and her husband."

Bao, her father, looked ancient. Not old, ancient. His features were those of a human fifty thousand years ago. His face was a cross between a lion and a monkey. Large cheekbones were far apart and pushed upward into the undersides of his eyes, which were like his daughter's. The bones above the eyes were sharp, giving them a sunken, dark expression. A long upper lip guarded a wide slit of a mouth and a small chin. Bao wore his hair long in matted curls that brushed the top of his chest. The girl's mother had a rounder face with her eyes closer together. The tension and exhaustion had deepened the wrinkles lining the corners of her eyes and mouth. The son was a younger version of his mother. The girl's husband was a powerfully built man with a muscular chest and long, corded arms. The only description that fit all of them was simian.

"They were working their fields late the day before yesterday. Bao says Lu Xi Liao was digging in the earth with a hoe-stick when there was suddenly a huge noise and fire. It threw her backward and set her afire."

"A napalm bomb?" Borjek wondered aloud.

"Bao says at first he thought it was the creatures that fly returning. Such white fires were dropped by them in the past. But they saw and heard nothing in the sky."

Borjek said, "Ask if the field where this happened was bombed in past seasons."

Seng said, "He says, 'Yes. Several seasons ago.'"

"My God," said Borjek. "An old bomb that didn't go off when it landed."

Sareno, looking as though he had been sick, slipped back inside the door.

The girl, Liao, spoke. Her words were dry and weak. Seng leaned over her mouth and listened.

"She says, 'Are you not the one they call the mushroom god?'"

"Me?" asked Borjek.

"You are," said Seng, and he nodded to the girl. She tried to smile, but it became a grimace.

Borjek asked Bo, "How can she stand pain like this?"

"I doubt there is much pain. She's got third-degree burns, which destroy the nerve endings themselves. She probably feels very little."

Sareno coughed and said in a reedy voice. "Is there anything I can do?"

An awkward silence was relieved by Seng. "These people have not eaten in more than a day. Perhaps you could ask Tsao's wife if she could prepare some rice. And bring some water."

Sareno nodded gratefully and left.

"Have they been walking for a day and a half?" asked Borjek.

"Nearly two days. It normally is a three- or four-day journey. The way was rough, and the rains made it difficult to walk in the mountains. Bao said they stopped only a few times to rest. He said they had heard there was a dalam in Sop Hao who could perform wondrous cures and that is why they came here. Because she is growing a baby inside her."

From the work counter, Bo said, "We're in luck. She has A positive. Borjek?"

"Hell yes. I got plenty of extra blood."

"Let me first get a drop and try a cross match for antibody reaction." Bo pricked his finger and pressed a drop onto a slide. A few minutes later he said, "It's okay. Not the greatest test in the world, but we don't have time for more sophisticated work."

"What about the baby?" asked Sylvia.

"That's who I'm trying to save. If we don't act now, it will be too late for both. Her blood pressure is falling. Come, Martin, let's get a transfusion started. Move a cot in here beside the operating table. I'm going to do a direct transfusion to save time. Sylvia, see if you and Seng can find out when the baby is due. And wet her lips and mouth with water, but don't let her drink any."

After a half-dozen exchanges among Sylvia, Seng and the girl's parents, it was determined that Liao had been pregnant for either seven-and-a-half months or eight-and-a-half months. It was her first child. She and Zhen, her husband, had been married at the end of the harvest season, about six months ago.

"Doc! Sylvia! I think she's in pain," said Borjek. The girl had pulled his hand to her swollen stomach. Her eye was clinched tightly, and she opened her mouth as if to cry out. Liao's mother came to her side and spoke with her.

"What is it?" Bo asked.

Seng said, "She says it is beginning. The child."

"Tell her to let us know when the next pain comes, the next time her stomach tightens," said Bo, working a needle into Borjek's arm. "Sylvia, get some water started, my delivery pack out and plenty of towels ready. Find out if she's had a discharge of clear fluid."

Her parents said she had, earlier that morning.

The next hour went quickly. Bo began diverting a pint of Borjek's blood into Liao. Between contractions that now came every three minutes, he examined the fetus. Its heartbeat was one hundred-and-forty five per minute, which was normal. The cervix was dilating, and the baby seemed to be positioned correctly.

The girl's husband, father and brother went outside the dispensary when it became apparent she was to deliver the baby. Although they said nothing to Bo or any of the other men, they were abiding by their own tradition that males do not attend the birth of a child. Wuan, the girl's mother, talked to her in a gentle, caressing voice. Seng said she was telling Liao to relax and be calm; that it was going as the gods intended and that the dalam was here. Normally the village midwife would be in attendance while the mother hunkered over a specially prepared cotton blanket beside a fire. During the birth, the mother would support herself by a rope hanging from the roof of the hut.

As the contractions closed in toward each other, Sylvia and Bo washed the girl's perineum and thighs, and readied the table with basins and towels. A stand for instruments was set up. While checking the cervix and the contractions, Bo also cleaned the burns and watched the girl's vital signs. Her blood pressure dropped to seventy over forty and then seemed to stabilize. She perspired heavily, and her pulse was weak and thready; Seng described it as feathery. She was in advanced shock. After Borjek's pint of blood had flowed into her, Bo started the saline solution again.

Liao seemed to rally a little as the contractions accelerated—two minutes apart now. Several times she asked for the mushroom god. Borjek moved to a stool beside her and held her hand.

Borjek had seen many men die in many different ways, but he could not remember having seen anyone as mutilated as this girl live. Her hand was cold and damp in his, but he could feel the tiny beat of her heart, even as his blood had flowed into hers. Except for those first few contractions, she had withstood the rest with no more than a stiffening in her neck.

As much to calm everyone as to explain, Bo told them that much of the pain of childbirth is a learned response, a fear of the unknown. Most primitive people, like the Man and the Lun Chun, were not afraid of birth, he said. They had seen it from the time they were children. Pregnant women worked in the fields until labor commenced. There was nothing unusual, strange or terrifying about it.

Sareno returned and said that several people were cooking rice for the visitors. He stood to one side, clutching the Bible as though it were the handkerchief of a lover who has gone away. In spite of having lived in Laos for more than eighteen months, he had never witnessed a birth before.

I should be praying, he thought. That poor, poor girl.

The rains started in the middle of the afternoon. Water tumbled off the dispensary roof and dived into puddles on the ground. The men from Ta Xai stayed outside, for rain was no inconvenience to them. Food was brought and they ate, except for the girl's mother. At some point, the indeterminate grayness of the day began to form into the dark of the evening and Bo asked Sylvia to bring all the lamps and candles from their house. Liao's contractions were scarcely more than a minute apart and her pulse beat was irregular and rapid.

"I think it's time," said Bo.

Liao was weak and pale. She moved her head from side to side. Her grip on Borjek's hand became surprisingly strong. He was transfixed by the serene beauty of half of her face and the scorched, nonliving mass which was the other half. He wanted to hit someone.

"I see the head," said Bo, placing his gloved hands around the wet skull.

Sareno took a step forward and opened the Bible to the book of John. "A woman when she is in travail hath sorrow, because her hour is come; but as soon as she is delivered of child, she remembereth no more the anguish, for joy that a man is born into the world. And you now therefore have sorrow: But I will see you again, and your heart shall rejoice, and your joy—"

Bo said, without looking up, "Reverend Sareno, please. That is more for you than her. She doesn't need you. Be quiet."

Sareno bowed his head and was able to pray, finally, for the lives of the girl and the baby.

"Here it comes. Its color is good. It was nearly ready for delivery. How is she doing?" asked Bo.

"Not good," said Sylvia. "Her pulse is blurring together, stopping sometimes and racing at other times. Right now, I can barely feel it."

Borjek asked, "Is the baby all right? Why is it so slow?"

"Birth is slower than most people think. It'll be breathing in a moment. Don't worry," said Bo, guiding the head out. The child turned and a shoulder emerged. Bo wiped its lips with a finger and opened its mouth. With an aspirator, he pulled the fluids from its mouth and nose. A moment later, the baby lay in his hands.

Borjek thought the baby ugly; it's hair was skimpy and stuck down by a light reddish mucus. It looked terribly vulnerable.

"That's it. Clamp and cut, Sylvia," said Bo. With both hands, he eased the baby upside down to force any liquids from its throat and lungs. "It's a boy. Come on, fellow, take a breath. It's not all that bad."

Seng smiled and pointed out to the girl's mother a bluish irregular circle at the base of the child's spine. "Anok ba yun," he said.

"What's that?" asked Borjek.

Bo answered, "Most babies among these people have a Mongolian mark like that. It's a racial characteristic of the Mongols and some Chinese people. It will fade away by the time he's two or three years old."

Suddenly the baby coughed and cried as if strangling. His face

125

flushed red. A second breath and another cry followed. "He's okay," said Bo, relieved and suddenly aware that his shirt was soaked through with perspiration.

Sareno thought, it really is a miracle. Birth is a miracle. It's true what they say. A moment ago, he wasn't here; he wasn't alive. Look, that tiny, pink hand is moving. I want a baby of my own, he thought in amazement.

Liao's mother smiled and told her daughter the baby was a son, and healthy. Liao gave a small cry and tried to raise her head.

Seng said, "She wants you to place the baby's ear next to her mouth."

"It should go to her breast to start the placenta," he said.

"Please, it is important," said Seng.

Bo stood and held the boy to her face.

Liao pursed her cracked lips and blew gently into her son's ear. The baby blinked.

"What was that?" asked Bo.

Seng said, "She blew into his ear to send the child's soul into his body. It is their custom."

Bo gave the baby to Sylvia. "Hold him to her breast while I check the placenta."

Sylvia started around the table when a noise from Borjek's throat stopped her.

"It's no use," he said, tears in his eyes. "She's dead."

CHAPTER XVI

A TRIP INTO CHINA

L EMON and lime parrots and long-tailed monkeys with shelflike eyebrows studied the slow procession of people through their woods. The figures appeared and disappeared in the thick morning fog like uncertain ghosts. With them floated a white-shrouded body, a lifeless cocoon bound by vines.

Here at nine thousand feet on the southern slopes of the Muong Tha Shan, the air was thinner and the white people—the doctor, the woman, the Baptist minister and the one called the mushroom god—were conscious of breathing. The others—the brown ones—walked with the jerky gait of mountain people and breathed without effort.

It was their third day on the trail, and they had met no one since leaving Sin Pak the previous morning. The valleys fell away as sharply as the Muong Tha rose. Travel from east to west was impossible. North, the direction in which they moved, led to the deserted plateaus of western China. They had been walking from dawn to sunset, except during the heaviest of the afternoon rains, and they were only fifty kilometers from Sop Hao. Today they approached the ridge of a mountain and the ground was firmer. Ahead rose gray cliffs of limestone, exposed by centuries of rain.

The vegetation was different from that around Sop Hao. Around them stood senatorial forests of cedar, corktree, juniper, oak and ailanthus. Crowded against the stream banks were rhododendron, gaoliang, ivy and wild orchids. In the open areas, elephant grass with its knife-edged blades and thick pollen collected water from the fog in yellow droplets.

Bo, walking behind Sylvia, noticed that even though the temperature was cooler, the back of her shirt was damp. His eyes slid to her hips, and he felt a twinge of desire, tempered by the observation that girls really did walk funny. Their hips, he thought, are higher and the ilium is broader and set more to the rear. For having babies. He looked ahead to Wuan, carrying her grandson in a back sling. The baby had been born healthy; he had weighed over five pounds and was fifteen-and-a-half inches long. Bo thought he was only a few weeks premature, at the most. A woman in Sop Hao who was giving milk was found to nurse the baby. Before they left, Liao's husband had sucked milk from her breast and spat it into a jar. The jar was now nearly empty. We have to reach the village today, Bo thought.

Bo was also remembering the baby he hadn't saved. The Montagnard baby whose life he had taken as surely as if he had strangled it, because he had prescribed the wrong medicine. He had delivered other babies since, but something, perhaps Liao's wounds or the presence of Borjek and his memories, had brought it all back. He hadn't realized how tense he had been at Liao's delivery until Sylvia's soft hand had told him his muscles were tight bundles.

He bumped into Sylvia, who had stopped.

"Whoa," she said, staggering. "We're taking a break." She dropped her knapsack and collapsed on the ground.

"Sorry," Bo said. The bottles and jars of medicine in his pack clinked as he set it beside hers.

"How much farther do you think it is?"

"Six or seven hours." Bo leaned his head back on his pack and looked at her profile. This lady is still going to be one handsome woman when she's fifty or sixty, he thought. "Say, did I ever tell you about a man in Charleston who once ran a classified ad asking for someone who could hypnotize him into forgetting the works of Charles Dickens. A reporter asked him why. The man said he loved Dickens and wanted to read him again when he got old."

"Wonderful," said Sylvia.

"Sometimes I think I would like to forget you, so I could fall in love with you all over again."

Ten feet away, leaning against his backpack, Martin Borjek was wondering when they would arrive at Ta Xai. The morning fogs made it hard to keep their direction straight, but, he thought, if we're finally on the ridge of the mountain, and if we're making two or three kilometers an hour, we should be near the border of Red

128

China. And still going north. At least, I'm doing something productive for the Agency. In his latest message, Willard said that reconnaissance planes had photographed mysterious construction activity just inside China. Land was being cleared and earth moved. It could be missile sites. Willard wanted to know what Borjek could pick up.

I wonder if it is military, he thought, and if we've been up to something no one told me about. I can still feel that girl's little hand as she lay there. At the end, when she was giving birth, Borjek thought he had never felt a grip as tight as hers. Then her hand had slowly relaxed and fallen limp. Even when Bao was covering the body to contain Liao's spirit, Borjek had not wanted to let go. He found himself praying for the first time in twenty-five years, praying out of anger and frustration to a god he had deserted long ago. That was the real reason Borjek was going with these people back to their village for the burial. He wanted to see the evidence, to see if his own Air Force had dropped that bomb, and if, in fact, it had been an old, unexploded bomb, not a new one. Though Borjek doubted he could explain the difference to the Lun Chun.

Nearby, Sareno hunkered beside Seng, who had been one of the men carrying Liao's body.

Dugpas Seng said, *"Dtohn sow,* thay mo."

"Sow, kunag," said Sareno, sitting. "While you are more than fit to continue bearing the weight of the litter, I feel a need to exercise my arms. Would you allow me to take your position for the next movement of the sun?"

"I would be honored, my friend."

The men from Sop Hao had been spelling the men from Ta Xai in carrying the platform. Sareno did not look forward to it. The picture of Liao's dying was too fresh in his mind. Worse, it brought back those few moments after she died, when he had thrown an enraged cry at God and had then crumbled inside; when he knew that his inner strength as a missionary was false. His bedrock was made of sand. When Liao died, Sareno did not see her lying there, but Tanna-li. They were the same age, and it could have just as easily been Tanna-li. The thought almost moved him to weep. The baby was so beautiful. Sareno had once read a poem about a robin so proud of a bit of blue in its nest and he wanted that feeling for his own. A man isn't too old at thirty-seven to have children, he told himself. Perhaps a man shouldn't even have children until he's old enough to feel that need. Was that why I skipped Sunday services for the first time? But that was the day we left and there wasn't time. I must stay with this event—"Suffer while you can, boy," daddy said—and these people until the end. The torment was comforting.

As if Seng were reading his mind, he said, "The parents of Tanna-li asked that I tell you they are deeply indebted to you."

"When did you see them?"

"Just before we left. They brought food for the trip."

"Tanna-li?"

"She came, too. I think to see you, but you had gone to see Ek Tho, I believe."

"Yes," said Sareno. He had hoped to find confirmation of his own worth, but Ek Tho had only talked excitedly about the baptism when he, Sareno and Borjek had fought in the water. Sareno had left Ek Tho more discouraged than ever.

"Tanna-li seemed, ki, ki, anxious to see you," said Seng.

"Really?"

"One method of allowing her family to settle their debt might be to accept invitations, which I feel will be forthcoming, to eat with them."

"I look forward to it. By the way, has anyone seen Oo?"

"The Lahu say he was seen going north. In this direction." Seng nibbled from a handful of mulberries, which he had found earlier. The possibility of finding Oo, or even hearing a report about him, was only one reason Seng had come on this trip. He also wanted to talk to the Lun Chun village chief about opium, to see if he had also received offers for its purchase. Seng did not want to move Sop Hao, but it might become necessary.

The landscape looked vaguely familiar to Seng. The trees on the slope immediately below them were not fully grown. The forest had been cleared in the past. Seng stood and walked into the woods.

Sareno followed. "You are looking for something, Kunag?"

"This place is friendly." He ran his hands over a tree, reading its history through his fingertips. "It might be a *k'sor*, a place where a village once was. Yes, there is a mark."

Sareno detected an old scar barely visible. Seng bent and dug at the base of the tree. In a few minutes, he had uncovered a small animal skull.

Seng laughed. "I forgot. This is where we once lived."

"You?"

"Sop Hao. Many fields ago, when I was young, we ate these forests and grew crops here. We marked the land so that it remains ours and so that no one else will eat the forest until it has regrown itself. I placed this pig skull here when we left."

A shout from the others told them it was time to go. Seng buried the skull again.

As they walked back, Sareno asked, "By the way, did they name the baby?"

"Yes. Ga tohng."

"What does it mean?"

"Tasteless entrails of crow."

"I don't understand."

"Children are given unflattering names so that a caak who should hear the name won't consider the baby attractive. Also, such a name protects children from caaks who might learn their real names and thus have power over them."

"He has another name then?"

"Yes. No one knows what it is except his father and Liao's parents. When the child becomes an adult, he will be given his own name."

Sareno thought about what name he would like to give his child.

CHAPTER XVII

THE BURIAL OF LIAO

SHORTLY before dark that day, six shadows emerged from a clump of bushes and materialized into Lun Chun warriors. After Bao, Liao's father, walked over to them, they stabbed their spears with points of chipped rock into the ground. In a few minutes, the warriors began calling a message back to their village, Ta Xai. The first man began a high-pitched cry, almost like a yodel. As he ran out of breath, the second man picked up the cry and the dispatch continued. Bao said they were telling what had happened to Liao, and who the strangers were.

Bo remembered that in South Carolina, back in great-great-grandaddy Bezel's day, hollering had been a practical method of communication. Bo's mother told of a man who could holler a request for a supper of turnips and pork across two miles of trees and fields. A community in the North Carolina sandhills still held an annual hollering contest, and Bo decided that these men would walk away with the prize.

Soon they were in Ta Xai. It was small, less than a dozen huts, and straddled a swift creek a few feet wide. In the light from pine-knot torches, the Lun Chun looked fierce and primitive. Their faces showed the same leonine-simian features as Liao's family, and the firelight turned their skin dusky bronze and sunk their eyes into black holes.

The village chief, a stern man named Yaksha, who seemed young for a chief, invited them to eat and then spend the night in the village longhouse. He took them to it. The longhouse was as wide as the average hut, but three times longer; at each end were small porches used for storing baskets, rope-vines and chicken coops. Steps to the porches were notched tree trunks. One end of the interior was for sleeping and the other was a community cooking area. It was used for certain religious rites and occasionally

132

by courting couples. The longhouse, Seng explained, was built on a north-south axis to distinguish it from the spirit houses on graves, which are placed in an east-west direction. Also, the prevailing winds, which blew from west to east, would take the smoke from cooking fires out through the side walls instead of carrying it the length of the house.

Two women from the village brought them bowls of rice and a dish of fried June bug larvae and red peppers. Even Borjek was too hungry and tired to do anything but eat and grunt occasionally.

After supper, they added small limbs to the fire for warmth and tea.

"Does anybody know where we are, exactly?" asked Sylvia.

"The end of the earth," said Bo.

Borjek said, "Near the Chinese border, maybe a few kilometers inside. On my map there's nothing marked around here but a river which eventually runs into the Mekong at the Burmese and Laotian border. And there's a mountain a few kilometers north-west marked at ten thousand feet."

"No wonder it's chilly," said Sylvia.

The fire was the only light in the longhouse. Pale orange flames tossed and danced from coal to coal.

"Fires are entrancing," said Sareno. "Like a stream or pond, you can stare into one for hours."

Sylvia said, "Maybe there is a racial memory in each of us that remembers when we sat around in caves and a fire meant protection and warmth."

Bo said, "Maybe it's also because fire was the first power man gained. It was the first thing in nature, or that was part of nature, that he got control of. The first harnessing—"

"Look . . ." Sylvia suddenly said in a cold whispery voice.

They followed her eyes to the fire, where the flickers of fire had joined together into one thin flame about a foot tall. It did not move or quiver, but hung there as though painted. Silence filled the longhouse and the burning wood smelled of nuts and leaves. The colors of the fire—gold, poppy-red and topaz—twisted upward through the stalk of the flame and faded abruptly into gunmetal-gray smoke.

"Jesus God," muttered Borjek.

Bo was the first to look at Seng, who had sat quietly through their talking, which had been in English. Seng was staring intently into the fire.

"Kunag?" Bo said.

The focus in the old man's eyes changed, and he looked around at the others. "I am impolite, but it has been a long day." He stood slowly. "I must sleep, but please continue, as the sounds of young people talking are pleasant." He spread his bamboo mat in the dark against a wall.

The fire burned normally again. No one spoke. The only noise came from outside the longhouse: the sound of axes hollowing the tree for Liao's coffin, a rhythm for the burial rituals that were beginning.

After breakfast the next morning, Sareno surprised Bo by asking to help with sick call. While they arranged the medicines on a porch of the longhouse, word spread through Ta Xai about the dalam who had saved Liao's baby. Those not helping with the burial preparations came to look at the two tall, white men and the woman with the lemon hair.

The villagers were shy, reluctant to come closer, until Sylvia squatted beside a small boy who had a puffy, red sore on one leg. She took his hands in hers and talked with him. Though the words were strange, her tone was calm and persuasive. Within a few moments Bo was cleaning and bandaging the cut. Soon everyone crowded around the dalam.

During the morning, Bo saw two more burn victims, who had been near Liao when the bomb exploded. They were not seriously injured and had treated themselves with lotus flowers and oil from the ta feng tze plant, a medicine which Bo knew and would have recommended himself. Several of the people there had advanced goiter, not rare among these mountain people who received little iodine in their diets.

In Yaksha's hut, Borjek, Dugpas Seng and their host were well into their third cup of tea and serious conversation. Seng said, "In my area, there have been requests for a large quantity of ty fong ki. If it would not be inelegant to ask, I wonder if this is true here?"

"The plant of dreams, ki? Traders from the north and west have put forth strong suggestions along a similar path. Our days and nights are anxious. We have offended the spirits in some manner. Liao is dead. Several men and women are hurt. The ground burns. I thought for a moment that the creatures had returned because they were angry that I had shot at them the last time they came."

"You shot at them?" Borjek said, amazed. "With what, and when?"

"Several seasons ago. Then they came and shot at the trees in that direction." He pointed to the east. "I remember one of them stuck its head down and, falling toward our fields, made a loud roar, shocking my heart. We are only rice farmers, and we did not believe it would shoot us. But it did shoot us, and our buffalo. Ours is an inconsiderable village; we only had one buffalo and it was the source of a hundred thousand loves and a hundred thousand worries. That field was the same field which turned upside down and burned Lu Xi Liao."

"You shot at it," Borjek reminded him.

"With my *na nying,*" Yaksha gestured at a crossbow hanging on the wall.

Borjek stared at the handmade weapon. He remembered the firepower concept of bombing in Viet Nam: The U.S. Air Force could not run out of bombs, so use whatever power was necessary, plus a little extra. A wooden crossbow vs. a Goddamn F-105 jet bomber. Borjek could find no words to bridge the contrast.

He finally asked, "Have there been any strangers in the village?"

"Several men with guns asked for rice and water. They were the ones who offered to buy the ty fong ki this harvest."

"Did you know them?"

"No. They were not Lun Chun. One was much too short to be Lun Chun."

"Too short?" asked Seng. "What was his name and where did they go?"

"I don't remember the name, but they were walking north, where, it is said, there are men in the Chin Army near Wehnshan."

Borjek leaned forward. "The Chinese Army. What are they doing?"

"They are said to be digging industriously in the earth."

135

They talked for another hour, but Yaksha told them little else about the Chinese or the man who could have been Law Dorje Oo. He said that Wehnshan was only ten kilometers away and that the journey was not difficult. Borjek decided to go to the village the next day because it could be the location of the missile site. To his surprise, Seng also wanted to go—to look for Oo, he said. Yaksha offered to send several of his warriors with them because even though Wehnshan was Lun Chun, the people there were dedicated to a long tradition of discouraging visitors. They accepted.

Later, under the long rays of the afternoon sun, Liao's family carried her coffin, carved from a teak tree, to the grave. The noisy procession made its way through the village and around a field. For the first time, the crowd became silent. Yaksha pointed toward the field. Near the center, so out of place as to insult even a stranger's eye, was a black napalm scar. The people skirted the field carefully.

Sunlight was caught by the white lip of rice glue which held the top of the coffin to the tree trunk. For a moment the chasm between the rice glue and the crater threatened to engulf Borjek. The disjunction of one culture imposing not itself, but the worst of its self, upon another culture was almost overpowering. Borjek fixed his eyes on the rattan cords around the coffin.

Liao was buried with her head to the east, so she would face the dying sun. The ceremony was brief and simple. During it jars of rice wine were passed around.

"What's going to happen to the baby?" Sareno asked Seng, who was standing beside him.

"I think her parents will take it as their own, raising it with Liao's husband until he remarries. Maybe they'll keep it even after that. If a mother dies in childbirth and the baby lives, most often the mother's spirit is reincarnated in the child."

The speeches ended and everyone placed a gift on the ground near the spirit house. One person brought jackfruit; another laid down a piece of red cloth. Most of the presents were rice in small bowls or leaves. These things would enable Liao's spirit to eat and survive during the next few months while it was changing over to a permanent spirit or finding its new home in the baby. Relatives and friends would continue bringing food and gifts daily until Yaksha decreed that the time of mourning was over.

After receiving Yaksha's permission, Borjek planted a small pois d'angola tree at the head of the grave. Someday, he thought, bees will come to steal the sweetness of its yellow blossoms.

CHAPTER XVIII

THEY GO DEEPER INTO CHINA

FAR to the north, confused in the clouds and the haze of distance, Borjek made out the giant snow-covered mountains which were the easternmost reaches of the Himalayas. Earlier that morning, Seng had pointed out a beautiful goatlike animal with golden fleece on a hill near them. Seng called it a *nyeuang,* a takin, which was an antelope with a highly treasured blond coat found only in this area of the world. The takin had briefly stared down its nose at them before bounding out of sight in long, stiff-legged leaps. Borjek had imagined he saw no fear in the takin's eyes, only inquisitiveness.

Borjek felt younger than he had in years. He knew he was physically in better shape, but his thinking seemed clearer, fresher, more interesting. He no longer found himself boring; and he wondered how much of his previous conceit had been a defense against new ideas, new people. He remembered trying to change his personality as a teen-ager. Every time he entered a new school, he would tell himself to be more relaxed, to open up, to enjoy people and their ideas, but it never lasted. Now, he was changing without trying. The isolation from his past had produced not fear and retreat, but a luxurious freedom and curiosity. And he had forgotten about himself. He wanted to know more about the ways of the Man, their language and the people here. Their view of the world fascinated him, and he was attracted by their acceptance of fate—an acceptance that was not a concession, but rather a courtesy extended to events. Like people, fate was due certain considerations. Borjek remembered how the Chinese had absorbed barbarians into their culture. He realized that he was geographically and emotionally removed from his past life, but that realization was not unsettling. I feel—he searched for the emotion and when he found it, he laughed aloud—I feel free.

Not far from Borjek, Seng worked around a clump of glaucous, lacy-stemmed plants, cutting finger-length shoots from them. Enough rice had been given to them at Ta Xai for the day's trip, but Seng enjoyed finding fruits and nuts in the woods. Also, some plants that grew here were medically important and not found lower down at Sop Hao.

The three Lun Chun guards hunkered nearby, gesticulating as they discussed the endurance of both the old man and the mushroom god. Every now and then one would glance at Borjek and, if Borjek saw him, would smile (inanely, it appeared to Borjek) to cover the effrontery of a direct look.

Seng soon had collected several handfuls of the plant. He returned and gave some to the Lun Chun, who tied them to their loin cloths with vines.

Handing some to Borjek, he said, "T'ien men tung. It is still young and can be eaten without cooking. It removes heat and pains in the feet and strengthens the lungs." He showed Borjek how to use his teeth to tear off the thick, outer skin and suck the pulpy fruit inside.

The plants tasted like young asparagus. "Thank you, kunag, they are very good," said Borjek.

After eating, Borjek unfolded his agency map, printed on thin rubber. It carried the legend, *Dresse, dessine et publie par le Service Geographique de l'Indochine en 1938. Reedition de 1964.* He pointed at a series of ridges. "Are these mountains the ones we saw earlier?"

Seng bent over the map a long time. Finally he said, "I do not understand this. I cannot read, thay mo."

"They probably are," muttered Borjek, embarrassed. He should have known.

"I wonder, if you have the time and do not find an old man's leaves too dry to respond to water, could you teach me to read?" Seng ventured a small smile. One of the few desires left in his heart was to learn to read.

"Your language has not been written, has it?" During Borjek's training, the Green Beret soldiers taught by repetition. There had been no textbooks.

"You speak so well I thought you had written it down. Or perhaps had seen it written." He paused and then added, with shame, "We had a written language once."

"Yes?"

"Long ago all peoples went to a certain place to get their written languages. Others took weeds on which to record their language, but the Man, hoping to impress, took a buffalo hide on which to write. After receiving their language on the hide, they returned to the village and left the buffalo hide hanging on a porch. That night while they were asleep, some dogs came and ate the buffalo hide; thus, the Man have no written language."

Borjek tried to imagine living without a written language: How could you pass along all the information from one generation to the next? How could you teach anything? So much would be lost.

"Perhaps someday we will be given our written language again," Seng said.

Borjek chewed on one of the green plants. They smelled like fresh green peas. The Man language does not seem that difficult, he thought, mainly one-syllable words with five tones, similar to the six tones of Vietnamese. Verbs appear to be invariable and tense is indicated by specific words, rather than a change in the verb. The sounds could be transcribed with our alphabet . . .

"Ki, ki, ki, thay mo," said Seng. "You have asked many questions about the death of the farang Treadmill. Have you any thoughts about why his health failed so quickly?"

Borjek recalled that Seng had been one of his earliest suspects. Seng and Treadmill apparently had barely tolerated each other, and Borjek wondered how much Seng resented Treadmill's interference in the village's affairs. Even though Seng was capable of violence—the image of this old man slashing the chicken's throat without hesitation was vivid—Borjek knew there was much evidence against Oo.

"A few, kunag. I am of the opinion that probably someone in Sop Hao was responsible." He hesitated to accuse Oo, a Man tribesman.

Seng finished the last of the plants and wiped his mouth with the back of one hand. He looked directly at Borjek. "Let us toss the rice, friend. Who?"

140

"Did you know that the night Treadmill was killed, Oo was supposed to be with Tanna-li?"

"She said he was."

"That was not the truth. Oo forced her to say that. After he attacked her the other night, Tanna-li told Sylvia that she was not with Oo the night Treadmill died. Oo came to her the next morning and made her promise to say that."

Seng stared at the ground between them. "I see. It is far easier to tear down a stranger's house than one you have built yourself. I asked Oo to submit to the test of the bamboo, but he refused."

"Where do you think he has gone?" asked Borjek.

"I do not know." Seng almost said Oo was likely to be here in China somewhere with his "Peoples' Liberation Army," but did not. "As you heard in Ta Xai, Oo may have passed through this area."

"Perhaps he won't come back to Sop Hao."

"He will return, for it is his home and he has . . . unfinished business there. Also, he must answer to the phi for his actions." Seng's countenance was somber—unhappiness had ambushed his eyes and anger pressed against his mouth. After a few breaths of silence, Seng asked, "And the nature of your concern about Oo?"

"Curiosity, kunag. I knew Treadmill vaguely years ago. Shall we continue?"

"Yes." Seng rose and motioned to the Lun Chun.

"What have they been talking about?" asked Borjek.

"You, esteemed mushroom god. They have been discussing what kind of powers you might have and the attitude of the spirit concealed within your body. They said they were doubtful at first, but now they think you have many strengths and powers inside that are yet untested and unused. They say you fell from the sky and yet came to no harm. You survived the poisoned arrow and the cobra."

Borjek said nothing and Seng added, "My people say they can talk comfortably and pleasurably with you. You often have good advice. Perhaps it will become true. It is said that one does not have to be born a god in order to be one, although it helps."

Two hours later, the Lun Chun began their high-pitched

yodeling, which was unearthly in the mountain stillness. It reminded Borjek of the night spirit now haunting Sop Hao. Minutes passed and they continued, taking turns, each picking up the note when another had exhausted his lungs.

Several dozen yards away, a small pond sparkled as a light breeze rippled the water. Sunlight danced and leapt on the water, as if the light trapped just under the surface was trying to escape. Since lunch, they had crossed several streams and creeks. Seng said the water came from the high mountains, which were beginning to shed their winter skin of ice.

Then an answer came. A quivering yell from beyond a hill to the east.

Soon they were in Wehnshan and seated in the home of Yungton Gyatso, the village's portly chief. He, too, was Lun Chun, and they emptied two cups of tea while the guides offered gossip from Ta Xai.

To Seng's disappointment, Gyatso said he had seen no one resembling Oo. The only strangers, he reported, were Chin, who had forced them to leave their fields not long ago. As a result, they were hard pressed to clear new fields in time to plant crops for this season.

"We had to abandon the land which was only four seasons old and still fertile. We arrived here"—Gyatso spat expertly between the floor slats—"during the new moon after the Chin came."

Borjek saw his opening, "It is reported the Chinese make holes in the earth and fill them again. Not far from here. On the Ssu-ching Shan."

Gyatso nodded. "Your ears are those of a new mother. That is where our village was. At first we tried to go back and work those fields, but it was too long and too difficult. Young Chin men in clothes of the same appearance came to the Ssu-ching Shan during the last harvest. They have been assaulting the ground with varying degrees of worthlessness."

Borjek asked carefully, "Is it noted how many holes their labors have been rewarded with?"

"They are not actually holes. Their effrontery is confined to altering the shape and flow of the rivers and creeks, which, unlike them, have been here since everything began. The Chin push huge rocks into the water in order to slow the current, to make dams and cause lakes to form where none existed before."

"What? I thought it was the Army," said Borjek. Perhaps, he thought, it is some grand scheme to dry up southeastern Asia.

"They are also attempting to clear the banks and round the corners of the creeks and streams, something I believe they call channelization. They drain the water from the pools that once bathed our rice paddies. Now they speak of flood-control projects in a tone of voice indicating that they consider each other sane. They call themselves the Peoples' Corps of Engineers."

"The Corps of Engineers? You mean they aren't building missile sites?"

"I don't understand all your words. Apparently, these men go from area to area, like petty warlords, insulting the spirits of nature. They are like small boys playing with pebbles in a creek. Except that they endanger all the life around them."

"There are others who have been concerned about their activities, too," said Borjek.

Gyatso bowed elaborately toward Borjek. "Is it true then? You are the one called the mushroom god?"

Borjek thought, maybe Seng is right. "Mushroom god is the illustrious title which some have used instead of the unmusical name of my gloomy family."

"The dams and rocks cause more flooding, and now we will not be able to build our homes as before, close to the water. The river is no longer predictable. It is justifiably angry, and the animals are in turmoil. I am old and my life has been filled with great happiness brought to me by these mountains. I do not want to die in a foreign place. It was our hope that the spirits might take some action . . . and . . . here you are."

"Are you suggesting that some interference with the Chin might be proper?"

"Perhaps it is so ordained," said Gyatso.

"I see."

"Should we interfere with the *dao?* We can not go back to our fields, and the Chinese have insulted our ancestors, whose resting places are being destroyed. It is said that you have contact with the creatures that fly. Perhaps they could make the Chin leave. One should not tamper with what might be the will of the spirits, unless it would be to guide the flying creatures to their intended location by means of very precise directions."

"I understand, Gyatso. Your idea is meritorious. But possibly another path would reach the same journey's end, revered one. If the Corps of Engineers is attacked, they will bring even more men, maybe armed with powerful weapons. We have another way of dealing with the Corps of Engineers."

Gyatso leaned forward expectantly.

"Sue them. Take them to court."

"I don't understand. We would like to take them anywhere else. But does this suing cause them to stop?"

"Rarely," Borjek admitted. "Who is responsible for this area in government?"

"I am."

"No, I mean, who is higher than you. Your canton, it is called."

"Except for the Bon lama tulka of the gompas of Yung-tien and Hsiang-jen, there is no one," said Gyatso, frowning.

Seng explained, "He only abides by the shaman who lives in the mountains of northeastern Tibet."

It dawned on Borjek that Gyatso was, in fact, the only man responsible to his people. "Did you ever hear of a man named Mao Tse-tung?"

"It is said he is the new ruler of the empire to the east. But he has not asked for, nor given, tribute. Indeed, the only sign of his new kingdom is the Corps of Engineers, and I suspect they might be merely rampaging madmen acting on their own."

"Perhaps then you are right about attacking the Corps of Engineers. I will think about it."

Borjek and Seng returned to Ta Xai late that afternoon with bellies full of rice and chicken.

CHAPTER XIX

THE LEGEND OF THE FUR HAT

THE figure was moving at what appeared to be a rapid pace from northeast to southwest on the *chang thang,* the Man word for high grassy area. The person was a quarter of a kilometer away, and coming almost directly at them.

"Who can it be?" asked Sylvia.

"I can't imagine," said Bo. "Nobody lives around here."

"Maybe we're needed back at Ta Xai," said Sareno.

Seng and Borjek had returned from Wehnshan the night before and earlier in the morning they and the others had left Ta Xai to return to Sop Hao. The morning air had been chilly and walking was pleasant along the plateau. The noon rains had thinned into fitful showers by mid-afternoon. Now the sun struggled to make a last-minute appearance before dark. They had stopped for the night and were gathering wood for a fire when they saw the figure. As he came closer, it was apparent that he moved with an unusual gait and was indeed running, in a graceful lope.

Seng, who had been watching the man intently, said, "I believe he is a *lama lung-gom-pa,* a Bon religious man adept in the internal air. I have never seen one this far from the high mountains. It has been a long time . . ."

The man continued toward them, and his curious stride and speed brought questions from the white people. Seng answered, "There are certain lamas who undergo years of lung-gom training. They develop a remarkable nimbleness and can take long walks with amazing quickness. As a young man, I became familiar with lung-gom, although I left the training before becoming an adept. Such men are able to tramp for several days and nights without stopping. It is a method of covering long distances in a short time, which requires endurance rather than particular speed."

"We can offer him some rice and find out where he's going," said Sylvia.

"It would be fascinating to talk—" started Sareno.

"We cannot," interrupted Seng. "Please. We cannot stop him or speak to him. He is in deep meditation and would be killed. The spirit in him will escape if he does not repeat the *ngags*—certain words. If the spirit leaves before the proper time, it will shake the body so hard that he will die."

"Like a sleepwalker, only more serious," said Bo.

"You mean you believe a spirit is in that man?" asked Borjek.

"He is probably in a deep trance with all his sensory and motor functions shut down, except those needed for walking. A sudden awakening, which I doubt would kill him, could nevertheless be emotionally and physically damaging. Perhaps it is a spirit," said Bo.

By this time, the man was quite close, less than a dozen meters from them. He wore an orange toga, which was dirty and ragged about the hem. His face was impassive and calm, and his eyes were fixed on some distant object high above the horizon. He appeared to lift himself from the ground, moving in slow-motion leaps. His bare feet seemed made of rubber, for he rebounded in a springy, elastic motion each time they touched the ground. The noise from his feet was no more than that of a leaf falling to the ground. His right hand gripped a fold in the robe and his left hand held a dagger. His left hand moved a little with each step, almost as if the knife were a cane; each time, its tip would be set at some imaginary point above the ground, and he would support himself by it.

Seng bowed his head to the ground as the lama passed before them. The man did not appear to be breathing hard and gave no sign that he was aware of their presence. He did not change his pace or his gaze, still bound to the sky, and within minutes he had disappeared into a wooded area half a kilometer away.

Later, after a supper of rice balls, ants' eggs and a sweet sauce Seng made from tamarind fruit, Sareno asked about the training of a lama lung-gom-pa.

Seng said, "The initial training concentrates on controlling one's internal air. A student of lung-gom spends three to four years performing breathing exercises in strict seclusion and in darkness.

For example, one exercise involves sitting crosslegged on a large cushion. The novitiate inhales slowly for a long time in order to fill his body with air. Then, holding his breath, he jumps up."

"Using his legs?" Borjek asked.

"No, from the sitting position, without using his hands or feet and with his legs still crossed. Only one who can jump twice his standing height in such a fashion becomes a true lung-gom-pa. The ideal time for tramping is early morning or early evening. A clear night is also excellent. You are taught to fasten your eyes on a certain star. Sometimes the star will set or the clouds will obscure it, but its image is so strong in your mind, you can continue on. A flat, open area, such as the chang thang, is the best place to tramp."

"With less distractions, it would be easier to run," said Bo.

Sareno said, "I've been here more than a year and a half and just when I think I'm getting to be at least familiar with everything, something new happens."

"Knowledge," said Seng, "is like a fruit. One must take it when it is full, else it soon returns to the soil."

Borjek thought that such a saying would certainly be true in a society without a written language.

Bo shifted so the smoke would not blow in his face and asked, "Kunag, if this is not an inopportune occasion, have you reached a decision on the planting of the opium? There has been much discussion in the village."

"Let us have more tea; I would like to tell an old story."

Sareno poured water from a canteen into the small brass pot nesting on the edge of the fire.

"This was told to me by my father and to him by his grandfather. Once a man was with a caravan traveling near a village in our land. A storm developed and the wind blew his hat onto a thorn bush near the path. According to some, it is bad luck to pick up a hat in those particular circumstances, so he left it. The hat was a fur hat with long flaps for the ears. As time and the weather came and went, the hat's shape became untidy and scarcely recognizable. Some time later, another traveler who passed near that place at dusk saw an unusual form which appeared to be squatting in the bushes. He hurried by, and later mentioned the occurrence to

147

people who lived in the village. Other travelers began to report a strange object they had seen along the path. As the seasons changed, the fur of the hat became yellow and the ear flaps took on the appearance of an animal's ears. Several of the more stout-hearted villagers went to look at the hat; they expressed concern, for it was definitely an unusual object."

Seng paused as Sareno poured hot water into his cup. He dropped in several dried leaves and stirred the liquid with a twig. "Traders and visitors to the village were warned to be wary of a creature that was neither man nor beast waiting in ambush near the footpath. Someone suggested the thing was probably a demon, and soon the object, which had no real definition until then, was raised to the rank of a caak, a demon. Moons crossed the skies, and more people in the surrounding areas talked about this demon. Some even went and watched the thicket from a distance, only to confirm the rumors. Then one day, some people who were passing by saw the hat moving. Not long afterwards, the hat tried to free itself from the thorns which had grown around it. Finally, it followed a group of passers-by who ran, panic-stricken, for their lives." Seng sipped his tea. "The hat had been given life by the many thoughts concentrated on it, and directed at it."

"We humans create our own demons," said Bo.

"And," added Borjek, who was staring into the fire, "they begin to exist independently of us. We can no longer control them." He was thinking of the Agency, and of the planes which had bombed villages in Laos. At the end of the war, Nixon had officially ordered CIA activities inside China and Laos stopped, thinking he could open diplomatic relations with China. But by word of mouth and with top-secret classification, the order came to continue operations with extreme discretion. Borjek doubted that Carter knew the CIA was here.

Bo asked, "Kunag, are you saying that the growing of opium has created so many troubles that . . . What?"

"Perhaps we should not grow it. It has taken on a life of its own. Unfortunately there are those who have threatened us if we fail to provide them with the plant of dreams."

Sareno cleared his throat. "I'm beginning to wonder if it's wise for one country to interfere in the affairs of another country." It was the first time anyone had heard Sareno voice a political opinion.

"It is easier to make love to a tiger than to understand the wishes of a government," said Seng.

The moon, pale white and in its last quarter, was rising behind a jagged mountain ridge east of them. The night air was soft but cool, and soon everyone except Borjek had unrolled his mat and gone to bed.

Borjek poked at the dying fire for a few minutes and, needing to urinate, walked some distance from the others. He was finding difficulty in justifying some of the actions of the Agency. The bomb left over from an out-of-date war had shocked him. How many more were lying around? To force these people to grow opium is wrong; perhaps Agency policy in the whole Golden Triangle is wrong. As he started to urinate, Borjek realized he hadn't had a drink in nearly three weeks. Out of habit, an old voice said that a drunken bash would be a fitting reward for his abstinence. Then another voice reminded him how much better he was feeling. The flab at the waist was gone, his muscles felt tighter and his mind was sharp—not webbed in hangovers. I haven't really wanted anything to drink, he told himself and then repeated it, because it was true.

A noise startled him and a voice said, "It's me, George. I have to pee also."

Sure, Borjek thought.

"Father," Sareno began, "have you ever, ah, had moments when you doubted your calling?"

"As a . . .?"

"Priest."

Why me? Borjek thought. "From time to time. I suppose it's human nature."

The noise of their urine splashing on the ground was the only other sound in the night. A faint warm and acrid odor drifted up.

"What do you tell yourself at those times?" asked Sareno.

Borjek felt a curious empathy with the Baptist minister. "Are you having doubts?"

"I didn't want to say anything to anyone, but as a priest, as a fellow minister of the Word, you might have experience in such matters. It seemed right to talk to you." Sareno was embarrassed that his speech was so stiff, but he plunged on. "I have not made as many conversions here in Sop Hao as I had hoped." Sareno was finally giving in to emotions that, like Seng's fur hat, had taken on a life of their own during the past year. Before that, his feelings had been subordinated to his sense of duty and rightness. His father's violent flares of anger and his mother's unquestioning submission to those emotions had scared him. When he was young, he decided that reason, based on the precepts of the Bible, was far superior to emotion. As he grew older, he realized that had been a rationalization for the fact that he didn't trust his own emotions; he didn't know how to read them. And so they were beaten back again. But here, in this wild country, his reason and his theology were failing him, and, as if to compensate, his emotions were breaking through, altering his perceptions.

"There are many demands on us," Borjek said. He finished urinating and stood uneasily near the minister.

"I find myself enjoying the company of Tanna-li," said Sareno.

"Did Dr. Caen tell you what Tanna-li said about the night Treadmill was killed?"

Sareno's voice was strained. "No, I don't really—"

"That Oo was not with her that night?"

"What?" Sareno turned to Borjek.

"Oo forced her to say that. She never saw him that night—and watch where you're peeing," he said, moving a foot.

"Sorry." Sareno shook himself and buttoned his pants. "No, no. He didn't tell me that. That's great. Then nothing . . ."

Borjek finally understood Sareno's concern.

"Do you think a man can change his life at my age?" asked Sareno.

"If it is what you really want to do. A man can change anytime; it's just hard to do. It gets harder the older you are." Borjek listened to himself and was fascinated. "So much of our life is habit. We go along, day to day, always telling ourselves we can change if we want to, but we never suspect how hard it is until we try. It's easy to fall back into the old personality and old habits. Often we wind up being what we have projected to others; if we're lucky, that is also what we really want to be. If there are sufficient external reasons—

and maybe for you at this time there are—it might be easier to change." He added vaguely, "Sometimes we just end up being what we were always going to be."

"But what about Him?"

"Who?"

"God."

"Oh, God." I forgot about Him. "We should do whatever we do well, and whatever makes us happy." That makes sense. I can't believe this is me talking, thought Borjek. "You haven't lost your faith?"

"No, praise the Lord, I haven't. I only question if I'm a very good missionary and, if not, perhaps I shouldn't be one."

"Not all men should be missionaries. Aung Ne Swe, the man who lives in the hog pen, one day said to me, 'Pigs are good at being pigs because they don't have to think about it.' I didn't understand what he meant at first."

Absentmindedly, Sareno had taken out his tin of Tiger Balm and was rubbing some under his nose. No wonder I'm not a good missionary, he thought. I can't give as good advice to people as this Catholic priest. "Your thoughts are well put. Thank you for listening."

"That stuff keeps evil spirits away?" asked Borjek.

"Yes."

"I would like to try some."

CHAPTER XX

AN EPIC SAGA OF THE MAN

THEY were back in Sop Hao the evening of the third day after leaving Ta Xai. That night Bo asked Borjek and Sareno to come to his house after supper. When everyone was seated Bo began, "I think Seng has decided, or is about to decide, to plant only a little opium this year. It won't be enough to sell. Since we're involved with these people and what happens to them, I thought we ought to talk it over."

"What if they don't grow enough to sell?" asked Sylvia.

"It's hard to say. The Burmese bandits and the Kuomintang both made threats, according to Seng. They may do something as an example to other villages. Burn everything down. Shoot people," said Bo.

Borjek said, "I'm betting Oo is fronting for someone. The Pathet Lao or the Red Chinese—"

"I doubt it's the Pathet Lao," said Bo. "They tried to come into this area last year—"

"Seng told me."

"The Pathet Lao were disliked because they were strangers. And their arguments fell a little short. They harangued the Man over land reform, but the Man have plenty of land; when it doesn't produce any more, they move on. The Pathet Lao talked about oppressive taxes, but there are no taxes up here. They talked about corruption in government officials, but there are no officials here. They preached collective land use and everybody working together, but the Man have been doing that for hundreds of years. Finally, the Pathet Lao have discouraged opium growing in the areas they control. Frankly, I think a better bet is the CIA."

Borjek said, "The CIA does not buy opium. The Agency has arranged for transport from time to time in—"

"In return for the warm bodies of young men to fight in CIA

152

armies. Martin, we both were in Viet Nam; we know how the game is played."

"The Agency is trying to obtain these people's loyalty."

"What you have is not loyalty, but submission out of fear."

"If somebody is going to buy the opium," said Borjek stubbornly, "why not have it arranged through the CIA so at least these people can be protected?"

Sylvia said, "Protected from whom? The only ones causing trouble are the ones trying to buy the opium."

Sareno coughed. "I'm afraid I don't understand, Father Borjek. You speak authoritatively about politics and the CIA. Is there something I don't know?"

Bo and Sylvia looked into their tea cups.

Borjek said, "Ah, yes. American officials asked me to report anything unusual in this area as long as I was here. I was in the Army once and it seemed proper. At the time."

Sareno briefly considered the enormity of the Vatican intelligence net. In spite of that, he accepted Borjek as an honorable man and decided to trust his judgment. He said, "It seems to me that if the village didn't grow opium at all, there would not be any trouble. Isn't that what Seng said?"

"That brings us back to where we started," said Bo. "Is there some way the Man can avoid growing opium and survive the consequences at the same time?"

Borjek said, "There are three groups trying to buy opium from Sop Hao: the Burmese bandits, the KMT and Oo, either for himself or the Red Chinese. We don't have to worry about Oo and—"

"Wait. Why not Oo?" said Bo.

"Just a feeling I have. I don't think he'll be around this fall. But there are the other buyers. Even if Sop Hao grew all it could, there wouldn't be enough for everybody. Unless . . . Here's what I've been thinking: Last year, the Agency spent fifty thousand dollars in this area on rice, guns, bribes, salaries and other things. The Man have been offered around sixty dollars a kilo and if they grow, say, four hundred and fifty kilos, that would gross twenty-seven thousand dollars—"

Bo interrupted, "Out of curiosity, how much would that be

worth once it got to New York?"

"Let me see. That would work down to about forty-five ki's of pure heroin at a street price of three hundred thousand a ki. That would cut into a couple million hits, so say, roughly, twelve or thirteen million dollars on the street."

"Good Lord," said Sareno, astounded. "I had no idea."

Borjek said, "Okay, in effect we have upwards of fifty thousand dollars to work with, thanks to Treadmill's exaggeration of the political situation up here. Here's my plan . . ."

Sareno, who was having trouble following the conversation, noted the importance which Borjek placed on himself and his reports to the CIA. He thought, the CIA asked me to observe for them and what did I say? I said my mission was religious not political. Yet, now, Borjek might be able to help these people because he had the foresight, the intuition to become involved. Suffer while you can, my son.

Less than an hour later, Sylvia was serving a fifth round of tea, and Borjek had explained his plan.

Sareno said, "I'm not sure I followed it all, but if there's a chance it will mean safety and happiness for Sop Hao, I'm for it."

Bo said, "You believe the Agency will go along with it? It's pretty bizarre."

"I doubt that they would," said Borjek. "That's why I'm not going to tell them about it. They'll only know what they need to know."

"This is May what? I can't keep track of dates. May twenty-fourth. Harvest is four and a half months away. Between now and then, maybe we'll think of something else, or the conditions will change." Bo added, grinning, "Father Borjek, welcome to Sop Hao."

The following night the Man Lan Mien, on advice from their Kunag, Dugpas Seng, made sacrifices. Seng knew his people were tense after the visits of the opium traders, the attacks on Borjek and the death of Liao, a stranger, in their village. Thus, after returning from Ta Xai, he examined the stars and the sun, and found what he knew would be there. This, the now-named season of the mushroom god, was in trouble and immediate attention must be paid to the phi or the crops would falter even before they sprouted.

Some said Seng's reading also involved Oo, and that the forecast had been without comfort. Others said Seng would announce that only enough poppy seeds would be planted to supply Sop Hao's own needs, and this rumor was received with mixed reactions. Chu-wei, a third cousin of Swe, was heard to say he was disappointed, because the opium brought fame and riches to the village. Chu-wei's wife was overheard to answer that such fame was as fleeting as the leopard, and riches would not lift a hoe-stick nor tend a stalk of corn. Tsao told his wife that he agreed with Seng, who was a justly venerated man and only incidentally her uncle.

By dusk, the fires were lighted and jugs of rice wine rolled into the center of the village. Ek Tho came with his Coca-Cola. Swe, the man who lived with the pigs, arrived, carrying a dark purple-stemmed plant with a delicate pink flower. Sareno, fooling no one, contrived to sit with Tanna-li and her family. Man women were allowed to attend certain sacrifices, although not to participate in them.

Tonight's ceremonies would be in two parts: First, a chicken would be offered to the maraw nats, those spirits which are less than the phi, but which influence most day-to-day living. The maraw nats serve as a go-between for humans and the phi. If events do not turn out as predicted by the local diviner, then the fault lies with the maraw nats, who are charged with opening barriers to the phi and smoothing the way. The diviner, himself, will tell you this. Being less powerful than the phi, the maraw receive a lesser sacrifice, such as a chicken or a small pig. In hard times, a large rat will suffice.

The second part of the ceremony would be a pig sacrifice to the uma nats, those spirits who were the ancestors of Seng himself. To approach the major phi who controlled the fortunes and fertility of the land and its people, one had to use whatever family influence one could muster. Seng alone would make this sacrifice to the phi of the first males of his lineage.

Borjek, who was sitting with Bo and Sylvia on a log near the front of Seng's house, said, "How come the preacher didn't try to get these people to stop sacrifices?"

Bo answered, "He did for a while, but customs are slow to

change. When you think about it, it's not so bad. It's one way of feeding the village. According to a fortuitous legend, the spirits are happy with just the souls, the nonedible essences of the animals. Sooner or later these animals were going to be killed and eaten anyway. Seng is just adding some rituals before supper."

While they were talking, Seng and the older males had seated themselves in a circle. They began telling the spirits exactly why they were being given these animals, and what some of Sop Hao's problems were. In a few minutes, a chicken with its feet lashed together was brought out and placed in the circle of men. The smell of burning wood filled the air, and orange light from the fire painted the men in dark ochres and blacks. The voices of the elders dropped to soft whispers.

"Why are they talking so softly?" Borjek whispered.

Sylvia said, "To prevent other animals, especially the wild ones, like elephants and boars, from hearing that another animal is being sacrificed. They would become angry and destroy the crops."

Seng, assisted by several of the men, held the chicken on its back and quickly cut its throat. The others placed bamboo straws in the neck and drew some of the blood into small bowls. Soon the bowls were nearly full, and the chicken had stopped quivering. The men placed the bowls in front of the candles which Seng had lighted earlier. The village chief himself captured a small amount of the blood in a clay cup and set it aside.

Speaking so everyone could hear, Seng began a recitation of a shortened version of one of the Man's five great legends. These sagas contained the history of the Man, and each was long in its entirety, taking half the movement of the sun in one day to be spoken. The saga which Seng was chanting dealt with the Man living in a land with water on three sides.

"I don't recognize those names. What's he saying?" asked Borjek.

"I've heard it several times and I've about got it figured out," said Bo. "Although the names are different, I think he's referring to the Indonesian Islands. In this saga, the Man travel south on a long, narrow piece of land where they live for a while before the floods begin. I think that place is Indonesia, when it was still attached to the mainland of Asia. After the floods, they decided to leave because they had never forgotten their original home, so they build boats to sail back to Indochina and eventually come here to the mountains."

Sylvia said, "It's really curious because that's exactly what some anthropologists think happened to many of these tribes. They spread out of central China down across Indochina and eventually to the Indonesian islands. Then they were driven back to the mainland by changes in the climate or by other people. That would explain why some of their physical characteristics are Malaysian and why their language has traces of Polynesian. The Maori tribesmen of New Zealand are physically very similar to these people."

She hesitated and went on, "Or, it could be that the migration is reversed. Some argue this branch of man began somewhere in the islands and migrated to the mainland." Sylvia accepted a small jug of rice wine from Tsao and sipped the liquid through a straw.

Borjek said, "These stories, I suppose, are the only way to keep their history."

"I think much more of their actual history can he found in the 'myths' than most people think."

"Come on, now," smiled Borjek. "Swe told me one story about how the world began with a man using a pole to push the sky up to where it is."

Sylvia said, "Several of the Man legends, including that one, mention floods. Isn't it curious how most of the religions of the world have stories involving floods? Maybe they're all based on the fact—"

"That God caused it to rain forty days?" said Borjek.

Sylvia ignored him. "—that after the last ice age, which was about two hundred thousand years ago, the glaciers began to retreat. They melted and caused heavy rains and flooding of most of the land area in the world. This went on for hundreds, maybe thousands, of years. There's another theory that I'm less certain about. It claims that the planet Venus was once part of Jupiter until it was thrown out in a cataclysmic explosion a million years or so ago. When Venus passed near Earth on its way to its present orbit, it tilted the Earth's axis and caused flooding."

Borjek stared at her. "You think these stories have been passed from generation to generation for two hundred thousand years or more?"

"The Man believe they are the oldest people on earth, and say that their legends go back to the beginning. To pre-history. One of the Man feast days, duan wu, involves making miniature boats from bamboo leaves and setting them afloat in the Mekong. It's a symbolic tribute, a payment to China. That ceremony has been performed for hundreds of years, unchanged."

They were interrupted by the loud squealing of a pig being lifted into the group of men. The pig's feet were tied together and a heavy stick ran from its front feet to its back feet. Seng stood in the center of the men and told his father's fathers why they were being honored with a pig.

Aung Ne Swe joined the circle and placed his purple plant before him on the ground. He began a litany of his own.

Seng finished calling his ancestors and, taking out a thin knife, began stabbing the pig in a deliberate pattern, avoiding the heart. The pig's screams became agonized shrieks. Finally, Seng inserted the knife into the base of the pig's throat and twisted. Sylvia covered her ears and turned away. Even Borjek felt repulsion at the sight. Blood pumped out of the severed carotid artery. The first blood was caught by Seng in a cup, and even as the pig kicked spasmodically, he drank it in several swallows. At last the animal shuddered and died. The remainder of the blood was collected by Seng in large bowls. As they were filled, young men carried them into Seng's house for private rituals later that night.

At the same time, Swe had slashed the stalk of his plant with a knife. A clear, thick fluid rose into a half-bubble on the cut stem. He laid the pink flower gently on the ground and implored his own uma nats to pay attention to the rituals.

During the ceremonies, the villagers had continued drinking the wine and chatting among themselves, commenting on how well the rituals were performed and how tasty the pig would be. Sop Hao enjoyed a meal of pork only once every few months. Already the pig was being hung on a tree limb, and the women were gathering to remove its intestines.

"I don't think I'll ever get used to it," Sylvia said.

"Talk about strange ideas," said Borjek. "Killing animals to make spirits happy . . ."

Bo said, "I used to think the same thing until Seng explained the purpose of the sacrifices. They are not performed to make the spirits happy, or because the phi are bloodthirsty. They are a way of indebting the phi to you. The same principle applies in everyday life. Pass the wine, please."

"It's good wine," said Sareno, who took a mouthful as it passed.

Bo continued, "For example, if I give you a chicken, you are then indebted to me and must pay me back in kind at some time in the future. Seng is always receiving gifts from the villagers because they want to ensure that he is indebted to them and will, therefore, take care of them. The same thing applies to the spirits. If you kill a pig and dedicate its soul to the phi, they cannot ignore it. They must listen to you and, depending on the nature of the sacrifice, pay you back eventually. You are liabling them."

"That makes it more understandable, at least," said Borjek.

"The Man think of movable property such as chickens, jugs, bracelets and things like that, as adornment. By giving one away, you don't relinquish possession of it, you acquire a debt. You trade an object for a debt. Trading also increases your status by implying that you are both rich enough to have something to give away, and humble enough to give it away. In fact, the more you give away, the more you gain in merit and prestige by the public knowledge that you are doing it."

Borjek said, "I'm beginning to understand. After tonight, the spirits will be obliged to repay this debt by looking after Sop Hao during the growing season."

"Yes," said Bo. "And the larger a person wishes the indebtedness to be, the more important the sacrifice must be."

CHAPTER XXI

THE HOUR OF THE HARE

IT WAS during the first hour of the hare on the second day of *da shu*, the great heat of mid-July, when the explosion shattered the dawn at Sop Hao. A wild pig snuffling for the tender roots of a calamus plant near Sareno's hut was blinded by a sliver of bamboo that pierced his temple. The pig screamed and crashed wildly into the jungle. Three tiny parrots which had been loudly complaining of empty stomachs suddenly found themselves without a nest. They fell in a fluttering rainbow to the ground.

The explosion demolished Sareno's spirit house shaped like a Baptist church. It tore off the steps of his home and sheared three of the six supports which held the house off the ground. The front wall and parts of the side walls exploded outward. The floor in the front room became splinters and disappeared into the mud underneath. Almost as an afterthought, the house tilted forward and the roof collapsed. The noise died away quickly, absorbed into the jungle like water into sand.

Borjek, his ears ringing and his face burning from the blast, dived through the rear door of the house. By the time he hit the ground, the safety was off the Walthur PPK pistol and he was looking for movement. Something shifted above him and he jerked backward, bringing up the gun. As he started to squeeze the trigger, he recognized Sareno stumbling down the steps. Borjek moved the pistol aside and motioned Sareno to be quiet.

He edged carefully around the house toward the front. Wisps of smoke filtered through the piles of bamboo. The air smelled metallic. Borjek felt vulnerable, not only because he was naked, but because there was a dullness of sound, as if his ears were stoppered. He checked the nearby bushes and found nothing, except two dead baby parrots and one yellow one which was still alive, trembling.

When he returned to the rear of the house, Sareno was sitting on the ground. Blood trickled down the preacher's face and he held his right arm tight against his chest. He wore only undershorts.

"Are you all right?" asked Borjek.

"I don't know. What happened?"

"C-four, judging from the smell. Let me see your arm."

"I fell on it."

Moments later, Bo and Sylvia arrived, followed by Seng and most of the population of Sop Hao. After Borjek explained what had happened, Dugpas Seng ordered six of the village's hunters to search the woods. The others crowded around, talking excitedly and examining the ruins of the house.

Bo took over the examination of Sareno. "Lean back. Relax. What hit you?"

Sareno closed his eyes against the throbbing in his head. He felt as though he were underwater; sounds and noises were muffled. "I woke up—" His voice sounded detached to himself. "—in the middle of the loudest noise I ever heard. A pot came through the wall, and the house started coming apart." Sareno opened his eyes as a memory returned. He tried to touch his forehead, but Bo gently held his arm. "My crucifix fell and struck me. Who—"

The cry of a girl stopped him. Tanna-li ran around the house toward him. He smiled at her. In the six weeks since the incident with Oo and the burned girl from Ta Xai, Sareno had begun to court Tanna-li. He was shy, and at first only sat in her parents' home discussing the crops, the weather and sometimes religion. Tanna-li's parents, while relieved that their daughter, who was past the ideal age for marriage, had found a man, finally could not disguise their boredom on those long evenings and took to slipping away on various errands.

Being an outsider was no drawback to Sareno. The Man preferred to marry someone outside the village whenever possible because of strict mores about incest. Of course, the mate should be a Man, but Sareno had lived in Sop Hao long enough to be accepted—especially since Oo, Tanna-li's second cousin once removed (a marriage which would have been permissible) and her best chance, was clearly out of favor now.

Sareno was infatuated with Tanna-li. There were times when he

161

physically trembled. The decision to see her was made on the trip to the Lun Chun in China. Or maybe, he thought, he had given in to a decision which his emotions had made even before that. He was unable to trace the logic of his heart. He was now filled with a sense of urgency; perhaps he was too old, or perhaps she would grow tired and find him dull. His personal sense of time had speeded up.

As yet Sareno was unwilling to resolve his other problem. Since he was a boy, his life had been the church. He swore faithfulness to God and the church when he was seven years old at a creek-bank baptism. More important, he returned to that creek when he was twenty, and, alone, repeated those vows. How could he renounce all of that? During the trip into China, he had missed two Sunday services; the next Sunday he had shocked himself—frightened himself—by not remembering the Sabbath until the night before. Since then he had skipped two sermons. The first time he had been sick with diarrhea, something which had troubled him on several occasions since coming to Laos. The second time he had had a headache. Besides, he told himself, the crops were up and the fields needed daily tending in the midsummer rains.

Sareno knew that Ek Tho was seeing Borjek. The first time he had seen them together he felt rage. His flock was straying to popery. But then he realized it was, in fact, his entire flock, and shame checked his temper. What surprised him was how fast his anger dissipated. He was not prepared for that, yet he decided to accept it, and therefore to accept Borjek's increasing spiritual influence in the village. In the past such an acceptance would have been a surrender to despair. But it was different this time. He was giving in because it didn't matter that much and the measure of that, he realized, was that after he made the decision, he felt good. He was frankly pleased with himself.

Tanna-li, smelling faintly of lemons, an odor Sareno found exciting, pulled him close to her.

"Ti hak, my precious, are you hurt?" she asked.

"A little." Looking over her shoulder Sareno saw, only a few feet away, a penis and a large pair of hairy testicles, which at the moment were being scratched with a pistol muzzle. Only later did he remember, and wonder about, the pistol.

Sareno blurted, "My God, man, cover yourself."

Borjek looked down. He grinned and restrained an impulse to shake his member at Sareno, who was pulling Tanna-li's head into his shoulder. Tanna-li nearly giggled aloud when she realized her man was trying to keep her from seeing the genitals of the mushroom god. But she didn't, because his concern made her warm inside.

Bo stepped around her and began working on the cut in Sareno's forehead. In a few minutes he finished, and started to examine Borjek.

As cold metal probed his ear, Borjek considered why the bomb not only caught him off guard but insulted and angered him. Like all white men who stay in Asia for more than a few weeks, he had lost track of the calendar—the other calendar, for he now marked time as the Man did. This was the time of the Great Heat, and when the jackfruit ripened the Beginning of Autumn would come. He had arrived in Sop Hao just before Pure Brightness and that was, he finally figured out, two and a half months ago. It seemed much longer. The bomb was an ugly intrusion; it pushed him back into a life, a set of attitudes, which seemed so remote as to be almost a dream—a time before this life, a time separate from this life. He realized he was angry because he didn't want to go back to that life.

After they returned to Sop Hao from China, Borjek had radioed Willard and told him that he would need money and raw opium later in the year for a trap involving Communist agents. Willard eventually agreed to the request. Borjek asked for two loose-leaf notebooks and also gave Willard the location of the flood-control project which the Chinese Corps of Engineers was building near Wehnshan. He described it as a small, non-missile, non-nuclear installation. It also occurred to him that the Kuomintang's 93rd Division might be interested in the same information.

All of that came to Borjek abruptly as he realized that instead of thinking about the Agency for the past month, he had been trying to analyze his feelings about himself, and his status with the Man— to examine and understand his new role. Borjek had never been a man who sought, or thought he needed or even understood the attention of other people. As a teen-ager he was the one at parties who leaned against the wall, with a tight smile. As a man, he was always in the background. As a drunk, it was easier. His voice, his manner, his eyes emanated nothing. Indifference scared people. He knew that, and it had been useful in the past.

But when he saw the girl who had been burned by the napalm, Borjek realized that he actually held the future of these people in his hands, just as Liao had held his hand when she died. That was a feeling he had never experienced in the Army or with the Agency. He had killed before, but only men like himself: professionals. The possibility of one's death, or the deaths of one's fellow soldiers, was the first thing an agent came to grips with. Not the last thing. But this was different. These Man had not asked to become involved; they were not part of the game. They were innocents and, among all the people here, only he had any chance of saving Sop Hao.

Strangely enough, the Man seemed to know that. Borjek found himself the center of people's attention for the first time. He had not trusted before, and he never expected anyone to trust him. Some of the Man believed in him, called him their mushroom god. Several weeks before, Ek Tho had come to explore the possibility of Borjek's baptizing him, since Sareno seemed reluctant and preoccupied. Borjek and Ek Tho had sipped wine from the Coca-Cola, and finally Borjek told him he would consider a baptism. Borjek was bequeathed with the dreams of a village. It scared him, and it thrilled him.

After Bo had finished with his patients, Dugpas Seng called everyone to the front of the house.

"There." Seng pointed. Splotches of blood were drying on the bamboo. Near the frame of the door was a chicken's head and a thin, shiny wire.

Borjek remembered one of his early theories, that someone was training the flying wild chickens to carry bombs. On the other hand, he also remembered that if the chickens had not warned him about the poisoned arrow, his toenails would be sticking up through the ground now. "Was this one of the herd of flying wild chickens?" he asked Seng.

"Yes. This was N'so." I set them free. Seng thought, so that they might be happier and able to fly in the forests like birds. Am I

164

making the same mistake with the people of my village? Was Oo right in saying that times have changed but I haven't?

Since Seng had decreed that only a medicinal amount of the poppy would be planted, the mood of the Man had been uneasy and tense. A gnawing sense of apprehension rose with the sun every morning and with the moon every night. Seng knew their concern came from a fear of what consequences his action might have that fall. Or maybe sooner, he thought, looking down at the dead chicken. This might be retaliation for not planting enough of the ty fong ki, although it may have something to do with the mushroom god. Borjek was a powerful man, and not everything he attracted was lucky.

The poppies, planted when the horns of the moon were pointed up, were already young plants. They occupied a space less than one-sixth of that cultivated the previous season. They and the other crops had begun well, Seng told himself in consolation. Also, the two white men were continuing to help in the fields, and that meant four extra hands to pull the weeds. One eager man can dig a water channel in the time that it takes two pressed slaves to discuss where it should go. But Seng still dared not believe that Borjek could handle the opium buyers after the harvest. That, he thought, will demand the assistance of all my ancestors, and the current generation as well.

Seng turned toward the jungle, willing it to reveal its secrets, but the green undergrowth answered not a word nor moved a leaf. Seng wondered if Oo was alive. He restricted his outer perceptions and threw out a seeking-message into the distance. Oo had not been seen since the night he attacked Tanna-li. Since then only one rumor—that Oo was trying to recruit tribesmen inside China—had reached Seng's ears. Seng was torn between wanting to see Oo again, to talk with him and change his mind, and secretly hoping that he would never return—that he would simply disappear. At the fringes of his consciousness, Seng sensed that Oo was still alive. He turned away from the silent forest. The plants had many moons to enjoy, and more rains would fall before the harvest.

"Here's how it worked," said Borjek, squatting near the remains of the door. "A trip wire was probably connected to the bomb—a nail, a spring and a bullet would have been enough. It was strung across the door to get one of us when we walked out."

"The chicken hit it?" asked Sylvia.

"They never come into houses, and rarely fly alone," said Bo.

"N'so deliberately flew into it," said Seng.

Borjek started to ask how he could be so positive, but knew the answer could not be put into words. Over the last month, Borjek had been with Seng on many occasions. The old man had invited him to his house and he seemed to enjoy, to be refreshed by, the visits. Borjek found in Seng a man whom he respected and admired. And there was something still mysterious and undefinable about Seng which remained fascinating to him.

As the villagers began cleaning up the house, Borjek went searching through the bushes. After finding the baby yellow parrot, he made a new nest for it in a broken clay pot.

That afternoon, under chilling, misting rain, Oo and eight men armed with ancient but deadly Russian Mosin Nagant 7.62 semi-automatic rifles, walked into Sop Hao.

CHAPTER XXII

GUNMEN THREATEN SOP HAO

CHILDREN were hurried inside and told to be still. Chickens and pigs were shoved into their pens under the houses, and the gates were latched.

The soldiers walked through the darkening twilight directly to Seng's house. They wore dark green pants, no shoes and no shirts. Their hair was long. The villagers noticed with dismay that the men with Oo were not Man, but Jing Po tribesmen who lived in Yunnan. The status of the Jing Po, according to all available Man legends, was among the lowest of the tribes. Seng often chanted the story of how at the great *te wa gan*, when the precedence of the clans was decided and when it was established the Man were the senior line, the Jing Po arrived after the feasting was over. They knew they had arrived too late for meat, so they collected the scattered bamboos in which the meat had been cooked, and licked out the insides. Thus, the Jing Po were given approximately the status of pariah dogs. "To this day," Seng always concluded his story, "people can insult the Jing Po by saying, 'You Jing Pos licked bamboos at the headwaters of the Mekong.' "

The Jing Po were more ominous than the Kuomintang's soldiers or even the Burmese bandits. More ominous because Oo was leading them, and his capacity for cruelty was suspected, if not tested. Too, he would have a personal interest in any violence. The soldiers held their guns carefully and talked low among themselves. One watched the rear of Seng's home and another the front. It appeared to those Man brave enough to glance out their doors that the Jing Po were nervous and worried, perhaps angry. A joss stick lashed to one soldier's rifle barrel burned through the grayness of the rain. Few lights appeared in homes at dark, and suppers of cold rice were eaten quickly and in silence. Some families hid their possessions in the woods.

167

After the soldiers arrived, Bo and Sylvia joined Borjek and Sareno at Tsao's house, which was located across from Seng's. Tsao told them that Seng had been in his house when the Jing Po arrived and had asked Oo to enter even before Oo was visible in the doorway.

Borjek paced the floor, carrying his carbine and pistol, the village's only weapons besides some crossbows and a few spears. He had been willing to allow the village's legal system, whatever it was, to handle Oo, but the eight armed men had changed that. Dammit, he thought, if only Oo had stayed away. In spite of his two thirty-round banana clips, Borjek knew he had little chance of taking out all eight soldiers.

In contrast to Borjek's constant pacing, Sareno, his forehead bandaged, stood back from the open door of the house staring across at Seng's home. When word came that Oo was in Sop Hao, Sareno's first thought was that he had lost, again. That he was going to pay now for his few weeks of happiness. That he deserved to suffer. Then a voice surprised him: Suffer, hell! Oo tried to rape Tanna-li, and the bastard—yes, he repeated to himself, the bastard—is back. Anger had rushed through him, flooding out despair and guilt.

"Suffer, hell!" he had said to Borjek as he decided to confront Oo. Only when Borjek had physically stopped him, did Sareno realize that he had no idea what he would have done had he met Oo. Almost abstractedly he had noticed Borjek was carrying two guns, and that seemed right somehow. Sareno no longer wondered over the resources of the priest. The impulse to face Oo had faded with Borjek's reassurances, but the anger remained, more controlled and more serious now that its expression could be planned. Earlier, Sareno had gone to Tanna-li's to make sure she was all right. She was, although her father was not himself with worry. In trying to calm him down, Sareno had calmed himself, at least to the point where he was willing to leave her. Sareno was going to watch Oo, and if he or his bandits made a move toward Tanna-li's house, he would do something. Somehow.

Only an occasional word filtered from Seng's through the gloomy night into Tsao's house. Seng and Oo must have lighted candles, for a faint flicker was visible.

"What do you think is going on?" whispered Sylvia to no one in particular.

Borjek slowed his pacing, but said nothing. In the quietness of his moves, she sensed for the first time, the danger of the man.

Sareno continued staring into the night. Earlier Sylvia had sought him out and taken his hand. His wrist had been like a hawser. She had told him to relax, that the villagers would protect their own. But even she didn't believe that.

Bo finally answered. "I don't know. Maybe they're talking about the opium crop. Or maybe Oo is recruiting soldiers."

No one said anything. The tension stretched on.

In an effort to relax everyone, Bo said, "Look, has anyone ever figured out how much urine there is urinated in the world every day? There are three-and-a-half billion people in the world, who each urinate, what? Ten? say, ten, ounces a day. That works out to be something like two hundred and seventy million gallons of urine."

Bo caught Sareno's silhouette turning toward him.

"Urinated every day," Bo said.

Borjek stopped pacing.

"In the world," Bo said, his voice fading as he remembered that Borjek once said something about a problem Sareno had with his urine or his penis.

"What are you talking about?" asked Sylvia.

"Never mind," said Bo.

Borjek said, "Maybe I could jump them. It's dark. I could slip up on those jokers under Seng's porch and get most of them."

Bo asked, "What if you didn't kill them? It would be all over for the rest of us."

"And," added Sylvia, "what if you hit somebody else in the dark?"

Tsao stepped out of the back room. "Please don't talk so. Aren't all of you getting sleepy yet? Don't you want to go home?"

Dugpas Seng had tried to ready himself for Oo. During the day a premonition that Oo was nearby had increased, and finally he stopped working on the repair of Sareno's home and returned to his own. He had smoked a pipe and considered how he might change the direction of Oo's feet. Seng remembered a story his father told him when he was young. Once in the Yun Ling Shan many, many seasons ago, Chinese soldiers were attacking villages ever closer to their own. A young man from their village disguised himself as on old woman and went out onto the road carrying an enormous stone on his back. The soldiers met the old woman, and, amazed at her strength, questioned her. She said that her strength was nothing compared to the young men of the village. The soldiers were so alarmed that they turned back. With weariness, Seng looked at the ginger leaves tied under the roof, signifying each of the New Years he had celebrated. There were too many leaves to count.

Seng was preparing another pipe when he sensed Oo was outside. He laid the pipe aside and asked him to enter.

The courtesies were as sparse as the words.

"Where is the opium planted, old man?" asked Oo, his face taut and drawn.

"Sit and have tea. And a pipe, son of Leua and Tsapos."

Oo hesitated and then sat. "Invoke the names of my parents carefully, elder. Their spirits became such reluctantly."

"Reluctance to become a spirit is a quality perhaps worthy of imitation," said Seng. Then more gently, "Their spirits are mine, too. Have you returned to Sop Hao to take the epa gie?"

Oo stared at Seng. Surely the old man was not serious, he thought. "Why should I, kunag?"

"For a number of offenses against the village, myself and your people. There must be a reading on the occasion of your attacking Tanna-li, and you must answer those words which position you in other violent acts."

"Children at play. I want to know where the opium is planted. I brought comrades from China to my village—"

"Comrades? The Jing Po?"

Stung by the implication, Oo said, "There are no classes of people. The Jing Po are not less."

"Is it to encourage harmony that your comrades carry weapons?"

"To protect themselves. If my men shoot at someone, then someone must be shooting at my men," said Oo.

"Oo, don't you believe that you should be accountable for your actions against Tanna-li?"

"It is truly said that a leech is easier to shed than a tenacious relation. I did not hurt Tanna-li, and I refuse to be tried. She is a silly girl and would have enjoyed it as much as me, had not . . ." Oo's voice trailed off, and he felt his shoulders hunching together as he recalled the image of the giant howling creature. ". . . the demon interfered. If she was hurt, the demon did it. Not I." Oo finally decided to take the pipe. Coughing several times, he lighted it with a stick from the fire. Above, the rain drummed softly on the roof, and outside, the light became scarce. Seng took the burning stick from Oo and lighted a candle.

"Again, where is the opium planted?" asked Oo. "I saw only a few plants in the mir not far from Treadmill's burial place."

"Then you observed the crop," said Seng.

"That is all?" Instead of passing the pipe to Seng, Oo laid it down.

"There is enough for our uses and a little extra, in case the next season should be unlucky."

Oo's face darkened. In the candlelight, Seng saw the boy as he would look many years from now. He will look a little like me, he thought, sadly. Neither of us is very handsome.

"I gave my word that Sop Hao would grow at least four hundred and fifty kilos of opium," said Oo, his voice rising.

"It was not yours to give. Your beard has barely begun to grow."

"And the people? Chu-wei? Swe? Tsao? What do they think?"

Seng lifted the pipe and inhaled slowly. "They took my advice."

"I brought these soldiers here to see the plants," said Oo, standing. "There is nothing for them to see. They will think me a fool."

"If the fruit which one is holding looks, smells and tastes like a banana, chances are it is."

"Old snail. I thought it was settled."

"It is settled."

"Age has decayed more than your body. There must be opium to sell this harvest."

"No," said Seng.

Oo clinched his fists. "Some can yet be planted. Still—"

"It is too late in the season, and I will not sanction it."

Mi gin bpa merk. Offspring of a maggot feeding on the corpse of a mad slave! You will regret this, kunag." Oo slurred "kunag" into an insult.

"Your eyes, Law Dorje Oo."

"What?"

"The whites show all around in your eyes."

"Stupid superstitions. Words. That's all, words. You yourself taught me they emanate from the mind, and into the mind they sink."

"Tell me, that from which you fled the night you assaulted Tanna-li, was that a man or a caak? Words?"

Oo stood and impatiently walked to Seng's altar, above which hung the ancient Tibetan knife. "Enough, old man. You will order the villagers to plant the opium tomorrow."

Seng said nothing but noticed that Oo picked up the knife and ran his fingers along the ivory inlay of the curved handle.

Oo returned the knife to its bamboo supports. "I understand an explosion killed two of the long-nosed ones—"

"No, they were fortunate. But you admit it, Oo?" Seng asked, standing with difficulty, his body trembling with anger and hurt. He walked to Oo and spun him around. "And the attempts on the mushroom god? The poisoned arrow? The cobra? Treadmill?"

Oo laughed. "Treadmill was too greedy."

A bitter coldness settled in Seng's chest. "I knew, but I put the knowledge in the ground and covered it."

"My men will listen to me, not you. I will kill the white men and, if necessary, I will kill you, too. Tomorrow morning, you will call the people and tell them to plant more opium. I will be watching and my men will be watching."

"No, Oo, no. Do not ask this," said Seng, trying to pull Oo to him.

"It is settled." Oo shoved Seng backwards, and the old man fell to the floor. "Tomorrow morning." He turned and walked into the black, wet night.

On the hillside above Sop Hao in the rain and the dark and the mud sat the Lahu chieftain, Chom-the-carver, and his five hunters. Before noon they had heard of the attempt to kill the mushroom god, and they arrived in Sop Hao in time to see Oo and his Jing Po march into the village. They noted the unusual quiet of the village and saw the white people go into a house in front of Seng's. After dark, the Lahu slipped into the bushes near that house.

"What if there is another great noise and fire?" asked Luba.

"What if our bows become vines in our hand?" replied Chom. "Hand me a betel nut."

Li said, "Here. And by the by, there is a strange noise coming from down the path aways."

"Go and see what it is, and set your feet to be quieter than your mouth," said Chom.

Li slithered into the dark.

Luba said, "The midget Oo and the old one, Seng, are having a loud discourse. Perhaps their ears have been removed. Do you think it involves the mushroom god?"

"I don't know," said Chom. "This," he pointed at Tsao's house, "is not the home of the mushroom god. The rain cannot cover the feeling of unrest. Whatever happens we will not let these foolish valley dwellers harm the mushroom god."

"Can he not protect himself? After all, it is said he has powers over the winds and sky."

Shay answered, "Ki, ki, ki, it was I who first saw the grand mushroom god flying hand-in-hand with a black cloud, and I said to my woman, 'We are highly honored—'"

"We know, Shay," said Chom. "He can protect himself, but by showing him that we are fearless and willing to ignore our safety to help him, we will perhaps gain some small remembrance. Maybe protection from tigers or perhaps he could bring some of our ancestors back from the land of Tai-wan. I told my uncle he should not go, but he—"

"Listen," said Shay.

The voices from Seng's house suddenly stopped. The silence ran through Sop Hao like a shiver. A moment later, Oo's voice muttered a few words to the Jing Po. Their voices moved toward the end of the village.

"Shay, follow them and see where they go," said Chom.

173

As Shay was leaving, Li returned from his foray.

"What were the noises?" asked Chom.

"It was the old one who lives amongst the hogs. He was burning incense and cutting up plants—"

"Plants?"

"Flowers, orchids and such. And all the while he was chanting and singing. Perhaps to the gods."

"It is fitting that the mushroom god begins here among the Man, for they are clearly most needful of help," said Chom.

A voice from Tsao's porch interrupted him. It was the one who had once been a candidate for the rebirth of Chyanun-Woishun. Sareno said, "I want to go to Tanna-li's to make sure she's all right. I'm scared as long as Oo is somewhere around here."

"Okay, but be careful," said Borjek. "I'm going to see Seng and find out what Oo wants. Maybe everyone should go to bed." So they won't interfere with me doing a little recon on Oo and the Jing Po later, he added to himself.

Sylvia said, "That's the best idea I've heard all day. Bo?"

"See you all in the morning. Let me hold your hand, Sylvia. It's slippery."

In the bushes nearby, Luba said to Chom, "What do you think they're saying?"

"Probably discussing how many pebbles will fill an empty head. How do I know? They speak a language even more coarse than that of the Man."

"It sounds like they're going in different directions. Also, what is that noise from the house here beside us?" asked Luba, cocking his head.

Chom listened. *"Sek, sek, gom. Sek, sek, gom.* You know what that sounds like?"

"I sure do. Let's move closer and see if we can see anything," said Luba.

Just then Shay returned. "The Jing Po savages and the midget Oo—"

"Quiet. We are listening."

"Listening to what?"

"Sek, sek, gom."

After a few minutes the noise came faster and faster, and finally a voice cried out. A female voice laughed, and the noises stopped.

"Now," said Chom, "where did they go?"

"They are sleeping outside the village near the trail. One man is sitting up watching while the others are sleeping. They made a small fire, although with considerable difficulty. I also saw the tall, white man—"

"The one who fought the mushroom god in the water?"

"Yes. He came through the woods and hid in the bushes and watched the Jing Po also."

Chom coughed. "It is my opinion that the Jing Po mean to harm the mushroom god; they probably caused the great noise and fire this morning. It would be honorable for our children to remember that we killed these Jing Po and ate them."

"Eat the Jing Po?" said Luba, with disgust.

"Surely their meat is as good as the large ground rat, which I have never noticed you turning down," said Chom.

"That is true, wizard," said Luba.

"We will need to gather onions and nuts and pepper," added Shay.

CHAPTER XXIII

OO IS KILLED

LAW DORJE OO would never know exactly what woke him. He came awake quickly, with the feeling that something was wrong. It was a faint impression, and the more he tried to remember it, the more ephemeral it became. Overhead the trees rustled in the wind. Maybe it was a dream, he thought. The wind and the rain had increased during the night, and Oo thought how much more pleasant it would be lying in a hut in the soft arms of a woman. He shivered and walked to the fire, kicking a half-burned piece of wood back into it. The fire sputtered in the rain.

The guard nodded at Oo.

"Has everything been quiet?" asked Oo.

"No. Some inhuman creature has been howling in the woods. It sounds like a wild dog, except I know the wild dog."

"Your gun is stronger than a demon," Oo said angrily.

"Also, there are strange birds in the trees. A while ago one flew across like a giant bat. It is a good night to be somewhere other than here." The guard opened a small tin of Tiger Balm and rubbed the salve around his nose. He offered it to Oo, who shook his head.

"Those are only the wild chickens. They live in these woods. Don't worry about them." Oo stared into the small fire, hissing in the rain. These kha were as frustrating as the people in Sop Hao, he thought. Even more so. The Jing Po doubted he would be a village chief soon, and they doubted he had four hundred and fifty kilos of opium growing, either. Oo chastised himself for worrying about the opinion of men who were scarcely trained Communist cadre. More properly, they are savages who have been given guns and assigned to me, he thought. Nobody takes me seriously. But that will be changing soon. Oo shook himself and tried to look into the blackness around him.

"There's nothing out there," said Oo to both of them. He returned to his mat, glad he had placed several armloads of cane under it. With the cane and a poncho tied above him, he had a dry though fitful sleep so far. He sat on his mat and felt something against his hip. A snake? He jumped sideways, but in the same instant he knew the object was hard and unmoving. He picked it up. It was a long knife with a curved handle.

The guard by the fire had sullenly watched Oo go back to his sleeping area. Even at that distance, only ten feet away, he could barely make him out. The fire was losing its half-hearted battle with the rain, and the guard was too wet and miserable to try and find more dry wood. He was about to shift his eyes back to the fire where there was a movement. He peered through the rain and the dark at Oo's shadow, now jerking around. The guard stood and hesitantly stepped around the fire.

Something flashed like glass or metal. The guard was unable to tell if Oo was alone or if someone else was there. A howl, the same unearthly howl that had occurred earlier, rose in the trees. The guard felt it run along his neck and down the backs of his arms.

"Oo?" he called in a hoarse whisper.

Oo said something; it was an exclamation in his own Man tongue. He seemed to be standing now.

The guard took another cautious step forward. Does Oo have a knife in his hand? he wondered. Something flashed overhead, and the guard ducked. A flying chicken disappeared into the dark.

"Oo?" the guard called again, louder, fear suddenly loose in his soul. Now he could see Oo's face, and Oo was staring with horror at the knife. "What is going on?"

"Help me!" Oo shouted. He staggered and fell to the ground on his back as if pushed. The metal glittered as it hung above him, the blade pointed at his stomach. It looked as if Oo himself were holding the knife. It must be someone else. It couldn't be Oo's hand, the guard thought, near panic. Why would Oo be afraid of his own hand?

Other Jing Po were waking up. "What's happening?" called one.

"It's Oo," the guard answered, relieved that his comrades were awake. "Fighting with someone. Or something. Over there." He pointed with his gun. Again, the howl of the creature clawed above the wind and rain. It was impossible to tell where the creature was, but it seemed closer than before.

Oo fought his way to his knees. He was holding the knife away from himself with one hand. Rainwater ran down his face. He screamed again. "Help me! He's trying to kill me!"

All the Jing Po were awake now, crowding near the fire. In the air was a strange smell, like the fusty mold of a place long closed from the air.

"Who is with him?"

"I can't see anyone."

"The knife is in his own hand!"

"But it is pointed at him. Look!"

"Something is trying to kill him!"

The guard raised his rifle nervously and aimed it at the darkness around Oo. He fired, but the bullet only tore emptily through the leaves.

Oo struggled in the shadows, trying to come toward them. Somewhere a rooster crowed.

"I can't hold out much longer," shouted Oo. He fought in the mud and rain, stumbling toward the fire. The Jing Po danced backward. Several looked around, and others began snatching up their bed mats and gathering the rifles. A muttering, born of fear and twin of horror, climbed among them. The guard fired again at the darkness. And again.

Several birdlike shapes flew awkwardly across the clearing, scattering the tribesmen. One swung his rifle at a chicken, but missed. Another shot at the sky. Their panic surged.

Oo's scream became one of terror and desperation. In the last flickering light of the fire, the Jing Po saw Oo's face, strained and frozen in convulsion. The muscles were corded in his neck and arms. The knife plunged into Oo's stomach, and he screamed for the last time. He wobbled toward them, eyes open but seeing nothing. No one was visible behind him. The knife stuck in his stomach and blood coursed around it. Oo's legs collapsed, and he fell at their feet.

"Ayi, ayi," the guard shouted and ran into the woods. The others raced after him. A moment later, the clearing was empty, save for a body.

The gunfire woke a lightly sleeping Sop Hao. Caen, carrying his medical kit, ran into Sareno in the village. Sareno said the shooting had come from the area where Oo's men had camped.

They found Oo lying face down beside smoking coals. Caen felt for a pulse in his neck and, finding none, turned the body over. The knife protruded obscenely. Oo's hand still clutched its handle, which was inlaid with seven different shades of ivory.

"Jesus Christ," muttered Sareno.

"He's not been dead long," said Caen, beginning an examination of the body.

A few minutes later, their way lighted by torches, Seng, Borjek, Sylvia and most of the village men were gathered around. The hunters carried crossbows, and several wore their war knives tied around their waists. Seng ordered three of the males to track the flight of the Jing Po.

"Who killed him?" asked Sylvia.

"I don't know," said Caen. "He was stabbed and he has a broken wrist. No other wounds except minor scratches."

"The Jing Po?" asked Borjek.

"Gone when we got here. George said he heard them running far off in the jungle. Either they killed Oo, or whatever killed him scared them." Caen stood and wiped the mud from his hands on his pants.

Seng, who had been standing behind them, walked forward and knelt beside Oo. He spoke in low tones, and the others did not recognize the language.

Caen pulled Borjek aside and whispered, "Martin, where were you about an hour ago?"

Borjek raised his eyebrows. "I didn't kill him. Although I thought about it. I was at the house, asleep. Ask Sareno . . . wait, he wasn't there when I woke up. Or when I went to bed."

While they were talking, Sareno had walked up. "When I left Tsao's house, I came here to see what the Jing Po were doing. They were all asleep except for one man, so I went to Tanna-li's house and stayed a few hours. After that, I stood around the woods, waiting, in case anything should happen."

179

Borjek said, "Seng told me Oo threatened to kill him and us today. Oo was going to order the people to plant more opium."

"Is that what they argued about?" asked Sareno.

"That's all that Seng would say. The Jing Po were apparently Red Chinese, and Oo was their team leader."

Sylvia, who had joined them, said, "Now, I remember where I've seen that knife before. It was in Seng's house."

Borjek looked at Seng, still on his knees beside Oo. Then Borjek realized he could see the trees more clearly. He glanced at the sky. To the east, the silhouettes of the mountains were distinct. The rain was turning to mist, and dawn approached.

Sareno said, "I don't think Seng left his house all night. I could see it from where I was hiding in the woods. He had a candle burning, and from time to time I saw him moving around inside. Most of the night he was chanting something."

"Anyway," said Caen, "do you think Seng could have broken Oo's wrist?"

Borjek said, "I don't know. There's still something between Oo and Seng that I can't connect."

Others from Sop Hao were arriving. Tanna-li came to Sareno and held his arm tightly. Her parents and Tsao and his wife knelt with Seng at Oo's side. A few moments later, Seng rose weakly and stepped back to face the white people.

Seng said, "The night is nearly over." His voice was weary and sad.

"Who do you think killed Oo?" asked Caen.

"There is a story that the ancient master was once traveling and met an old, thin adept living by himself in a hut. The master stopped and asked the man how long he had lived there, practicing austerities. 'Twenty-five years,' the man said. 'And have you acquired any powers from such long and serious contemplation?' the master asked. 'I can cross the river by walking on the water,' the man proudly answered. 'Oh, my poor man,' said the master sympathetically. 'Have you really wasted so many years for only that? For a small coin, the ferry man will take you to the opposite bank.' "

Sareno said, "I'm not sure I understand that."

Borjek said, "Perhaps it means one should never lose sight of the practicality in life. Direct action is sometimes the best course." He turned to Tanna-li and asked, "Why is Tsao kneeling beside Oo?"

"He is part of our family," she answered. "Tsao's wife was a cousin to Oo's mother, Leua."

With excitement in his voice, Borjek said, "That's it. Seng, kunag, you are uncle to Tsao's wife?"

"Yes," said Seng.

"And you are uncle to Tanna-li's mother as well?"

"I was uncle to her grandmother. Tanna-li's grandmother's mother was my sister."

"Then you are Oo's grandfather."

"Yes. I thought you knew. My daughter Leua was Oo's mother. Oo was my grandson, and, therefore, next in line for village chief."

Seng turned and walked alone into the dripping forest.

CHAPTER XXIV

THE LEGEND BACK TO PRE-HISTORY

IN THE early morning, when the rain had thinned to a fine mist, as it had the day before and the day before that, Oo's body was carried to the porch of the house where he had lived. It was a small hut near Seng's and not well-tended, since Oo was away so much. The neighbors had commented to Oo in the past how pleasant a groomed house could be, but his ear flaps had been closed.

Oo was laid on a low platform made from bamboo laced together with sturdy grape vines. Abject horror was still etched in his face even though Swe, who helped prepare bodies for burials, had closed the eyes and tried to straighten the gape of the smile. Oo's feet were bound at the ankles, and his big toes tied with white cotton thread. His pipe and tobacco pouch were placed near his head. A dummy kitchen had also been set up on the porch for use in the afterlife.

At mid-morning, the men went into the forest to prepare a coffin. Coffins were not made in advance because it was thought that their presence in a village might give lurking spirits a desire to create more death. After the burning of incense and a wine offering to the tree spirits, a cedar tree, as big as the stomach of a buffalo, was cut down. One section, a little longer than five feet, for Oo was not a man of great stature, was hacked off and split lengthways. The hollowing out of the two halves began.

At noon a blue sky appeared, but it only lasted the length of a betel nut chew. By early afternoon the rains had started again. During the middle of the rainy season, from mid-July to mid-August, the weather was like this. During the previous season, it had rained nearly continuously for six days.

As the preparations for the funeral took shape, so did the anger, fear and frustration of Sop Hao's people. Though the Man considered Oo scarcely more than a renegade, he was still their renegade. The cause of Oo's death was mysterious and therefore threatening to all. Early theories had it that Oo killed himself because he realized that by refusing to stand trial for his crimes, he could never become village chief. Others considered the significance of what Dr. Caen had observed: Oo's wrist, the wrist of the hand which even in death had gripped the knife, was broken in a strange fashion. After a further examination of the body, Caen said it looked as if Oo's own muscles had snapped the bones. Like an animal caught in a trap, Oo had pushed against something or someone so forcefully that he had shattered his own wrist. Thus, according to some, there were several spiritual suspects. Among them were a *yu* caak, which would mean that Oo's soul had been taken over by rats and that he was not himself; and a *mayu* caak, a spirit which might have been set in motion by Oo's ancestors.

A growing number of others put forth arguments for a more temporal solution. Possibly the Jing Po, incited by their own worthlessness, killed Oo. But, these people were asked, why stab him? Why not shoot him? Anyway, what had the Jing Po been shooting at?

Dugpas Seng was mentioned as a suspect by a few, but he was the village chief and more important, he was Oo's grandfather. Also, Oo was younger and stronger than the old man.

Of all the suspects, Sareno had the most visible motive, but his character and temperament, as observed by the Man for nearly two years, seemed wrong for the planned violence of the act. Some said that if Sareno had, in fact, killed Oo in revenge for Tanna-li's mortification, he should be punished by forgoing three meals and presenting a small jar to the village. Tanna-li's father suggested that even that seemed severe for the crime.

However, the name most often mentioned as the likeliest contender was Thay Mo Martin Borjek. He was new to the village; he was big and looked strange. He owned guns. It was known that he believed Oo to have perpetrated the attempts on his life. The possibility that Borjek had supernatural contacts did not mitigate the supposition; indeed, it enhanced it. Caaks and phi had personalities both as lofty and as squalid as humans. This theory would explain Oo's terror and the Jing Po's inability to stop the attack. If Borjek had killed Oo, it would be a great effrontery, and the Man would have to consider which of many hideous agonies would precede Borjek's passage into the realm.

Seng, who had remained silent amidst the speculation, finally announced that Oo's death required the sacrifice of a buffalo. Bway, one of the buffalo owned by Seng and, therefore, by the village, would be slain tonight. Oo would be buried tomorrow, and tomorrow night the epa gie would be taken by all the likely males in the village. At the least, a secular offender could be identified.

In mid-afternoon Seng joined the women holding wake over Oo's body. Since he was the closest blood relative, this was proper. The women continued their rituals.

"Oh, Oo looks rather thin," said one.

"He was always small," said another. "I suppose he is truly dead, now."

Tsao's wife leaned across the body and tapped the forehead with a pipe. "Are you dead, Oo?"

"Surely he is dead."

"He was the youngest to die in a long time."

"He was killed." The speaker shook herself and pinched her shoulders to repel any nats who may have been awakened by the word "kill."

"They say he stuck himself. Look at his stomach."

They had discussed and examined the wound as well as all the events surrounding Oo's death many times that day, but they inspected it again. Several ran their fingers along the cold, torn edge, and they shuddered.

"But if he killed himself, why do his eyes appear as though he were summoned before all the spirits of the dead?"

The women were conscious that Seng sat among them, and their words were designed as much to be overheard by him as for tradition.

"It will take a powerful sacrifice to placate the spirits."

"Once the Man sacrificed people to build houses. There was little trouble with strangers then," said one woman, spitting loudly off the porch into the mud.

"Oo, are you really gone? Are you dead?"

"He is dead. He is already dead."

"See his wrist."

His hand was turned in an impossible fashion.

Seng gave forth a gutteral cry of anguish and fell forward with his forehead touching the edge of the burial platform. The women wailed and cried with him.

The casket was finished by late afternoon and carried to Sop Hao. Oo was not put in the coffin; that would come later that night or the next day, depending on the number of sacrifices and how long the ceremonies lasted.

Shortly afterwards, the men whom Seng had sent to follow the Jing Po returned and said that the Jing Po seemed headed back into China, in as straight a path as could be made. They had met a woman who said Lahu warriors, led by Chom-the-carver, were close behind the Jing Po. The Lahu had told her they were going to eat the Jing Po.

At dusk in the center of the village, the sacrifices began. The rain was falling lightly, and a large fire was stacked and lighted. Seng, alone, killed a chicken and quickly opened its heart. He held the fowl over Oo's body, and the blood splattered onto the chest and stomach. His navel filled with crimson. When the blood had slowed to a few drops, Seng threw the chicken aside. Someone picked the bird up, for it would be eaten later. With his hands, Seng smeared the blood over Oo's body.

As Seng was completing this first sacrifice, which served to notify the spirits that a larger sacrifice would be forthcoming, Bo and Sylvia joined Sareno and Tanna-li at the edge of the crowd.

"Where's Borjek?" asked Sareno.

"At the dispensary. Praying." said Bo.

"Do you think he killed Oo?" asked Sareno.

"I'm not sure. It did occur to me that maybe Oo was killed because he was interfering with the opium deal. Or deals."

Sylvia said, "Martin said he was coming down here after a while."

"Is it safe for him? I've heard some talk . . ." said Sareno.

"Seng told Borjek he wouldn't be harmed. Seng also said that Oo would 'dance' later tonight," she said.

"What does that mean?"

"I don't know. I suppose something to do with the burial or funeral. By the way, they found a bag of peach pits in Oo's house."

By the time Borjek arrived, jars of rice wine had been tapped, and most of Sop Hao's people had overcome their visible mourning. It would be an insult to the spirits not to partake of the wine and no one wanted to rile the phi further. Borjek wore his cassock, as had become his custom at the more formal village ceremonies. He sat between Sylvia and Sareno.

Swe, sitting beside Seng near the fire, placed a yellow marigold potted in a bamboo section in front of him. Without introduction, he began to chant, and the people became quiet.

"The first epoch is the creation of everything and the legend of H'Bia Ngo. In the beginning of time, animals and man spoke the same language and lived together. The emperor of heaven saw . . ."

Most of the villagers listened attentively, occasionally drinking wine or eating a betel nut rolled in hickory ashes and wrapped in an areca leaf. Borjek realized this story was a longer version of the one Swe had sung to him when he first arrived in Sop Hao. Seng sat behind Swe, close to Oo's body, and stared beyond the focus of his eyes. Now and then, Seng would add a sentence or a word to Swe's account—a correction in the narrative. The man who lived in the hog pen would thank him and continue.

"Every day Tum Nduu and the woman hunted wild animals and looked for fruit, but they were troubled because they had no children. One day as they wandered in the woods, H'Bia Ngo met them and promised them children. His promise was fulfilled, and the woman gave birth to eight sons at once. But as the children grew, they ate more and more and began to quarrel among themselves. Then a great magician came through and wanted to become the tribal leader. He turned water into a solid so that it could be sliced, and thus proved to be worthwhile. He rode a great hairy creature like an elephant but with long hair and teeth as large as a man's leg."

Sareno stared at the fire, emotionally and physically drained by the night without sleep and the day's events. Swe's words penetrated into his mind and moved slowly there, word by word. Sareno could summon no strength to fight the legends or even to disparage himself. He thought, a great hairy creature like an elephant but with long hair; it must have been a mastodon. How old can these stories be? Turning water into a solid. Ice? A reference to glaciers; the last ice age? Turning water into wine. That's one of my stories, our stories. His thinking was slow, but sure. Tonight there were no fuzzy images and undefined words flying around the edges of his thoughts.

He remembered thinking that the Man believed he was telling their own stories but with different names. Maybe, he thought with sudden clarity, they're telling our stories, but with different names. Earlier in the saga, Swe said that in the beginning man and animals spoke the same language. In the Garden of Eden man lived with all the animals and the serpent could speak to man. Not my stories and not their stories, but *our* stories, Sareno thought with growing excitement. He had an emotional vision of all people having descended from a few a long time ago, passing down their stories as best they could. And we called our stories the Bible, and they call their stories epic sagas—but they're really all the same.

His thoughts raced, clear and uncluttered. We in the West weren't given the only truth, the only salvation. Each people works for its own salvation as its heritage and community dictates. He uncrossed his legs and glanced at Tanna-li. She was watching Swe, her lips mouthing some of the words along with him. Sareno felt almost certain now: We abide by right and wrong and these people have a right and wrong, which really, when you consider the incredible differences in culture and time, are not very different from ours. God is working His will here. Through them.

He reached over and took Tanna-li's hand.

Swe was continuing with the legend. "After a time, one of the younger brothers acquired a precious and beautiful sword having remarkable powers. When the handle was grasped securely, rain would fall; when the blade was held, the sun would shine. One day the boy who owned the sword became very hungry, for man did not know how to grow rice then. He went looking for food, and on the bank of a river, he saw a fig tree and a civet cat eating the figs. The

187

boy went to the civet cat and asked for something to eat. But the cat said, 'This is not your kind of food. If you want to eat these figs you will have to become a civet cat like me.' With that, the cat brought out a civet cat skin and the boy put it on. He became a civet cat, eating figs and sleeping in the shade of the tree.

"And Nayn fell in love with the civet cat which was really the boy. And H'Bia Ngo commanded the civet cat to grasp the precious sword by the handle several times. A violent rainstorm followed, and it rained for so long that the waters destroyed everything on earth. The waters rose to the heavens, and the fish nibbled at the stars.

"Everything was flooded except two mountains, Goong Din and Goong Dom. On Goong Din lived Nayn and the civet cat, who had removed his disguise and was now a man. On Goong Dom lived a woman and a dog. The woman mated with the dog, and her son mated with her, and the people from that mountain became the people who live in the lowlands.

"Nayn and the man who had been disguised as the civet cat mated and had four daughters and four sons, and they allowed their sons to marry their sisters. For a long time, brothers continued to marry sisters, but their children were sickly and skinny, and many died. The head of the clan then said that H'Bia Ngo revealed to him that marriage between brothers and sisters must cease. The next morning, the head of the tribe and his relatives fixed the following fines for incest: three buffalo for a marriage between brother and sister, two buffalo for a marriage between two persons with the same grandparents, two buffalo for a marriage between parents and children, one—"

Sareno had not heard this part of the saga before. He realized it was the passing along of mores, rules for living together, right and wrong—even as Moses took down and passed along our own commandments. It's all fitting in, he thought. They had their floods, we had ours. The same. Sareno felt very secure all of a sudden. He kissed Tanna-li's palm, and she smiled.

The story continued for several chews. Children began to fall asleep and were either left on the ground or taken to bed. The night was warm and humid, for the rain had finally stopped.

As Swe neared the end of the epoch, Seng got up slowly and

joined the white people. The firelight deepened the wrinkles in his face. He seemed lifeless.

Sylvia placed her hand on his arm. "Are you feeling all right, kunag?"

"It has been a tiring day," said Seng, with a little smile. "But I will live as long as I should."

Swe completed the story and cut the marigold petals into small flecks of yellow. He dipped them in rice wine and spread them on Oo's chest, now brown from the dried blood.

Seng nodded toward Swe and said to Sylvia, "We have argued many times, but he is convinced that one should not sacrifice animals. He is a good man and a friend."

Swe retired to the crowd, and Seng stood as a buffalo was led in by Pakse and tied to a pole. Seng walked to the buffalo and talked gently to him. Bway was old, perhaps a dozen seasons old, but Seng remembered when he was born; it seemed only a harvest ago. Bway had had a birth defect, a crooked front leg, and only by the persuasion of Tanna-li, who was then a little girl, was Bway allowed to live. The leg never hindered the animal's walking or working in the fields. Eventually, the crooked leg became a good luck symbol for the village, and the buffalo became a playmate for the children.

Seng looked into Bway's huge black eyes, sparkling with tiny reflections of the bonfire, and he knew that Bway did not understand what was going to happen. Seng unsheathed the sacrificial knife which his father had given to him. At least, he thought, it's only water buffalo now. He remembered the woman's words at the wake. There were rites, and not long ago, which meant the killing of young people. One of the first things Seng had done as village chief was to dream about a message from Ten Luong, representing H'Bia Ngo himself, that henceforth buffalo were decreed a sacrificial animal equal to humans. Buffalo would be sacrificed so humans would not be. After much contemplation, the Man Lan Mien came to accept Seng's dream.

Seng stepped behind Bway and slashed the hamstring tendons in the animal's back legs. The water buffalo can make no sound, but air rasped through a wide-open mouth as Bway collapsed clumsily to the ground.

Except, Seng thought, there were certain crimes for which the sacrifice of a water buffalo was still insufficient.

Would there ever come a time when there would be no sacrifices? Seng wondered. When Swe would be right, and only flowers offered?

Seng moved in front of Bway and pulled the animal's head up so its throat was exposed.

CHAPTER XXV

THE DANCE OF DEATH

AROUND midnight, long after a quarter moon had risen to light a playground for the black clouds chasing one another northward, the public ceremonies ended, and Oo's body was carried inside his house. Most of the villagers returned to their homes, some because they were too drunk to continue and some because of rumors about the ritual yet to come.

Seng, wearing his long, white robe, had lighted three candles and made seven five-pointed stars from bamboo splits, each with a circle in the middle, which he hung around Oo's room. He had removed the ankle bindings and the fatigue pants from the corpse.

For more than an hour, Seng had been chanting the same series of sounds, barely audible to those outside the house. The words were not Man, at least none of the white people sitting outside near the fire recognized them. Through the door, they watched Seng, backlit by a faint yellow glow, as he knelt beside the body.

"Is this it, or is something more going to happen?" asked Sylvia.

"I'm not sure," said Bo. "Swe was the only one who admitted having seen this before, and he called it 'demon magic.' It's used only on very rare occasions. Swe seemed upset, and I noticed that he's not here."

"Did he say anything about what the ceremony means?" she asked.

"When a person dies, his soul becomes a *ma*, a ghostly, errant spirit and potentially dangerous. Part of the ma goes to heaven and another part remains near the corpse, hovering around the body and later around the grave. This disembodied soul remembers its earthly existence and has the same needs as the living body. That's why the Man take offerings of food to the grave. The ma are miserable in this transitional state and will often try to snatch other souls which are about to leave the world of the living. The longer a ma is in this transitional state, the more dangerous it is for those around the corpse. If the ma does not return to the body in a few hours, or if the person was murdered—especially if he was killed in an unexplained and strange way—magical means are necessary to coax the ma back into the body. Since Oo was killed this way, it's necessary to perform the 'dance of death' as Swe called it. It's all very complicated and somehow bound up with Seng being Oo's grandfather."

Sareno, sitting alone since Tanna-li had left with her parents earlier, stood. "Excuse me. I have to . . . I'll be back in a minute." He walked to the edge of the trees when suddenly something appeared from the shadows, and he stumbled backward.

"Do not be afraid, thay mo," a voice said. "It's only me, Ek Tho." A Coca-Cola bottle flashed in the moonlight.

"You frightened me," said Sareno, grinning at his mistake. "Excuse me." He went into the bushes. To Sareno, Ek Tho was, in fact, a caak of sorts, reminding him of his failures, but the reminder was not so bitter nor so personal anymore. He had given himself over to a life with Tanna-li, to a life of acceptance, not struggle. Sareno felt awkward but not threatened.

Ek Tho approached the others. "Esteemed white ones, does your placability extend to this lowly creature at an hour of the night most frequented by bats, caaks and turtles?"

Borjek answered, "Indeed, it would be an insult, though such are well known to my family, if Ek Tho did not share his illuminating aura with us."

Ek Tho hunkered beside Borjek. "Worthy mushroom god, in my evil and sinful way, I have forgotten the lamb again. Evil thoughts have pounced on me. I must be saved once more, and to be baptized by your celebrated hands would be more than I deserve."

Borjek lowered his voice, "What about Reverend Sareno?"

"I think he is entering another phase of life. He has discovered the torturous ways of the flesh," he said sadly. "When I asked him recently, he was hesitant about the baptism. And there is a more compelling reason." Ek Tho stopped and toyed with the Coca-Cola.

Borjek was filled with the radiant thought that this old man needed him. " 'Seek the Lord while He may be found; call upon Him while He is near.' Have faith in me." The act of asking Ek Tho to believe in him gave Borjek a sudden rush of belief in himself. His heart swelled.

"Then you, too, see why a baptism tonight would be prudent," said Ek Tho.

"Tonight?"

Before Ek Tho could answer, a howl erupted from the darkness. It began deep within the being of its maker and rose higher, up through loneliness and pain, rounding at the end to "ooooouuueee."

"Sounds like an old coon dog to me," said Caen.

After several moments, the howls ended; the remaining villagers muttered to one another and left quickly for their homes. Borjek threw more wood on the fire to replace the limbs taken by the villagers to light their way.

Borjek asked, "You were saying . . . tonight? Why not wait until a more equitable moment? Perhaps one favored with the light of day?"

"Ignore my indiscreet haste, but it is said that anyone indebted to you who wished to absolve the debt before you joined your worthy ancestors, would be advised that tonight is propitious." Ek Tho offered the Coca-Cola to Borjek, who noticed for the first time that it was filled with an amber liquid.

Inside the house Seng moved closer to Oo. The orange light from the fire deepened his wrinkles and illuminated his black, filed-down teeth, giving him an ancient and monstrous countenance.

Borjek took a mouthful of the wine. "You want me to baptize you tonight because tomorrow I might pass beyond? Have I got it?"

"The tree does not always die of old age; sometimes it is cut down." Ek Tho retrieved the bottle and drank from it. "Also, I wondered, if we baptized tonight in the dark, could I go without my cloth? The water is so refreshing."

"Ek Tho, my friend, Kunag Seng has assured me that I shall come to no harm tomorrow. He will perform the epa gie. This is good wine, by the way. A new batch?"

193

"Yes. I put it up only a few days ago. I did not know that Seng had said that. Although a heathen, he is an honest and a good man. The epa gie will fix the truth. More wine, thay mo?"

"Don't mind if I do."

When Sareno returned a few minutes later, Caen asked, "George, did you hear that howl—"

"My Lord, look! Seng is laying down on the body," interrupted Sylvia.

Through the doorway they watched Seng lower himself gently onto the corpse. The night was suddenly chilly, and everyone became aware of the silence, made more intense by the low chanting within the hut. No wind stirred, and even the clouds stopped their games; one covered the moon, sending darkness around them. The lighted doorway in front of them was a window into another world.

Seng's chignon rested on the back of his neck, and his shoulders trembled with the effort to position himself on Oo's body. He seemed to be trying to match their limbs exactly.

"I think that whatever is going to happen will happen soon," said Sylvia. Standing, she walked to within a dozen feet of the door. After a moment, the others joined her, instinctively staying near each other.

Apparently Seng had finally placed himself as he wanted on Oo's body. So exactly did they match up that no light shone between the bodies. Only their heads were separate. They seemed to be one creature.

Seng's chanting stopped, and he slowly dropped his lips to touch Oo's, like a lover. They were mated head to foot.

Someone tugged at Borjek's arm.

Ek Tho whispered, "Come quickly. Baptize me, for now I am afraid as well as full of sin."

"Don't worry. I am with you now and evermore." Borjek took Ek Tho's hand and held it.

"In Tuscaloosa?"

"Especially in Tuscaloosa."

"Will you all hush," muttered Bo.

Time eked by. Even though Seng lay still, they watched

transfixed by the strangeness of the scene and the night. The air felt odd; like the air before a thunderstorm, it was filled with a subtle quivering of electricity.

Minutes passed.

Sylvia finally said, "Did Swe say what would happen next?"

"He said that if the ritual works, the corpse will become animated and dance," said Bo.

"You mean . . . dance?"

"Dance was the word he used. He also said it was very dangerous."

Something occured to Bo, and he leaned close to Ek Tho. "Does Seng have any other grandchildren?"

"No, he had only the one daughter, and she and her worthless husband were killed as Oo was beginning his manhood. Seng took care of Oo for a few years, but the boy inherited nothing from him. So little, in fact, that some have questioned the fidelity of Oo's immediate female ancestor."

Bo remembered when his great-grandfather, Matthew Caen, died in a room that smelled of stale tobacco, unwashed clothes and sickness. A fire had burned low in the wood stove and Matthew lay under a mound of quilts. A full head of white hair had pillowed his head. Bo had stared at his great-grandfather's mustache, which was dirty and stained brown from tobacco juice.

Bo had been petrified when his mother placed his hand in Matthew's cold and shaking palm. Matthew had said, "Son, you are the last male in this Caen family. The name should be carried on." Matthew's eyes were brown and didn't focus. They were teary from pneumonia that filled his lungs. Later that night, while Bo slept in a chair in the next room, Matthew died. My great-grandfather was trying to pass something along to me, much as Seng is doing with his grandson. To give me part of his spirit, his person, his being. Only it's too late for Seng.

Ek Tho interrupted his thoughts. "By the by, dalam, have you been baptized?"

"Sort of. I was a Methodist, and my head was sprinkled with water."

A frown formed on Ek Tho's face. "Sprinkled? That would be like calling snail meat leg of buffalo. Surely—"

"Seng is moving," said Sylvia.

Seng's arm's were twitching and his legs trembling. From their viewpoint, it seemed as though Oo's body were also moving, but the light from the candles was uncertain and the shadows deceptive. Seng's lips remained pressed against the mouth of the corpse.

A gutteral cry rose from the old man's throat, and the twitching and jerking became more animated. Seng's entire body shook as if he were having spasms.

"He might be having a stroke or a heart attack," said Sylvia, starting forward.

"No, don't go. I think it's the ritual," said Caen. "The dance is beginning."

The hut was camouflaged in ocher and black, and through the door the bodies, one living and one dead, moved in concert. Suddenly the figures rose, still locked in an embrace. The platform on which Oo had lain was kicked aside in their struggle. As Seng tightly clutched the hands of Oo, the bodies began to weave and turn in the yellow and orange light in a *danse macabre.*

"Oh, my God," said Sareno. "It's eyes are open!"

Inside, Seng was almost overwhelmed at the power in the body. Had Oo been a normal-sized person, Seng thought, I could not contain him. The dance began sooner than I thought it would; Oo's ma must have been close, and my ancestors must be helping out.

Seng had performed the *ro-lang,* the dance of death, once before and then it had taken nearly half a night. And he had been much younger. Although he had been expecting it, Seng was terrified when he saw Oo's eyes open. At first, they had been glazed and uncertain; the movements of his body weak and feeble. Now the body was gaining strength, and the eyes were clear and yellow with venom. Seng had been unable to prevent the creature from coming to its feet, and it struggled, now with more maneuverability, to free itself. Seng interlaced his fingers with those of the corpse to better hold it, but the body raised their entwined arms and flailed about.

Seng fought not only the ma, but also to keep his concentration. It was vital to repeat the magical words in his mind. He hooked a leg around one of the corpse's feet to trip it, but it was alert and strong now. Seng felt the muscles in its thighs and stomach knotting in determination to become free. The critical moment was approaching. Seng knew he could not hold the being much longer. If it freed itself, he would die, and all the lives of the people in Sop Hao would be threatened.

They whirled together, grotesque lovers in a ballet of death. Around the room and against the walls. Seng rode the corpse as it leapt high into the air. Seng's head brushed the bamboo roof. I can't hold it much more, he thought. The lips and the hands, which had been cold, were becoming warm. They crashed to the floor, but seconds later the creature was up and the dancers reeled around the room again.

The lips of the corpse began to part, taking Seng's with them. At last, he thought, the moment is here. Seng was no longer aware of the floor or the room or the night. Only the lips and the repetition of the magical words. Seng's neck ached as he pressed his mouth against the open mouth of the corpse.

There. There it was. Oo's tongue issued forth into Seng's mouth. It was hot and cold at the same time. Seng was repulsed, yet knew what must happen. The terrible moment was upon him; if he failed to conquer it, the being that was not Oo would overpower him. The corpse's tongue pushed itself into his mouth so far that he nearly gagged. With the last of his strength, Seng bit into and through the tongue. His teeth grated together and the tongue wiggled loose in his mouth.

The body stopped moving and collapsed under him. Seng lost his balance and fell across it. He looked at Oo's eyes; they were closed. The face had lost its hardness and malevolence. The body was a dead boy again; his grandson.

Exhausted, Seng took a white cloth from his robe and spat the tongue into it. His hands were shaking violently.

CHAPTER XXVI

THE TEST OF THE BAMBOO

I WILL flee far from the haunts of the White Ant. I will turn aside from the dwelling places of demons and spirits. Sloping places I will shun as well as men with hair in their ears and officials of the government. In short, I will never be found where evil is to be expected."

"And that's all?" asked Borjek.

Seng said, "Yes. That is what you must say aloud when you are selecting the location of your house. After the epa gie today, you will be free to build it. Swe can help you chose a place that—"

"I would be honored if you would lend your knowledge to such an important event."

They were standing before Seng's house, having just returned from the funeral of Oo, who was buried alone in the woods, for his parents' graves were too far away. Oo's feet were also buried since Seng declared that his spirit had found peace at last.

The sky was clear for the first time in days, though no one tended the crops. That would wait until the events surrounding Oo's death were settled.

To Borjek, Dugpas Seng looked weak and tired. His eyes were dark with fatigue, and his arms and legs blotched with dark purple bruises from the dance of death. Borjek wondered how the old man could have done so much over the past days. Tsao said he didn't think Seng had slept in three nights. At the funeral, Seng had groped for words several times and moved hesitantly. Borjek detected a slight wobbling of Seng's head; an involuntary shaking, as though his neck muscles could no longer carry the burden.

Borjek didn't want Seng to age this fast. He was only beginning to know him. He had not gotten to know his parents in time, and now the same thing was going to happen again. Borjek realized he held himself away from people, and, on the few occasions when at last something inside opened up, it had always been too late. Life is too short for that kind of fear, he thought. Or maybe we never know another person in time.

Seng said, "I must go lie down. I have told the others that you will be accepted into the village. You may build your home here."

As Seng turned back toward the steps, Borjek touched his arm. Seng looked around. Borjek had intended to promise him that he was going to write the Man language down, that he had already begun trying to come up with a system for matching the sounds consistently with letters, that he wanted Seng to help him. Instead he said, "I'm sorry about Oo, kunag."

"My ancestral line is ended, and Oo should not be buried alone."

Borjek could think of nothing to say.

"It's the same in this culture, too. Look here," said Bo, offering the microscope to Sylvia. "Could you see my colleague's face in Charleston if I prescribed radish seeds and a dab of mud for ringworm?"

"You're right. It is clear. Why do you think it works?"

"More and more researchers are finding a scientific basis for many old superstitions. Radish seeds must have a chemical in them—I could identify it if I had more sophisticated equipment—that is fungicidal and selectively antibiotic. The moisture in the mud loosens the seed's covering in preparation for sprouting and that releases the chemical."

Bo moved another slide into the microscope while Sylvia wrote the results in a notebook.

"Are you supposed to take the bamboo test today?" she asked.

"Yes. Me, Sareno, Borjek, Tsao—all of the males in the village who had, or might have had, any cause to kill Oo."

"Seng looked terrible this morning at the funeral."

"I asked him to let me examine him, but he said he was only tired from lack of sleep."

"No wonder," she said. "What do you think about the incredible dance of death?"

"I honestly don't know. My mind tells me it had to be Seng in some sort of trance, pulling the corpse around with him. That the dance was caused by him."

"But those movements? The leaps? Even when Oo was alive, I doubt he could have jumped like that. And could Seng, as old as he is, move that way, plus carry another body?"

"You've read about men lifting wrecked cars off accident victims, and things like that. Maybe that's what's wrong with Seng. He exhausted himself."

"And the tongue?" asked Sylvia.

Bo shook his head. "I don't know."

"I think maybe there really was something supernatural going on." Sylvia picked up a test tube. "By the way, as soon as we can get a message out I'm ordering some books on ancient Eastern myths and prehistoric anthropology. I'm convinced there is a thread linking the Man's tribal myths with prehistorical times."

Bo raised up from the microscope, and pulled her to him. "You may be on to something, Watson. My God, stories about when we were jumping from tree to tree—Ouch!" She bit him on the chest.

Sylvia said, "At least, it's better than trying to figure out why women are women and men are men."

"Speaking of which, I had another thought. Women never have to suffer, at least not as much as men, the indignity of territorial imperative. It's the male dogs that stake out their bounds by urinating—"

"Do you realize how much you and Borjek talk about peeing?"

"Us? Sareno's the one that pees all the time."

"Don't you think it's a bit strange? I mean you shouldn't have penis envy." She pulled his pants out and looked inside. "Hey there, little fella, you want to stake out some territory?"

"Uh, Sylvia, the two of you get along pretty well . . . uh, how do you feel about, uh, the rest of me?"

Why is he acting so nervous? Sylvia wondered. I think Bo is trying to say something and doesn't know how. She had never seen him hesitant in expressing his thoughts before. She tried to look into his eyes, but he was looking down.

"Ah . . . see," he stuttered. "Have you thought about us having a baby or something someday?"

"Or something? You mean maybe a water buffalo or a pig? Kinky sex is okay, but—"

"I'm serious, Sylvia," he said, looking up.

"I love you," she said simply. "I hope I always will."

Nervous but determined to show the depth of his commitment, Bo returned Sylvia's words, making them his own: "I love you."

There was no more talk of water buffalo.

At the other end of Sop Hao in Tanna-li's home, the Reverend George Saint Sareno sipped tea with Kwan Nam, her father. They had been discussing the weather for many minutes, and Sareno was searching for a way to turn the conversation to the purpose of his visit: He wanted to ask Kwan for Tanna-li's hand. The request wasn't necessary with the Man, but that was the way it was done in Tennessee. Sareno felt like a teen-ager. His speech was awkward, he had spilled his tea twice, and his long legs would not stay still.

Kwan poured another cup of tea and wondered when this tall man who obviously wanted to marry his daughter would get to the point. Kwan thought about bringing it up himself, but that would be impolite and he didn't want to interfere with any rituals of Sareno's own tribe. Among the Man, the courtship was initiated and settled by the female. Only after the marriage was agreed upon did the families become involved, and then only to arrange the exchange of gifts and to assist the sorcerer in selecting the proper wedding date. Apparently, white people handled it differently, and Kwan did not want to harm Tanna-li's chances.

"The crops are doing well so far," said Sareno for the third time.

"Yes. They are coming up straight," said Kwan.

Sareno was taking the first big step in his life. Divinity school and even his mission here in Laos had been set in motion at a time distant and distinct from now. For the first time he felt he was living his own life, and he was invigorated. Once he admitted to himself and to Tanna-li that he loved her, his love grew in his heart until it hurt. It was astounding: He wanted to be with her all the time, to touch her and talk with her. She said they would make a basket together, and that thrilled him. She said they would farm, and that excited him. He had been trying to remember all that he could about his father's farm. The crops and techniques were not the same, but he could learn. He was already learning.

"The *sa li* which you planted is getting its adult leaves," said Kwan, pouring more tea."

"The corn? Yes, I thought the rain might hurt it, but the soil drains fast."

Last week, Sareno had written a letter, as yet unsent, to the Mission Board, telling everything—about Ek Tho and the Coca-Cola, about the fight with the priest in the baptismal pool and about Tanna-li. He couldn't bring himself to say outright that he could no longer be a missionary, so he had requested a year's leave of absence and hoped the board would realize what he was trying to say. But Sareno had already released himself, and that was more important.

Sareno said, "In my land, we use fertilizer—"

"What?"

"The leavings of animals—it replenishes the soil and replaces the things which the crops take out."

"Perhaps it could be done. The phi would be consulted, of course."

This morning, before Oo's funeral, Borjek had said he would be building his own home soon. That was good, because he and Tanna-li were going to repair the damage from the explosion and live in his house after the wedding. It's funny, he thought, Father Borjek asked if he could have any extra Bibles I had. What if, out of all the people here, I made a convert out of him? Anyway, I must get on with the reason I am here. I have to urinate and Kwan seems ill at ease.

"Kwan Nam, about, uh, your daughter . . ."

"Yes, I know," said Kwan. I shouldn't have said that, he thought. Maybe I'm not supposed to know and what is it that I know?

What does he know? Sareno thought. "She, Tanna-li and I . . ."

"I'm happy," said Kwan. What's the matter with me? This tall man is so distraught. It's catching.

"Then . . . ?" Sareno asked.

"Of course . . ." said Kwan.

"Even. . ." said Sareno, uncertain.

"Naturally . . ." said Kwan, feeling closer to the point.

"As it should be . . ." said Sareno, with more confidence.

The Test of the Bamboo

"More, in fact," Kwan concluded, smiling.

"And now . . ." Sareno said, smiling and rising. That wasn't so hard, he thought, relieved.

"Indeed," said Kwan, standing and starting toward the wine jug.

"I must go. I have to, ah, urinate," he said.

What am I supposed to do, wondered Kwan. "I, too, in that case. We will signify the new relationship. Father and son-in-law together."

Sareno paused. "I would be honored," he said, bowing.

Tanna-li and her mother, who had been waiting discreetly outside, anxiously watched the two men come down the steps. The men turned and walked into the bushes.

"Where are they going?" asked Tanna-li, worried.

"I don't know. Men are strange, sometimes. You must let them be themselves and when they aren't, help them gently. Don't worry, though. It went fine. I could tell from your father's expression."

The epa gie was held in mid-afternoon in the place where Oo was killed. Those spirits which knew the truth and would determine the length of the bamboo were still likely to be in the vicinity.

The rains continued to hold off as the men cut bamboo the length of a man and as big around as a thumb. Swe supervised the preparation since Seng was resting in his house. As the people began gathering for the trial, there was a question as to whether or not Seng would attend. There was also a question about when all these sacrifices would end. Sop Hao was now down one buffalo, three chickens and a pig. Plus two chickens from the flying wild herd, which was considered a reserve supply of food.

Unable to walk but insistent upon performing the ceremony, Seng was placed on Bo's examining table and carried to the area. He wore his white robe, which was stained from the dance with Oo the night before. He seemed shrunken and smaller.

The entire population of Sop Hao was present. For once the children were quiet and stayed by their mothers' sides. The men, standing up front, wore their hunting knives, except for Ek Tho, who carried his Coca-Cola bottle and hunkered near Borjek.

Tanna-li's father leaned against a walking stick, one foot braced against the thigh of his other leg. He looked like a brown, hairless stork. Next to him were Sareno and Tanna-li, holding hands. Sareno wore no shoes or shirt, and his bare shoulders were already topped with pink from the sun.

When Seng was situated, Bo went to him and talked with him. While pretending to hold his wrist, he had taken his pulse and felt his blood pressure as Seng had taught him.

"How is he?" asked Sylvia when he rejoined her.

"Not well. There doesn't seem to be anything specifically wrong. His blood pressure feels empty, like an onion stalk that is hollow in the middle and firm on both sides. I've never seen his eyes so weak and unresponsive. It's almost as if he were willing himself to die."

"He's going on with it?"

"He said he's always read the bamboo."

The ritual began when Nam Kwan, Tanna-li's father, whom Seng had asked to help, killed a chicken. At the same time, Swe sprinkled orchid petals on the ground near Seng. Seng dictated the order in which the men were to be tested. Each came forward and held his left arm out from his side. Swe placed a length of bamboo underneath it, touching his armpit. The wood was marked carefully at the tip of the man's longest finger. While it was cut, Seng began the questions in a voice barely audible to the crowd. "This is the epa gie. Those phi which are always with us and which witnessed the death of Oo control the length of this stick. You must speak only that which is true. Should you not, the stick will be pulled longer, representing the truth and the knowledge of the spirits. Do not anger them, and do not fail to speak what is true."

The stick was placed under the man's arm again, while Seng asked if he had killed Oo and if he had any knowledge of Oo's death. As each replied, Seng and Swe would examine the stick.

Man after man took the test and the bamboos never changed their length. When Swe took the test, Nam Kwan assisted. Finally Dr. Caen was called forward. While the stick was measured, he looked at Seng and suddenly he knew the old man was dying.

"Kunag, forgo these tests. Let me give you medicine, and allow yourself the rest of several days," said Bo.

A frail smile appeared around Seng's mouth. "No medicine will help. This must be done for my people. Otherwise there would be suspicion and fear. Now I will ask you the questions."

The stick remained the same.

He turned to leave, but Seng stopped him. "You will have a male child and he will be healthy," he said.

Caen started to ask how he knew they had even decided to have a baby, but Seng was calling Sareno forward.

The people watched Sareno intently. Swe cut the stick, which was the longest one by far. Seng said in a voice so soft Sareno had to bend over to hear him. "Thay mo Sareno, the san pa-ku of your eyes is healthy. As is Tanna-li's. She is the great-granddaughter of my sister and will bear you beautiful children. You are becoming one with yourself."

The stick did not change its length.

Borjek walked to Seng's side even before his name was called. He rolled one sleeve of his cassock back for a measurement. There was no noise from the people of Sop Hao.

Borjek said, "Oo's killer is unknown, kunag. Maybe it was the Jing Po. Do not put yourself through this."

Seng looked at him with watery eyes. "Do you remember when Swe told you to speak louder to me?"

"Yes. I realized later it was a little joke he played on me."

"Now is the time to speak louder. Your voice is a whisper. You have become involved with the spiritual affairs of our village and with those of your own life. This is good. Too often men leave the understanding of the spirits to others, but ultimately we each must deal with our own."

"This is what I am humbly trying to do, kunag."

"It is said that no one is more surprised when a worm turns into a butterfly than the worm himself," said Seng.

Borjek thought, I came in search of Treadmill's murderer and instead I found myself. Or, is it that people like me caused people like Treadmill? There is still time, Lord. Thy will can be done.

Seng said, "My only regret is that I never was able to read the writing."

"Kunag, your spoken words are like a thousand fireflies lighting the darkness of our misunderstandings."

"The length of your bamboo will not change."

205

It did not, and words rustled in the crowd.

Sylvia said to Bo. "Then no one from the village is guilty."

"One man has yet to take the test."

The villagers pressed closer and Swe took the length of the last stick.

In a voice for only Seng's ear, Swe said, "Old friend, it was an act which can be and has been forgiven. A man's life is measured by his years and yours do not have to be counted yet."

"Aung Ne Swe, companion of my heart, we both know this must be done, even as Oo had to be dealt with. Do you have one of your flowers?"

"Yes."

"Then sacrifice it and place it on my grave. Bring my spirit and Oo's spirit a little rice from time to time. Place the stick under my arm and ask me the questions. I shall deny them, and the integrity of the test will be maintained."

Seng closed his eyes and his heart beat slower. A cold nausea grew in his stomach. He was a little boy again, and he wanted his mother to take him in her arms. His father's face was so strong and handsome. A great fear swept over him. Dimly he heard Swe repeat the questions.

Seng said he did not kill Oo, and the bamboo grew longer. Longer until it was nearly a half-inch past his fingernail. His hand stopped trembling. His chest heaved, and he died.

CHAPTER XXVII

THE HARVEST

THE rains in northwest Laos taper off in August and by mid-September the air is dry and cooling. The winds shift from the south to the east and that is one reason the harvesting of the rice starts on the western side of a mir: The uncut crops shield the workers from the winds. Another reason is that the spirits of the mir follow the sinking sun. Thus the rice is cut opposite the path of the sun, in order to prevent the sun from carrying away these spirits.

The Man harvest their rice by the *puot* method; they grasp the stalk below the seeds and pull the grain off in an upward motion. The grain is thrown in a woven basket carried on the back. Later, the rice is spread in large, flat winnowing baskets to dry in the sun. One of the chores of the children is to stir the rice several times a day to speed the drying.

The rice harvest takes about a month, and by then the poppy fields are olive and aquamarine. The petals have dropped from the poppy, and only the ovoid pods are left. The oldest of the farmers decides when to make the cuts, for if the pods are slashed too soon, the sap will be more red than brown, and too thin. It will drop on the ground instead of oozing slowly out. If the cuts are too late, the morphine will change to codeine.

Cutting the pod is an art, for the incision must be exactly so deep and must circumscribe only three-fourths of the pod. Two or three quick little cuts are made, and those who are adept can work so quickly that they seem never to pause from plant to plant.

Women and men make the cuts in the late afternoon and early evening; the next morning, the congealed sap is collected. One must be tall enough to stand above the plants, which are about four feet tall. Children cannot help because the fumes of the poppy are so strong that they may fall into a sleep and become suffocated.

Flat, dull knives are used to collect the sap by scraping the sticky chocolate exudate off the pod. The sap is put into small brass cups carried on vines at the waist.

In the fall as the opium crop was being gathered, a number of unusual events occurred in Golden Triangle. The Central Intelligence Agency will deny that they happened, but then the CIA never admitted flying Lahu tribesmen disguised as Kuomintang soldiers from Burma to Taiwan.

On October 18, over ninety years after the French bombarded the imperial Vietnamese capital of Tonkin in search of a back door to China, and eighty years after the French captured Laos, still in search of a back door, an Air America C–130 airplane parachuted four hundred and fifty kilos of opium into the jungle near Sop Hao. At first the CIA was reluctant to make the drop, but their agent, Martin Borjek, had been convincing and he had done a good job in securing the loyalty of the local tribes. The opium had been discovered less than a month before in Bangkok in a crate marked "Diplomatic Corps." The box had been the property of Prince Petsai, Laotian ambassador-designate to France and president of the Lao Bar Association.

The Agency also dropped into the jungle a smaller package, an assortment of currencies totaling $34,000.

The opium was carefully unpackaged, rewrapped in banana leaves, and tied with vines. Aung Ne Swe tested the opium and proclaimed the quality fair, though not as good as that grown by the Man.

A few weeks later, General Yone-fu, whose bandit army was said to be the third largest in northeastern Burma, arrived in Sop Hao with seventy men and twenty-three mules. He was distressed to hear of the death of his old friend Dugpas Seng, but overcame his grief enough to proceed with the negotiations. He bought four hundred and fifty kilos of opium at sixty dollars each, for a total price of $27,000. He also traded sixty pounds of sugar, ten iron axheads and a dozen metal bells. Handling the transaction was Kwan Nam, Tanna-li's father, who, as the closest blood relative to Seng, served as temporary village chief.

Nam gave the $27,000 to Borjek, who added it to his $34,000, making a total of $61,000. The Man kept the sugar, ax-heads and bells.

Two days out of Sop Hao, on the Burmese side of the Mekong River, General Yone-fu's caravan was stopped by a white man in a cassock. Yone-fu recognized the man as the white priest whom the tribes called the mushroom god and whose imperviousness to poisoned arrows and cobras was well recounted. A young yellow parrot rode the man's shoulders. He offered Yone-fu eighty-eight dollars a kilo for four hundred and fifty kilos. That was, it occurred to Yone-fu later, the exact amount of opium he had purchased at Sop Hao.

Yone-fu rubbed the black mole on his cheek and considered the offer. The profit was about two dollars less per kilo than what he expected to make in Keng Tung. On the other hand, it was money now and it freed up five mules. Furthermore, Yone-fu's soldiers were nervous about the mushroom god and the several dozen nearby flying chickens apparently under his command.

Yone-fu was pleased with the $39,750 he received in kyat and dollars. Even subtracting the four hundred and fifty kilos, his caravan had collected nearly a thousand kilos of opium. It was enough to buy the guns to capture Sam Kiao and with it, the head of his worthless one-eyed cousin. Yone-fu was tired and had already decided this would be his last run. He would establish Sam Kiao as his own, build a fine home there and retire. Well, he thought, perhaps I'll trade a few guns in the dry season.

That night the mushroom god and fifteen Man warriors loaded the opium into packs and began the walk back to Sop Hao. Borjek had $21,250 left.

Less than a week later, Colonel Ming Su-wen of the dread 93rd Kuomintang Division arrived in Sop Hao with a platoon of soldiers and a caravan of thirty-five mules. He paid fifty-five dollars a kilo or a total of $24,750 in kyat, kip and dollars for four hundred and fifty kilos of opium. He also left thirty pounds of salt, six fine cow hides and fifteen hoes, which were well received. There were no problems and Su-wen and his mules left the same day they arrived.

Borjek now had a total of $46,000.

Colonel Su-wen was also stopped several days out of Sop Hao by a man in a cassock. The man was the legendary mushroom god, who controlled numerous spirits, not the least of which were the airplanes. The white priest offered Su-wen eighty dollars a kilo for four hundred and fifty kilos. Su-wen counselled briefly with his lieutenants. The deal was made.

Su-wen was pleased with the thirty-six thousand dollars he received in several currencies. In fact, he tried to interest the mushroom god in even more opium, but he declined. Borjek had only $10,000 left and he had plans for it.

As they finished a last cup of tea, the mushroom god said, "There is something else which is on my mind, Colonel. Something which could add a sentence or two to your already impressive fame."

"Split the bamboo," said Su-wen, caressing his ivory walking stick.

"A few days' march across the Chinese border is a certain contingent of Chinese, the number of which is less than the brave and diligent men who have pledged their livelihood to you. These Chinese are Communist—"

Su-wen spat.

"—and could be persuaded with your help to alter their viewpoints. The Lun Chun, who live in the area, do not like the Chin. If someone should rid them of this infestation, it would certainly not harm the Nationalist Chinese Army's chances of returning to the mainland."

"Such a journey would be long, and my men are poorly clothed . . ."

"These Chinese carry few weapons and are ill-prepared for repelling an attack," said the mushroom god, flicking a leech from his arm.

"How ill-prepared?"

"They are not soldiers but call themselves engineers and seek to change the contours of the land. And," he said, removing a roll of money from his robe, "this small token of five thousand dollars could purchase sufficient clothing for your men."

"Ah," said Su-wen. "Perhaps it would seem less small if a similar amount were available to buy boots for my men . . ."

Another pile of money joined the first.

"Where exactly are the enemies of the people located?" asked Su-wen as the money disappeared into a sleeve.

Sometime in November the first chill of the year slips down the Muong Tha Shan and into northern Laos. The temperature drops so low as to encourage two-coat days and four-coat nights. The harvest is over, and the families use their time to repair tools, make clothes and baskets, and to work on their homes. By mid-November it was apparent that the Red Chinese, or whomever Oo had been representing, were not going to show up for the opium, and Father Martin Borjek arranged for a helicopter to take back the four hundred and fifty kilos of opium.

The Chinese did not return to Sop Hao because the Jing Po, who controlled the border and knew the trails, would not cross into Laos. The Jing Po said that Law Dorje Oo, who had been assigned as their cadreman, was viciously disemboweled by a ghost before their eyes. Worse, five of their men had been killed and eaten by the fierce Lahu tribesmen who lived in the hills near the Man. In fact, the Jing Po did not even want another cadreman working with them.

Since smuggling was the avocation of only one particular Communist district officer, there was no need to report the incident. Indeed, it verged on never having occurred in the first place. Furthermore, several companies of the dread Kuomintang 93rd Division had attacked and wiped out a Corps of Engineers unit near Wehnshan. That incident was reported to Peking, but the American Secretary of State Henry Kissinger was meeting with Premier Chou En-lai at the time, and it was conveniently concluded the Engineers must have accidentally strayed into Burma. Anyway, it would have taken weeks to get soldiers into that remote area.

The marriage of Tanna-li Nam and George Saint Sareno also occurred in November. For several weeks prior to the wedding, Sareno and others in the village worked on his house, adding a kitchen room and a larger bed. A small hut was also built for Borjek near the dispensary.

The wedding was a two-day affair and brought much excitement to the village. On the morning of the first day, Dr. Beauregard Caen and Sylvia Karman, acting as intermediaries for Sareno, carried trays of presents to Tanna-li. On the trays were bananas, a brass bell, a comb and a tiny jade bracelet which Sylvia had given to Sareno for his bride. Tanna-li's father received the gifts in her name. After examining them closely, as was the custom, he called for a jug of rice wine. There were a great many spirits to be toasted, but then the whole afternoon was before them.

Tanna-li did not emerge from her room on the first day. That afternoon a married woman, Tsao's wife, and a married man, Chu-wei, went to her and cut and shaped her hair. Sareno spent the day gathering baskets of areca leaves. After dinner, Aung Ne Swe went to Tanna-li's house and tied a thread of raw cotton, for purification, on her wrist. Afterwards, he went to Sareno's and tied a similar thread on his wrist.

Before dawn of the second day, Sareno woke and dressed in his finest clothes: a seersucker suit, which was the only formal clothing he had brought to Laos, a white shirt and tie. His leather dress shoes had long ago disappeared beneath a green mold, so he wore crepe-sole canvas loafers. In front of Sareno's house, Swe laid a mat and on it he placed an overturned mortar, a pitcher of water, an offering of puffed rice, a pig's head and a yellow orchid. Sareno sat on the mortar, not without some difficulty, until Swe hit a gong, indicating the rising of the sun. Following the ritual taught to him by Swe, Sareno raised his hands, touched the mat with his forehead three times and turned his palms around three times.

Sareno then proceeded to Tanna-li's house, carrying the baskets of areca leaves with him. He sat on the mat in the center of the Nam's front room and greeted those present by turning his hands around. Gathered around were Tanna-li's family, Swe and the Americans, who represented Sareno's family.

Tanna-li walked from behind a screen which had shielded her room. She wore a plain white skirt and a white cotton blouse. Her breasts were covered for the first time in the courtship. In her hair was a tiara of scarab wings. Sareno thought he had never seen anyone so beautiful in his life.

She sat on the mat beside him and they joined hands. They

bowed forward to the guests. Sylvia, forearmed with the details of the ceremony, noticed that Tanna-li kept her head slightly higher than Sareno's to ensure having the upper hand in the household. Although, she thought, perhaps Sareno lowered his more than necessary.

The guests passed a cotton thread from hand to hand, eventually encircling the couple. Three candles were lighted and these, too, circulated from guest to guest, with each person blowing the flame toward the couple. Sareno and Tanna-li then stood, and Swe tied their wrists together with cotton bracelets and dropped areca flowers on their heads. One by one, parents and friends came up to them and bound their hands with thread, scattering flowers on them and placing gifts on the mat.

Tanna-li snorted once behind Sareno's ear, and he blushed uncontrollably.

The Man ceremony was officially over, but before the celebrating began, Borjek, in his black robe, stepped forward and performed the marriage according to the Christian rites. Sareno had explained to Tanna-li and her family that this ritual was his tribe's custom, and they had agreed to it without hesitation. During the reading, Kwan Nam whispered to his wife that it was a rather colorless rite.

Sylvia was so taken with the proceeding that she and Bo were married in an identical ceremony in December.

Sop Hao persisted and grew. The next spring, a healthy baby boy was born to Sylvia Karman Caen. He was named Brieng Dai, malformed leg of warty lizard. At puberty, or maybe before, he would be told his real name, Bezel Matthew Caen.

Father Martin Borjek, the mushroom god, coexisted with the Man's religion and spread a gentle kind of Baptist-Catholicism in the hills. Oh, he held a few baptisms from time to time, occasionally for someone other than Ek Tho. But he never attempted a formal church. He and his yellow parrot lived among the Man, worked in the fields and gave what everyone agreed was sage advice. Now and then he reported to Willard that the Pathet Lao were being beaten back into the jungle. At the end of Borjek's first year in Sop Hao, Willard passed along a guarded compliment on his work and offered to send in a replacement. Borjek declined, quoting, "He who teaches men knowledge, the Lord, knows the thoughts of man, that they are but a breath." Although Willard could not match the sentence with any of his codes, he decided there was no reason not to let Borjek stay in situ. Whatever deal Borjek had made involving the four hundred and fifty kilos of opium the previous fall must have worked, since the opium was returned. Also, except for the one-time drop of $34,000, Borjek had not requested any additional money, and that amount was considerably less than Treadmill had been spending annually. Willard had sent along two notebooks with the opium, and later Borjek ordered thirty more. The CIA wasn't worried; it had plenty of paper.

The Lahu continued their protective, if unseen, watch over the mushroom god. They came to know the white, bushy-eyebrowed one better and found him worthy of his godhood. Once the Lahu killed a rogue tiger that had gone crazy in his old age and was raging about in the woods near Sop Hao. They discovered a Jing Po patrol of fifteen men that had come too close to the Laotian border and had so terrified them that two Jing Po were said to have died of fright. Before they were eaten.

Sop Hao still had a demon that occasionally shrieked in the night. Curiously enough, not long after the wedding of Tanna-li and George Saint Sareno, a second demon joined the first. Some said the voice of the second caak was softer, even feminine, and together the howls were less strident, almost joyous.

By then, though, the Man had accepted the demons as their own. They were rather fond of them.